A WINTER'S WEDDING

Emily loves Dylan. And Dylan loves Emily. Their relationship is rock solid. There's just one tiny fly in the ointment: Emily hates weddings. Which is fair enough seeing as she was jilted at the altar years ago by Alex, her supposed soulmate. Still, Dylan isn't Alex. He's gorgeous and sexy and scruffy and kind. But what happens when the ghost of Emily's Christmas past threatens to ruin everything? Can Dylan convince the love of his life he's different and that their wedding day will be remembered for the right reasons?

A WINTER'S WEDDING

A WINTER'S WEDDING

by

Sharon Owens

Magna Large Print Books
Long Preston, North Yorkshire,
BD23 4ND, England.

British Library Cataloguing in Publication Data.

Owens, Sharon
    A winter's wedding

    A catalogue record of this book is
    available from the British Library

    ISBN   978-0-7505-3569-4

First published in Great Britain 2010 by Penguin Group

Copyright © Sharon Owens, 2010

Cover illustration © Helene Havard by arrangement with
Arcangel Images

The moral right of the author has been asserted

Published in Large Print 2012 by arrangement with
Penguin Books Limited

Magna Large Print is an imprint of Library Magna Books Ltd.

Printed and bound in Great Britain by
T.J. (International) Ltd., Cornwall, PL28 8RW

For Dermot and Alice

1. Trapped in the Doll's House

Christmas Day was just two days away and London was shivering in the coldest December for thirty years. Nobody could remember a winter that had been so disruptive or where the sky had been so relentlessly grey. Windows were running with condensation, radiators were rattling with fatigue, and worn-out boilers everywhere were giving up the ghost. Fresh snow was falling all across the city and by mid-morning it was six inches deep, but thankfully it was dry and fluffy rather than icy and slippery and treacherous. Snow-covered gardens sparkled like spilt sugar in the weak morning sunshine.

Emily's trusty little car crunched slowly up the pristine driveway to the Diamond residence. She noticed a meandering set of tiny paw prints near the front gates. Emily supposed that Mr and Mrs Diamond must have a cat. That was good, she thought to herself. A nice shot of a pampered, contented cat curled up in its cosy basket always went down well with the readers. Finally, she turned a corner in the driveway and saw the house itself. It was set in a small clearing amid a cluster of snow-laden evergreen trees.

'Oh wow, it's so, so beautiful,' she said softly, though there was nobody there to hear her. She parked the car a little way back from the house, careful not to make any ugly tyre tracks near the

9

front door. For this house was so amazing it would surely make the cover of their next Christmas issue. Arabella would be delighted. She always liked to have the prettiest Christmas cover in the industry.

Quickly Emily checked her make-up in the rear-view mirror and then opened the car door. A blast of icy wind went rushing straight up her nostrils and she sneezed loudly several times. The inside of her nose was suddenly alive with angry prickling and soon she was sneezing non-stop. Blinking rapidly, she felt a layer of mascara melt into her eyes. They began to sting fiercely and go red at the edges.

'Perfect timing,' she said. 'This is all I need. Trying to take some decent photographs and conduct a vaguely interesting interview in the middle of a sneezing fit.'

Emily closed the car door again and began to dab at her nose and eyes with a clean tissue from the glove compartment. Her skin was snow white and her lipstick was an easy-to-wear bronze. Emily didn't slavishly follow the latest fashion trends so there was no fake tan or dark-red lips for her. Everyone in the London media was obsessing over their looks these days, but so far Emily had remained relatively immune. This was not just because she was usually fairly easy-going but also because she didn't have the money to indulge the fashion-loving aspect of her nature. She had big soulful green eyes with hazel flecks in them, and hair the colour of dark chocolate that she wore in a simple ponytail. Her only concession to high fashion was a glossy fringe that

10

she set on a large roller every night before going to bed. She was tall and slim and a girlish thirty.

'Right, that's enough of your silly antics,' she said, holding another tissue to her nose until it had warmed up a bit and she stopped sneezing. Just as she was contemplating adding a slick of mascara to her watery eyes, the front door of the house opened and a tall, good-looking man wearing a white crew-neck sweater and immaculate white cords waved out at her. With his healthy pink skin tone and the kindly twinkle in his eyes he looked a well-preserved fifty. He also looked a bit like a sweet little snowman in those all-white clothes, Emily thought to herself. She opened the car door for a second time and tested one boot on the glistening drive.

'You found us without too much trouble, then?' the man said cheerfully.

'Yes, no trouble at all. Mr Diamond, I presume?'

'Yes, do call me Peter. And you must be Emily?'

'Indeed I am, and what a truly fabulous house,' Emily said, stepping out of the car at last, her camera bag and handbag looped over one arm. 'Your email didn't do it justice, Mr Diamond. It's just heavenly. I really love it. No, please don't come out. I'll just take a shot here of the outside of the house before anyone walks on the snow.'

'Okay, carry on, just knock when you're ready,' he said, closing the door softly again.

And Emily did love the house. Tall and narrow, it looked almost regal standing here in its own grounds. Four storeys high, and everything that could be painted white had been: house walls, garden walls, window frames, front door. There

11

was a pretty carriage lamp hanging above the door and a small potted lemon tree on either side.

'It's just like a doll's house scaled up to life-size,' Emily said suddenly.

Perfectly proportioned, beautifully presented and so self-contained, it felt as if the building were alive in some way, and expecting her visit. She took a few dozen shots with her digital camera and then rang the doorbell. By this time her nose had gone so numb that the sneezes were frozen inside it.

'We have a pot of tea and some freshly baked mince pies all ready for you,' Mr Diamond said, opening the door at once.

'Thank you, how lovely,' Emily replied, stepping gingerly into the hallway and shaking the man's hand warmly.

She thought she felt his arm flinch slightly when their hands locked, and a brief flicker of anxiety passed across his narrow, blue eyes. But the moment passed and then he smiled again, the corners of his eyes folding up into very attractive crow's feet. There was something warm and re-assuring about this man, as if he would be good at looking after a woman. Emily could usually sense when someone had a kind heart. She had always had a sixth sense about people, and a feeling for whether or not she could trust them. It was a useful talent to have when she worked so much with strangers. Emily's special talent had only let her down badly once; she really hadn't seen the end coming to her relationship with her ex-fiancé, Alex. But then there were a lot of things about

Alex that she had chosen to overlook during their years together. So she really couldn't blame her instincts for failing to protect her from Alex; she'd never given them a chance to rally against him in the first place.

'I expect you'll want to take a picture of the tea things before we tuck in?' Mr Diamond added, pulling Emily out of her reverie.

'Yes, I always like to get a shot of the teapot if there's a brew on offer,' she smiled.

The carpet inside the house was the purest white. Up the stairs and in the rooms on the ground floor all was a sea of perfect uninterrupted white. Everywhere was vacuumed smooth with no footprints or vacuum tracks visible. Emily supposed they must have a special technique of backing out of the rooms as they cleaned. Emily had a white carpet in her bedroom back at the flat, but the walls were navy blue so the effect wasn't nearly as ethereal.

'I love your home, Mr Diamond,' she said brightly. 'The light is so soft. It's like Narnia in here.'

And it did feel like Narnia in the Diamond house. Even the walls were white, and there were few pictures – instead delicate Venetian mirrors reflected back the light from the white-painted furniture, the collection of glass candlesticks on the hall table, and the massive glass chandelier hanging up on the landing. Heavy drapes muffled any sound of distant traffic.

'Thank you very much,' the man said brightly. 'It's all my wife's doing. And do call me Peter, please. My wife's name is Sarah; well, of course, you know all this already from my email. Now, would you like that tea?'

'Lead the way. Are you regular readers of *Stylish Living?*' Emily asked.

'We never miss it. It's the highlight of our month.'

Emily nodded. She didn't doubt what Peter said was true. In the ten years she'd worked for the magazine she'd met hundreds of people who lived for their homes rather than just in them.

'Hello, you must be Sarah?' Emily said as they went into the conservatory kitchen together.

A beautiful woman in her early forties was standing by an exquisitely laid table. Even the white linen napkins had been carefully folded into miniature swans.

'Yes, I'm Sarah,' the woman said. She was dressed in a white shift dress, with her long blonde hair pinned up.

Emily could sense that both this lovely man and his beautiful wife were very nervous about her visit. She got out her camera and began clicking immediately. From experience she knew that most people relaxed a little when the shoot got underway quite quickly. The light was just right in this all-glass extension and the snow-covered garden outside was the most romantic backdrop possible to the white china on the table.

'It's our wedding anniversary today,' Peter said brightly. 'It was snowing the day we got married too. A real blizzard it was. I had flu. We had to walk the last mile to the church because the wedding cars got stuck in traffic. I arranged this photo shoot as a surprise for Sarah.'

14

Sarah blushed as Peter took her hand and kissed her on the cheek.

'That's lovely,' Emily said, taking a quick shot of the couple as they held hands by the massive fridge. 'Okay, that'll do for now.'

The three of them sat down at the pedestal table and Peter began to pour tea while Emily smiled encouragingly at both of them and got out a notebook and pen.

'Not a tape recorder, then?' Peter asked.

'No, I prefer shorthand,' Emily said, helping herself to a mince pie and a spoonful of cream. 'It's less intimidating, isn't it?'

'Yes,' Sarah smiled.

'So first things first – what do you both do?'

'I'm an accountant,' Peter said shyly.

'And yourself, Sarah?' Emily asked.

'I'm just a boring old housewife,' Sarah said quietly, and her pretty smile faded away.

'Nothing wrong with that,' Emily said quickly. 'This gorgeous house must take a lot of looking after. Have you any children?'

'No, we haven't,' Peter said matter-of-factly.

'Okay, so tell me when and why you bought this house,' Emily said.

'My wife fell in love with it the minute she saw it,' Peter said tenderly. 'Ten years ago it was. We got a bargain really, because there was so much work to be done. The whole place was derelict, but Sarah brought it back to life.'

'How lovely,' Emily said. 'Now, shall we get those all-important pictures of your Christmas tree?'

'Yes, of course. It's in the drawing room

upstairs,' Peter told her. 'Luckily it's still got all its needles, even though it's been up since the first day of December.'

'I can't wait to see it,' Emily said. She was also secretly eager to get a peek into all the other rooms. She never got tired of looking round other people's houses.

'Let's go up,' Peter said, showing the way.

Sarah remained sitting at the table as Emily followed Peter up the stairs and into the drawing room. He switched on the tree lights.

'Well, that's just splendid,' Emily said, awe-struck at the sight of a ten-foot Blue Spruce covered in hundreds of white lights and handmade fabric love hearts.

'My wife did it all,' Peter told her proudly. 'She hand stitched every one of those little hearts. She's so creative.'

'She could be a stylist, you know,' Emily said softly, clicking the tree from every angle. Again, everything in the room was white, elegant and perfectly arranged.

'This house truly is the most amazing home I've ever set foot in.'

'You are too kind.'

'No, really, your wife has a genuine flair for interior design. I'm not just saying that. She ought to be a professional stylist.'

'Sarah was an interior designer,' Peter said sadly. 'She was one of the best in London at one time.'

'I see,' Emily said, though she didn't quite see.

'I thought your boss might have heard of her?'

'Well, I'm sure she has.'

16

'You don't have to say that.'

'Arabella probably meant to mention it to me,' Emily faltered. 'She's terribly absent-minded about names. I mean, I'm sure she would have come herself today if she'd put two and two together. Arabella loves to meet the real talent as well as the celebrities, and the regular readers, of course.'

'It doesn't matter,' Peter said gently. 'People tend to forget someone when they've been off the radar for more than six months.'

'Tell you what, I'll ask Arabella if she knows Sarah,' Emily offered. 'Maybe they can have lunch sometime?'

'No, really, it doesn't matter.'

'Look, I'm very sorry if any offence has been caused.'

'Dear me, no, there's no offence taken. It's just that Sarah is acutely agoraphobic, I'm afraid,' Peter said, turning his back to Emily and gazing out of the window. 'She never meets anyone for lunch any more.'

'Oh dear...'

'Yes, well, that's life, I suppose,' he said.

'I had no idea anything was the matter. She seems so... I mean, what happened?' Emily said before she could stop herself.

'My wife was physically assaulted in an underground walkway near a Tube station. That's what happened.'

'Oh, how awful. How absolutely awful for her,' Emily said, not knowing what else she could say. She discreetly put her camera away.

'Some evil lowlife punched her to the ground

17

and stole her bag and keys. Pulled the jewellery off her hands and cut her quite badly. He was a determined sort of chap by all accounts. It could have been much worse, I daresay, but some people came along and scared him off. Sarah was in too much shock to ask for help so she just staggered all the way home. Five miles it was, and then she waited on the doorstep for me to come home from work. She hasn't left the house since.'

'I'm so sorry. When was that?'

'Nine years ago, just when the structural work on the house was nearing completion. I asked my company if I could work from home for a few weeks until she got her nerve back, but she never did. She had to give up her own work. The stress of getting around London on her own was just too much for her.'

'Well, I suppose it would be.'

'And we decided as the years went by not to have any children. It would have been too difficult, as you can imagine – to bring them up without Sarah ever leaving the house.'

'Indeed, yes.'

'I rarely go out myself any more,' he added in a faraway voice. 'It upsets her so much to be here by herself. And she doesn't like anyone else but me to keep her company.'

'But I'm sure you must be able to get help? Surely there must be all kinds of help for people with agoraphobia nowadays?' Emily asked, her nerves beginning to jangle. She wondered if she had enough pictures already for a ten-page feature, or if it would seem terribly rude of her to ask Peter for a swift look around the rest of the house.

Emily needed some upstairs pictures for her feature, otherwise Peter's hopes of having their house in the magazine might come to nothing.

'We've tried medication, counselling, neurolinguistic programming, cognitive behaviour therapy, hypnosis, exposure therapy, an organic diet – and even healing crystals – but nothing helps.'

'That's just terrible ... and to think it was all the result of a random robbery.'

'Listen to me telling you all our woes. I wasn't planning to reveal any of this. But I thought it would give my wife a boost if she could see her handiwork in print one more time. She used to get so excited whenever one of her projects made it into a glossy magazine. Please don't say anything to Sarah about this. She's so embarrassed about her illness. That's the crux of the whole problem, really. If only she could accept that people would be sympathetic, I'm sure she could begin to go out again.'

'Yes, I understand.'

'But she won't believe me. So you will be discreet in your write-up?'

'Yes, of course I will. And I'm pretty sure my editor will want to put your fabulous home on the next December cover – if you're still interested in the project?'

'Yes, please go ahead with the feature. I just worry about what Sarah will do if anything happens to me. That's what keeps me awake at night nowadays,' he said in a flat voice.

'I'm sure she'll get better one day. Just as suddenly as she became, well, like this...' Emily said hopefully.

But Peter Diamond just shook his head, as if he'd never heard of anything so unlikely. Then he turned to Emily and told her to go round the house taking shots as she pleased, and that he'd see her downstairs again when she was finished.

Emily looked at her watch and shivered. What had seemed like the most perfect house in the world only thirty minutes ago now seemed like a luxury prison.

'Trapped in some sort of giant doll's house,' Emily whispered to herself. 'That's what they are. Not that I'll be mentioning any of that in the feature.'

She took one more look around the majestic drawing room and hurried on up to the next floor to look for one master bedroom and one deluxe bathroom shot. Then she made her way back to the ground floor and said goodbye.

'Can I email you if I need any more information?' she asked, pulling on her coat in the hallway.

'Certainly,' Peter said warmly. 'You still have my email address, yes? Thanks for coming, Emily, and a very merry Christmas to you.'

'Goodbye, Sarah,' Emily said, kissing her briskly on the cheek and then shaking Peter warmly by the hand, 'and a very merry Christmas to you both.'

'Goodbye,' Sarah said. Already she was retreating into her shell.

It began to snow again as Emily did a three-point turn and headed back to the magazine's offices. She was halfway there before she even remembered about the cat. There'd been no sign of a basket, but in a house that big she could easily have missed it.

'The poor man,' she said to herself. 'That gorgeous house ... such a beautiful wife too ... and yet he must be in agony.'

She switched on the radio for company. 'Hey There Delilah' by the Plain White T's was just beginning. By the time the song was finished Emily was close to tears. And not just for Peter and Sarah Diamond trapped in their doll's house. She was sad for herself too, and for her poor mother and father back home in Belfast. For all the mistakes they had made – the chances they had missed – and because she had decided not to go home for Christmas, yet again.

'Would you stop it, you great big stupid eejit,' she said to herself. She switched off the radio and wiped her eyes with the back of her hand. 'Stop that sentimental old nonsense and get a hold of yourself. You're thirty years old; you're not seventeen any more.'

Arabella was smoking a cigarette on the rickety old fire escape when Emily got back to work.

'Did the shoot go all right?' Arabella asked when she came inside. 'It's freezing out there. Don't be cross with me, Emily. I only had two puffs, I swear to you.'

Emily took one look at Arabella's petite frame shivering violently in a fur-trimmed cardigan and felt very protective of her. So what if Arabella was a bit of a drama queen with her cigarettes? Pretending everyone was always on at her to stop smoking! She was the nicest boss possible in

21

every other respect. 'Okay, then, I'll say nothing. And the shoot went fine; more than fine. It was a super house and I think we've found our next Christmas cover, actually.'

'Good work – let's see.'

'Look, there...' Emily said, showing her boss some pictures on the camera.

'Okay, you're right, what a lovely house. Emily, you've got some fabulous pictures. Good girl. Well done. Yes, that's definitely our next December cover – either the house itself or the Christmas tree.'

'Thank you, Arabella.'

'What were the owners like?'

'Lovely couple – Peter and Sarah Diamond.'

'Never heard of them. Are they anything special?'

'He's an accountant and she used to be a top stylist, apparently.'

'Was she? Oh dear, I can't say the name rings a bell.'

'She doesn't get out much nowadays,' Emily added.

'Is that right?' Arabella said, only half listening now. She was still scanning through Emily's photographs. She was not interested in the owners – not really.

'Fancy a decent coffee?' Emily asked.

There was a Starbucks next door.

'No, thanks. I'm far too nervous to enjoy it. We have our IVF thing this evening. You know? The meet and greet part? I want to have a relaxing bath and make myself all calm and positive.'

'Right, of course. Good luck, Arabella; I'll be

thinking of you.'

'Thanks, Emily. Can you load those shots and I'll have a proper look at them next week?'

'Sure.'

'And can you finish the write-up for that barn conversion in Surrey? I know I said I'd do it, but I was on the phone to our advertisers all morning.'

'Of course, it's no problem.'

'Thanks, Emily. You're just brilliant.'

Then Arabella collected her coat and bag, and swept out of the office in a cloud of Coco Chanel and stale cigarette smoke, leaving Emily alone with her thoughts.

2. Emily's Wardrobe

When Emily got home from work that evening she was in a contemplative mood. There was no sign of the snow melting and little hope of the temperature creeping above zero. Her third-floor apartment in a Twickenham town house was delightfully bohemian in the summer months when the sun came streaming in through two large dormer windows. But in the depths of winter it could feel positively Dickensian with its exposed ceiling joists and wooden floors. And compared to the Diamond house (which Emily would now forever think of as the Doll's House) it was nothing but a draughty old attic. Not that she was grumbling about where she lived; she definitely wasn't. Some of her contemporaries had had to move back in with their parents because they could no longer afford to rent a place to live and pay off their debts at the same time. Luckily, with careful budgeting, Emily was just about able to keep on top of her own finances. She had a roof over her head and she was more than grateful for it.

She switched on the lights on her own Christmas tree, a white artificial fir with several glass angels hanging on it. The sitting room was painted a calming shade of cream, and looked reasonably pretty with several plump sofa cushions embroidered with teacups and roses.

'But where am I going?' she asked her reflection in the mirror above the tiny faux fireplace in the sitting room. 'What will become of me?'

Would she end up as just one more homesick Irish immigrant, hurrying along the streets of London with a half-pint of milk in a Tesco carrier bag? No longer remembered back home in Ireland? But never really belonging in London either? Well, she thought sadly, what did it matter? For she was never going home to Ireland again, was she? There was nothing in Ireland to go back to any more. There never had been, really.

'This flat could do with a good clear-out,' she said to herself, more to keep her own thoughts at bay than anything else.

The flat was actually spotless, but to Emily's expert eye it was still far from perfect. She pre-pared some coffee and then settled down in front of *EastEnders* with a fleece jacket over her jeans and vest, and her laptop balanced on her knees.

'Right,' she said firmly.

She'd order a pizza and browse the sales pages of John Lewis for some homely bits and pieces. And then she'd do some serious de-cluttering. For what was the point of buying new rugs and lamps and maybe a couple of side tables if the effect was going to be ruined by the accumulated junk and possessions of several years? And wasn't that the whole point of living on soup and baked beans all the time? So that she could afford the occasional splurge on a takeaway pizza?

By midnight she had filled several cardboard boxes with unwanted gifts, unread books, un-worn clothes and unwatched DVDs. Most of her clutter had been donated by Arabella, she realized, for Arabella's hedge fund manager husband was incredibly wealthy and Arabella thought nothing of spending several thousand pounds on gifts every Christmas. She also gave Emily lots of things she didn't want or need any more. And that was how Emily had ended up with several complicated kitchen gadgets she'd never used, some designer shoes that were too nice for any place Emily ever went, some signed books and modern art prints she had no interest in, and eleven special-occasion hats. She really ought to sell it all on eBay, Emily thought to herself, but she didn't want the worry of Arabella finding out. It would really hurt Arabella's feelings and might even ruin their friendship. So Emily set the boxes neatly by the front door and vowed to take them all to the charity shop at the end of her road. That little place, what was it supporting again? Was it a hospice of some sort? Or was it for homeless dogs? Anyway, it didn't matter, she decided, because all charity shops were in support of something good. She washed her plate and cup and put them back in the cupboard. The pizza box she added to the recycling basket.

Then Emily brushed her teeth, set her fringe on its large roller and climbed into bed.

'Some day that thing will be thoroughly decluttered too,' Emily said, looking over at the large antique wardrobe in the corner of her bedroom. 'Some day I'll be in just the right mood to give it a proper clear-out.'

The wardrobe had been the inspiration for the

decor in Emily's bedroom, even though she never opened its doors any more. The navy-blue walls and the white carpet made the wardrobe look as if it were standing outside in the snow on a winter's night. Emily didn't know why this idea pleased her so much; it just did.

She switched off her bedside lamp, curled up into a tight ball and waited for sleep to come. But despite the long drive that morning to the Doll's House and all the editing work she'd done in the afternoon (and the pizza that she'd eaten) she could not sleep. Emily sat up in bed and stared at the imposing wardrobe in the corner of her bedroom. A huge thing, it was part of the fittings and furnishings in Emily's rented flat. Emily suspected the waxed oak wardrobe might be worth a lot of money because it had some very intricate carving and a bevelled mirror on the door front. But no doubt it had been so difficult getting it up three flights of stairs in the first place, the landlord had just decided to leave it there. And Emily had promptly filled it with all the things she didn't wear any more. The very day she'd moved in, she'd filled it to the brim and turned the key in the lock. And in doing so, she'd also put an awful lot of painful memories into hibernation.

'Is this why I feel so stuck? Have I got too much emotional baggage? And too much physical baggage stuffed into that thing over there?' she asked herself. Her voice sounded very small and vulnerable in the witching hour between midnight and one. 'Is that why I never go on dates any more? Why I never make plans for the weekend?

Why I never go home for Christmas?'

She suddenly felt alone in a way she never had before.

'But this is what I wanted. This is it,' she reminded herself. 'This is my life. This is the path that I chose for myself. Remember that. An independent, single girl working in magazine publishing in the coolest city in the world – with no ties, no responsibilities, my own car, my own flat and my own rules.'

The wardrobe stood solid and silent in the corner, not giving her any clue as to what she should do next.

'Isn't it a pity the wardrobe isn't haunted or something?' Emily said then. 'I bet it would have a few interesting stories to tell...'

She got out of bed and ventured across the soft white carpet in her bare feet. Her fingers fastened around the tiny bronze key in the door. It felt icy cold to the touch. Emily could detect the faint aroma of ancient beeswax. Maybe she could reach in and take one thing out? Just one single, solitary item – any item at all. And she could add it to her pile of boxes for the charity shop and she'd be one step closer to becoming unstuck? But her hand remained frozen and the impulse passed.

'I can't do it,' she said. 'Not yet, not yet.'

And so she went sadly back to bed and forced herself to go to sleep.

In the middle of the night Emily's mobile phone began to ring.

'Hello?' She yawned.

'Emily, it's me. Are you awake?'

Well, she was now.

'Arabella, are you okay? What on earth's happened?'

'Nothing's happened, but I'm really fed up. It's David. He didn't show up for the IVF appointment.'

'Are you serious? Did he have to work late?' Emily asked, sitting up in bed.

'He sent me a text to say there was an emergency in their Hong Kong office, but I didn't believe him.'

'No? Why didn't you?'

'Instinct, Emily. Just a woman's instinct.'

'So did you have the consultation, anyway?'

'No, I was far too upset to go ahead with it on my own. I ran out of the place in floods of tears when I got his text. They'll think I'm crazy now. They'll probably ban me from having IVF.' Arabella began to sob down the phone.

'Arabella ... you poor thing. Is David not there with you now?' Emily asked.

'No, we had a massive fight. He said he couldn't bear to spend one more Christmas with me. He said I was obsessive and nagging and he couldn't stand it any more.'

'He said that? But that must have been terrible for you, coming on top of the missed consultation and everything.'

'Oh, I went berserk. I lost my temper and slapped his face. He's gone to a hotel, but he won't say which one. And he's switched off his mobile phone. I've been crying for hours.'

'Arabella, I'm so sorry.'

29

'That man. He's been so difficult recently.'

'What do you mean?' Emily asked, pushing a strand of hair out of her eyes and trying to see her clock in the dark. She could never remember her phone showed the time.

'He snaps at me constantly. He has no sympathy for me when my period arrives each month and I cry because I'm not pregnant yet. He used to send me flowers and take me out for dinner and spoil me with chocolates and perfume and little gifts on my pillow, but not any more.'

'Well, maybe it's the recession? Maybe he's distracted by work?'

'Maybe,' Arabella admitted. She rarely asked David specific questions about his work.

'He's responsible for an awful lot of money, isn't he?'

'Yes, though it's not all that high-risk any more, I don't think. They mostly handle property port-folios these days in his department. Of course, David saw the crash coming and recession-proofed his assets while everybody else was still swilling Bolly in the strip clubs. I could throttle him, actually, for not coming to the clinic. I felt so humiliated. No wonder I'm not pregnant yet if this is his attitude. I'm not sure he even wants to have a baby with me any more, to be honest.'

'I'm sure he does, Arabella. I'm sure you're just imagining it because things have been pretty stressed lately. Look, are you okay on your own or do you want me to come over and keep you company? It'd be no trouble for me to nip over.'

'No, I'll be okay. I'm looking through some old magazines and eating an entire apple pie.'

'Are you sure you don't want me to come over? I don't mind.'

'No, I'll be fine – and it's snowing again too. The roads might be treacherous.'

'Look, tomorrow is Saturday. Will we meet up for an early lunch?'

'Were you not planning anything else?'

'Not really, I'm just taking some stuff to my local charity shop.'

'What stuff?' Arabella asked. Not that she really cared. She just wanted to keep Emily on the phone for another little while.

'Just some odds and ends,' Emily said, beginning to perspire at the back of her neck. She always did that when she was nervous. 'Nothing significant, just a few boxes of really ancient bits and bobs.'

'Shall I come to yours tomorrow and give you a lift? My car boot is much bigger than yours.'

'No, please don't do that.'

'But why can't I help you, Emily? I'd like to help.'

'I want to do it myself. It's a Zen thing, I read about it in a magazine.'

'What magazine was that? Are we missing a feature idea here?'

'I can't remember what the magazine was called,' she said at once. 'But the feature said it was very soothing for the soul to de-clutter one room or memory at a time, and to fill and seal one box at a time. You know, so you won't feel wobbled by losing too much stuff at once?'

'Yes, I see,' Arabella said flatly.

Emily thought she sounded rather put out, and

she felt guilty all over again about giving away Arabella's generous gifts.

'You have to do it by yourself because it's symbolic, do you see? It means you are responsible for de-cluttering your emotions at the same time. A lot of nonsense, no doubt, but you know me – I'm a sucker for these things.'

'No, it all sounds very sweet. Although, personally, I'd settle for better storage. Please try and remember the name of that magazine, won't you? I'd love to read the article in full.'

'Okay,' Emily lied. 'Though I think it might have been an imported magazine, actually. Or a really old one I saw at the dentist's. What will you say to David tomorrow when he comes home?'

'I don't know, I might go away by myself for a few days. I need to stop thinking about babies for a little while before I go completely mad.'

'Do you think it's wise to take off in the middle of a domestic?'

'Yes, why not? If David can swan off whenever it suits him then so can I. I've got three days' worth of spa vouchers in my handbag. So I can stay away for three days, if I fancy. Teach that husband of mine a lesson. He takes me for granted, that's the truth of it. He thinks I'll always be here for him – basically, because I always *have* been here for him.'

'Well, that's up to you, Arabella.'

'Emily, that's a bit of a lukewarm attitude, I must say. I didn't expect you of all people to go and take his side. You sound just like my dreary old dragon of a mother, if you must know. She's been telling me for years to take a career break and have a baby, or else David would leave me. She never listened to me when I told her that David didn't want us to have children before we'd got a good whack of the mortgage paid off. But what would my mother know about anything? She describes my career as *messing about with pamphlets*.'

'Look, I'm sorry. You know I'm completely on your side, Arabella. It's just that I'm not very good at knowing what to say in these situations. And you know what happened with me and Alex, what a total and absolute fiasco that was. Right up until the wedding was cancelled, I thought he was the love of my life. Just goes to show you what a fool I am where love is concerned.'

'You're not a fool.'

'Well, really, the last thing I should be doing is giving anyone advice on relationships.'

'I think you're very wise, actually,' Arabella said kindly.

'But I'd die if you took any heed of my opinion and then it turned out to be the wrong thing to do, that's all,' Emily said.

'That's okay, darling, I do understand. You've had your own troubles, nobody can say you haven't. But it would help if you called David a selfish little toad every now and then – and used his full name too.'

'Okay. Mr David Harrington is a selfish little toad. Fact.'

'Ha! He is a toad, isn't be? Thanks a million for your support. You know what, Emily? I know I'm a bit tipsy here but I was half considering just having an affair or even a one-night stand with a good-looking younger man.'

'No comment, even though you're my dearest friend. You're on your own with this one.'

'No, listen. We had all the tests two years ago, David and me. And there's nothing wrong with me. And there's nothing wrong with him. So I think it's a Zen thing. You know, like in that magazine you were reading? I think we're both too stubborn, too Alpha in our personalities. And that's why our genes can't combine. Because neither set of genes wants to make the first move.'

'I'm not sure it works that way.'

'And David's so strange these days. He's distracted all the time, checking his phone constantly for messages and worrying far too much about work, in my humble opinion.'

'I'd really think twice before doing anything too dramatic, seriously I would, Arabella.'

'But I'm thirty-seven, Emily. Time is running out for me. It's a miracle the clinic even agreed to see me at all. Mind you, we're willing to pay anything they ask – so maybe that helps a little?'

'Well, listen, really and truly it's your decision to make. I won't breathe a word of this to anyone, you can be sure of that. And you shouldn't tell anybody else either. Just in case David finds out you were even thinking about being unfaithful to him, and that leads to another argument. I'm sure you two will be madly in love again by this time tomorrow, in any case. You'll probably be cross with me for calling him a toad.'

'I don't know if we will make up. I just keep thinking I should stop dithering and take affirmative action. The guy who works in our local petrol station is quite sexy.'

'Is he gorgeous? What's he like?' Emily said, trying to inject some humour into the conversation.

'He's about nineteen years of age for starters. He's got lovely firm arms in that red T-shirt they have to wear. I bet he'd have no trouble whatsoever getting a girl pregnant. I'd love to see him naked, actually. I haven't seen a naked man in ever such a long time. You know, properly gloriously completely naked? I don't count having a quickie with David, with his T-shirt on and his shorts around his ankles, as seeing a man properly naked. I want to be swept away, Emily, instead of just begging for crumbs.'

'Oh, Arabella, what am I going to do with you?'

'I don't know. Last night I dreamed about the guy from the petrol station. I dreamed that I went straight in there – and propositioned him in broad daylight. Just told him I wanted a baby, and could he please oblige me? There was nobody around, and it was a gorgeous sunny day. So we just kissed and then lay down in the flower bed and got right on with it. And five minutes later, what do you know? I'm on my way to being a mother.'

'You really are a closet hussy,' Emily said affectionately.

'I know, I know. But does it really matter who the father is? It's only a little tadpole, when all's said and done. Men are so arrogant, aren't they? We women are the ones who have to suffer with IVF injections and morning sickness and epidurals and childbirth and C-sections and breastfeeding and bleeding nipples. All they have to do

35

is make love to us.'

'Yes, but what if David decides to have a DNA test done some day, if the baby turns out to be a gorgeous male model or is no good at mathematics? I don't think he'd think it was just a tadpole – and not care whose. Men tend to care rather a lot about DNA, don't they? I wouldn't want him to walk out on you.'

'I never thought of that.'

'Lucky you have me, then,' Emily said, 'to do all the worrying for you.'

'You're so sensible, Emily.'

'I know, it's a gift,' Emily said sarcastically. She wished she could be more carefree sometimes.

'And also a curse. Am I right?' Arabella said. She was nothing if not perceptive.

'Yes, sometimes it is a curse,' Emily admitted. 'Look, I'll try and get some sleep now. And when you've dropped off your Zen-box things to the charity shop tomorrow, will you call me? And I'll meet you at the McDonald's near your flat.'

'Do you really mean that?' Emily was incredulous. 'McDonald's? As in fried food?'

'Yes, I fancy a dirty great double cheeseburger with pickles and fries and a strawberry milkshake. Sometimes I get tired of rabbit food and white meat and all the things that are supposed to help me conceive. I just want a good old burger dripping grease and melted cheese all down my chin.'

'I know what you mean. I had a massive pizza tonight. Listen, Arabella, you must get some sleep now. I think a good night's sleep would do you the power of good. See you tomorrow, then?'

'Yes, call me when you get back from the charity

shop. Yes?'

'Okay. Goodnight, Arabella.'

'Goodnight, Emily. And thanks for listening. It means a lot.'

'Don't mention it. What are friends for?'

Emily stayed sitting up in bed for a while afterwards. She knew she would never get to sleep now that she was thinking about Arabella. And she was hungry again too. The pizza must have increased her appetite, she thought to herself. Pulling on warm socks and her fleece, she padded into the kitchen to prepare baked beans on toast. She might as well go back to her usual diet before she got a hankering for the fancy stuff. David and Arabella Harrington might be able to afford the finer things in life. But she definitely couldn't. Not when she still had a cancelled wedding to pay for. An absolute fortune spent on a Vera Wang dress and all the trimmings – and all she'd got for her trouble was an anxiety attack in the church porch.

Oh the shame of it...

3. Donations Urgently Required

It was Christmas Eve. It was still snowing. People were beginning to tire of the beauty of their all-white cityscape and instead spent a lot of time moaning about frozen pipes, slippery pathways and the soaring cost of heating bills. Emily's attic apartment felt as cold as the North Pole, and the accumulated snow on the skylights was blocking out almost all the daylight from her bedroom. Still, she was determined to press on with her de-cluttering project. And maybe somebody in the neighbourhood would be glad of her cast-offs this Christmas. Emily picked up the first box and took a deep breath.

'Never mind my fake Zen theory,' she said to herself. 'If Arabella ever finds out I gave all this stuff away, she'll never speak to me again.'

But what was the use of having a pasta maker the size of a mangle, and a complicated coffee maker, and all of these lovely high-heeled shoes if she was never going to use any of them?

'Come on, then. Let's do it,' she said, pulling the door closed behind her and going carefully down the dimly lit stairs. 'I dare say Arabella has more on her mind than what I do in my spare time. With luck she's forgotten about most of these gifts, anyway.'

The snow on the path outside had been pounded to a slush-coloured blanket. The parking spaces for the flats were just off the main road and, luckily, all the principal roads in Emily's neighbourhood had been gritted. She said a brief hello to the owner of the hair salon next door.

'Merry Christmas, you lot.'

'Merry Christmas, Emily. How are you?'

'I'm great. The salon looks even more gorgeous with that tree in the window.'

'Thanks. See you soon?'

'You bet.'

The *Rock & Fairy* had become a bit of a fashion destination ever since it had opened for business a year earlier. And quite a few A-list celebrities had been seen gracing the black leather chairs. The gorgeous mirrors were a real talking point, and that chandelier with its rainbow-coloured droplets was just so divine. Emily vowed to treat herself to a new hairstyle in the New Year.

The car started first time, and Emily could have kissed the steering wheel. There wasn't much traffic as many of the usual Christmas Eve shoppers had opted to stay in bed. So in less than five minutes, Emily was pulling up right outside the charity shop. The lights were on, and she could see a young man busily sawing pieces of wood. He had his back to her, so all she could make out was a very nice bum and a pair of long legs in black combats. The ancient shelves in the shop were only half filled with bric-a-brac. There was a poster in the window. It said: DONATIONS URGENTLY REQUIRED.

'Good, then,' Emily said, feeling suddenly quite virtuous and smug.

Through force of habit she checked her make-up in the rear-view mirror and then hopped out of the car, fetching her box from the back seat and closing the car door with one elbow. The box was very heavy, but she managed to lock her car and open the shop door without too much trouble.

'Hi there,' she said cheerfully as the door pinged shut behind her.

'Be right with you,' the man said, setting down his saw. Then he straightened up and turned to face her.

'Hi again,' Emily said, blushing furiously. For if Arabella were ever to set eyes on this specimen of male beauty, she would have him stripped and tied to her bedposts without further delay. And not untie him until it was confirmed by a doctor that she was expecting triplets.

He was utterly gorgeous. Broad shoulders, narrow waist, mischievous blue eyes, tousled blond hair. He was wearing a washed-out rugby shirt with the collar turned up in a casual way. He looked posh. And his nose was slightly dented, so maybe he was an actual rugby player, Emily thought to herself. But then, if he were really a posh rugby type, why would he be sawing wood in a shabby little charity shop on a freezing cold Christmas Eve?

'I see you've got something for me?' he said, nodding at Emily's box of donations.

'Yes, yes, I've been tidying up,' Emily said, setting the box on the counter.

'Thanks a million, yeah. A designer pasta maker ... nice one, thanks. There's some great stuff here. Did you see our poster or something?'

'No, I just felt like de-cluttering,' Emily admitted. 'But now you mention it, I'm sure you'll be swamped with unwanted gifts in the very near future.'

'Hope so. Or maybe people will just take everything back to the shops for a refund. You know, with the recession and everything?'

'Yes, well, maybe they'd feel better giving stuff to charity. What charity are you supporting here, by the way?'

'Retired horses, it is. Some lovely old horses – about thirty of them, so far – and it costs an absolute fortune in vets' bills. We haven't got the shop sign up yet. We only opened for business three months ago.'

'But I thought this shop was always here?' Emily said, gazing around at the various shelves. Most had warped slightly and turned yellow with age.

'It has always been here in one form or another, yes. But my sister has taken over the lease now,' the man explained. 'And she's in the process of setting up her own charity. Sylvia runs a stable for retired horses – it's all her project, really. I'm just helping her out for a while and putting up the new shelving, and so on.'

'I see.'

'Yes, I'm going to take down all these tragic old things and put up some funky cube-type arrangements. You won't know this shop in a few months' time. Sylvia's got big plans for it.'

'Sounds great. Well, good luck with the shop ... and merry Christmas,' Emily said, backing reluctantly to the door. She wanted to stay longer and go on gazing at this divine vision of a man, but

41

she couldn't think of any legitimate reason for hanging around – unless she was suddenly to develop an acute interest in cube shelving.

'Same to you,' he said, smiling warmly at her.

They stood looking at one another, neither one wanting to be the first person to say goodbye.

'I've got some more boxes at home, if you'd like them?' Emily said in a flash of inspiration.

'Sure, the more the merrier,' he said.

'I'll drop them off later today, then,' Emily told him. She had one hand on the door handle.

'Thanks again. I'm going to stay open until six. I'm Dylan,' he said.

'Okay, right. And I'm Emily.'

'See you later, then, Emily,' he said, beginning to unpack the box. He lifted out a pair of gemstone-encrusted stilettos and raised one eyebrow. 'And if I don't see you again before Christmas ... well, merry Christmas.'

'Yes, merry Christmas.'

But she definitely hoped she'd be seeing him again, she thought to herself.

'Nice shoes,' he laughed.

'I didn't pick them myself. They were gifts from a dear friend. Bye for now,' she blushed.

Emily slipped out of the shop and went tripping giddily to her car. She could barely feel the cold wind snapping at her heels. It wasn't often she felt so attracted to a man. Of course, he was unbelievably good-looking. But there was more to it than that. Clearly he had a strong social conscience, working in a little charity shop in the suburbs when he could have been a model, or something much more ambitious – a stockbroker, or whatever. It was nice to fancy a man again after all that had happened with Alex, she thought to herself. It was nice to know she might be getting over her very major romantic setback. Even if it was hopeless – knowing her luck, Dylan would turn out to be married, engaged, in love with an old flame, or gay. Still, there was no harm in getting rid of those other boxes. The shop was clearly in dire need of new donations. Oh, she was so transparent! She'd wait until later on that afternoon, she decided.

No need to go back straight away and risk looking totally desperate.

By the time Emily returned at four o'clock, the light in the sky was beginning to fade. She'd had lunch in McDonald's with Arabella, who was still fuming about her stubborn husband David decamping to a mystery hotel. For a full ninety minutes Emily had had to console poor Arabella as she ranted and raved about how it was okay for David to dither and dally about making a baby, but how every single day that passed without a pregnancy was a huge setback for her. And then Arabella had flirted shamelessly with the mortified teenage boys working behind the counter, going up several times to ask for extra sachets of sugar. And they weren't even having tea. In the end Emily had had to beg her boss to behave herself.

After lunch Emily had gone home and relaxed in a bubble bath. And simply daydreamed away the afternoon, imagining Dylan and herself strolling along a beach somewhere with the sun

43

beating down on them. Somewhere very far away from this endless London winter. Then she'd blow-dried her hair into a sleek ponytail, curled her fringe, painted her nails, applied full make-up and swapped her old anorak for a smart denim jacket with a soft pink beret and matching scarf.

She carried the rest of the boxes down to her car and loaded them into the boot. It took ages to make everything fit. She'd have liked to just pile it all up on the back seat, but she was wary of an opportunist thief smashing the window and leaving her with the hassle of booking the car in for repair at the height of the breakdown season. Sometimes it *is* a curse being so sensible, she thought to herself. Then she drove back to Dylan's shop with her heart racing, her mouth going dry and her neck perspiring like a honey roast ham.

'Hello again,' she said lightly.

'Hey, it's my lucky charm come back to me,' he smiled.

'What did you say?'

'All that stuff you brought in this morning, I've sold it.'

'All of it? Even the shoes?'

'Yes.'

'Wow.'

'Yes, wow. It all seemed to be in good working order, so I set it in the window and within two hours it was sold. We've made over two hundred pounds. You really should have put it on eBay.'

'That's okay. But I didn't think you'd sell the shoes so quickly. They were, um, quite a niche size.'

Dylan threw back his head and laughed out

loud. 'Niche, did you say? Size nine? Yes, I did notice.'

'Just call me Bigfoot,' Emily said, and she went bright red.

Dylan buckled up with laughter. 'You'll be enjoying this snowy weather, then?' he spluttered.

Emily couldn't help laughing too. 'Yes, I'm feeling right at home in these blizzards,' she wheezed.

'What's wrong with being a size nine, anyway? You're really tall, aren't you? What height are you? Five ten?'

'Yes. Five ten.'

'Well, then. Stands to reason, doesn't it? You'd look all wrong with tiny feet. And it's got to be fun leaving your footprints in the snow and keeping the Bigfoot hunters guessing...'

'Very funny, but who bought the shoes? Was it a transvestite?'

'Actually, yes, it was. He said he had lots of Christmas parties to go to, and a posh wedding on Boxing Day.'

'Are you kidding me?'

'No, he took the lot. Five pairs of designer shoes for twenty quid each. He said his guardian angel must have guided him down this street today.'

'But they were all covered in gemstones and, um, very sparkly.'

'Yes, I know. He was almost crying with joy.'

'Well, I'm very happy for him, then. Actually, Dylan, would you mind helping me in with the rest of my clutter? So sorry to ask. Only I've nearly done my back in, going up and down the stairs to my flat. My car is right outside the shop.'

'Of course, no problem, just give me one second.' He opened a narrow door behind the counter. 'Sylvia, I'm nipping outside for a minute,' he called.

A bossy-looking girl with a bleached-blonde pixie cut came bustling into the shop, carrying a tray with two mugs of tea on it and a packet of pink wafer biscuits.

'Hello,' she said, plonking the tray down on the counter.

'Emily, this is my sister, Sylvia. Sylvia, this is Emily, one of our chief patrons.'

'Hi, Emily,' Sylvia said kindly. 'Thanks so much for your very valuable support. Every little helps – and your donations helped a lot. Any sign of that plumber yet, Dylan?'

'Not yet,' Dylan said

'He's an hour late,' Sylvia declared. 'Pipe's dripping all over my fresh paintwork!'

'Look, I just came to drop off some more stuff,' Emily explained. And then wondered why she'd said something so silly. For why else would she be standing in a charity shop, chatting to a man she didn't know? 'I ... um ... I don't want to keep you back, but I've six more boxes with me.'

'Let me,' Sylvia said, already halfway to the door. 'I could do with some fresh air. That storeroom has a whiff of mould in it. Can I have your car keys, Emily?'

Emily barely had time to say yes, before Sylvia took them and breezed out of the door. Within seconds she was back, carrying not one but three boxes.

'Five years of motherhood,' she laughed, seeing

Emily's chin drop. 'I've got arms on me like a lumberjack.' Soon she had the other three boxes stored safely behind the counter. 'There's your keys back, thanks. Have my tea,' she said brightly. 'By way of thanks. It's not easy finding good-quality donations at this time of year. And I'm told it doesn't get much better in January – mostly bath salts and novelty socks.'

Emily looked longingly at the tea and biscuits, and even more longingly at Dylan's perfect lips and his lovely broad shoulders, but then decided with great reluctance that she should let him and his sister get on with their work. They'd be closing the shop soon, anyway, and heading for home. Suddenly Emily felt rather melancholy that she had nobody to share Christmas Eve with – or, indeed, Christmas Day.

'Listen, I'd love to stay and chat. But I've loads of things to do,' she lied, 'and I'm sure you have too. So anyway... I hope you sell the rest of that stuff as easily as the first lot. Bye, then.'

'Do drop by again, won't you?' Dylan said, offering his hand for Emily to shake. 'I'd like to know the hunters haven't got to you.'

'What are you talking about?' Sylvia said, mystified.

'Nothing; it's a secret,' Dylan told her.

Emily's heart turned over as she placed her hand in his and felt his warm fingers close around hers. The skin on the back of Dylan's hand felt incredibly soft, covered with a delicious layer of translucent blond hairs.

'Maybe I will drop by sometime,' Emily said.

'Yes, you've got to see how we do this place up,'

he added.

'Drop by any time,' Sylvia said knowingly.

Dylan reluctantly let go of Emily's hand.

'Okay, then. See you soon,' Emily said as she left.

'Merry Christmas,' Dylan said.

'Yes, merry Christmas,' Emily replied.

Sylvia and Dylan exchanged knowing glances. Sylvia winked at Dylan, and he laughed and shrugged his shoulders.

Later that evening Emily lay on her sofa, wondering what Sylvia's little wink had meant. Did every woman who came anywhere near Dylan end up falling hopelessly in love with him? Did Sylvia spend half her life talking Dylan's ex-girlfriends down off various window sills? Or had Sylvia simply been aware of a little spark of mutual attraction in the air? Emily wasn't sure. But she sensed they were good people, and that took away some of the niggling fear that Sylvia and Dylan had been laughing at her instead of with her.

At nine o'clock Emily's mobile phone rang.

To her amazement it was Dylan.

'Emily? I hope you don't mind me calling you on Christmas Eve,' he said quickly.

'Dylan? Well, no, of course I don't mind. But how did you find my number?'

'Sylvia found your business card in one of those handbags you donated.'

'I thought I'd emptied them all out.'

'You did; it was in a side pocket.'

'Sorry,' Emily said, feeling embarrassed and yet

hugely pleased at the same time.

'No need to apologize. I was going to ask you for your number today, anyway. But you left the shop so quickly that I didn't get the chance. I'm calling to ask if you'd likc to have a drink with me sometime.'

'Oh, now let me see,' she said, feeling slightly flustered.

'I mean, obviously, if you're not already seeing somebody? And if you're not interested ... then I'm sorry for bothering you.'

'No, it's no bother.'

'It's just, I thought it would be nice to make some new friends.'

'New friends ... yes, that'd be ... well, nice.'

'I mean, I'm asking you out on a date. Yes? But if you'd rather not go on a date with me, then maybe we can still be friends – or, at least, acquaintances? I mean, I'd really like to stay in touch with you. If that's okay?'

'Well, that'd be lovely. I mean, yes ... thanks.'

'Why don't you come to the shop for a coffee?' Dylan said, detecting a hint of reticence in Emily's voice. 'Sylvia can chaperone us. As you can see, she's a real no-nonsense sort. She won't put up with any funny business, so I won't be pouncing on you or anything. Not unless you want me to,' he added playfully.

For a moment Emily was terrified. She'd love to go on a date with Dylan. Of course she would. But what would happen if it turned out to be a proper falling-in-love date, and then a proper grown-up relationship? Emily wasn't sure she was ready for that. Not after Alex had left her standing at the altar the year before. The humiliation of that day was still seared into her soul. Or would she make a fool of herself if it turned out that Dylan only wanted a casual sort of romance? Would she be able to think of a single thing to say on their date? Would she be able to keep up the façade of the strong, independent woman for more than five minutes?

'Emily, are you still there?'

'Yes, sorry, I was thinking.'

'Were you thinking yes or no?'

'I was thinking ... maybe.'

'Maybe you'll call in next Saturday?'

'Next Saturday?'

'Well, yes. I presume you'll be working all week? It says on your card that you're the chief features writer for *Sylish Living*.'

'Yes, that's right.'

'Hey, that sounds pretty impressive.'

'Um, thanks.'

'And, of course, I'm sure you have plans for Christmas Day tomorrow, and so on? So shall we say the first Saturday after Christmas?'

Emily closed her eyes. She didn't have a single plan for Christmas Day, but Dylan didn't have to know that. She'd give her parents a quick call, of course. But that was about it. For the rest of the day it'd just be herself and her Christmas tree, a ready meal and the *Radio Times*.

'Okay, then,' she heard herself saying. 'I'll see you, then.'

'Great. Bye, Emily.'

'Bye, Dylan.'

Emily shut off her phone and went into the

50

bedroom. She sat down gently on her unmade bed and looked pointedly at the wardrobe.

'Yes, I know,' she told it. 'I'm not quite ready yet. But if I don't do something soon, I never will be ready. I don't have to throw myself at him, you know. I'll just go along to the shop for an innocent cup of coffee and see what happens. And if he turns out to be as lovely as he looks, that'll be brilliant. And if he turns out to be a let-down ... well, I'll just deal with it, okay?'

She crossed the floor and turned the small bronze key in the wardrobe lock. With a tiny squeak the door opened. Inside, folded neatly into a hundred layers like a cross-section diagram in a geography book, were all the clothes and keepsakes that were holding Emily back. Things she hadn't looked at in years. She could almost smell the disappointment lingering on everything like brick dust or mothballs. So many things, going all the way back to her insular childhood on a Belfast estate. She was thirty years old, she reminded herself. A milestone year. Surely she was not going to let a milestone year go by without at least making some changes to her safe (but stuck) life? And was it better to be safe and stuck or vulnerable and free?

A life coach would have described Emily as a butterfly. But was she a cowardly butterfly that was going to remain safely in her little glass box for ever? Or was she going to bravely take flight up into the bright blue sky, with all the possibilities – both good and bad – that might await her there?

Emily closed the door again and went to bed.

51

She listened to the radio for company and was glad she hadn't told Dylan she'd be on her own for Christmas. It was too soon to burden him with her various little family anecdotes, none of them pleasant.

Emily was still awake and thinking about Dylan when Christmas morning dawned. She got up, went into the sitting room and switched on the lights on her pretty tree. She made a cup of hot chocolate and listened to a carol service on the radio. She rang her parents in Belfast to wish them a merry Christmas, but nobody answered the phone – even though she let it ring for ages and ages before she gave up. Wondering what might have happened to her flaky mother and father, Emily opened the sitting-room curtains to find it was snowing heavily, yet again.

'Oh, I don't believe it,' she murmured. 'Not more snow! Will this winter never end?'

4. Tea and Biscuits

Dylan set the two mugs on the counter and offered Emily a broken biscuit.

'Sorry, I dropped the packet on the floor,' he said.

'Better than dropping the tea on the floor,' she replied.

'So, Emily, is that a trace of an Irish accent you've got there?' Dylan asked brightly.

Emily laughed in spite of her nerves. She was wearing skinny jeans, brown boots and her warmest jacket.

'It's a Belfast accent,' she said carefully. 'That's in *Northern* Ireland, by the way.'

'Um, I know where Belfast is. I'm not completely thick, you know.'

'You'd be surprised how many people don't know where Belfast is on the map. And then they start all this *top of the morning* stuff. We don't say *top of the morning* in the north of Ireland. I'm not sure they say it in the south either, mind you. Maybe it's just something that American film makers think we say? So then I remind them that I'm from Northern Ireland and they start shouting *No Surrender!* into my face – you know, like Ian Paisley? We're not all like that. Actually, most of us are very shy and softly spoken. It's only a handful of nutters and narcissists that give us all a bad name. And now I'm rambling again. Anyway,

53

I thought I was doing a great job of covering up my accent.'

'It's not on a par with that Paisley chap,' Dylan agreed. 'You're not scaring the living daylights out of me, I'll give you that. But it's still there. It's very nice, actually.'

'Ha, you don't expect me to believe that, do you?'

'Of course I do.'

'I don't like my accent.'

'You should. It is *way* nicer than the LA whine that's taking over the planet these days, not to mention our very own Essex cackle.'

'You say the nicest things, Dylan. But then again, that's easy for you to say because your accent is nice and clear and easy to understand. And people don't make fun of it all the time.'

'Fair point,' he had to admit.

'If you're interested in accents, I can tell you that every neighbourhood in Northern Ireland has its own very distinct accent. Especially in Belfast – the accent changes slightly with every street corner. I can usually tell a lot about a person by the way they pronounce certain words. As well as their appearance, obviously...'

'Can you really?'

'Yes, I can.'

'What's it like over there? I've never been to Ireland. Sorry ... Northern Ireland.'

'It's a very complicated society in many ways. People grow up with a heightened sense of danger. Their trouble radar is never switched off – even nowadays. Although most of the really scary stuff ended over a decade ago.'

'But you live in London now, yes?'

'Yes. I left Belfast for good when I was eighteen.'

'Why? Was it for work?'

'Yes, mainly for work. But I longed for the anonymity of London. Back home everybody knows everybody else, and it's a bit claustrophobic.'

'Same here. I'm from a little village in Surrey, called Appleton.'

Emily and Dylan were sitting on two old chairs in the charity shop. Dylan had bought a packet of chocolate biscuits in honour of Emily's visit. But he'd dropped them twice on the way back from the shop and consequently most of the biscuits were in pieces.

'What can you deduce about me?' Dylan asked, still fascinated by Emily's strange talent. 'I know I'm not from Belfast. But have a try, anyway.'

'You won't be offended?' Emily asked carefully.

'I promise,' he said firmly.

'Well, from your accent and the rugby-shirt collar being turned up, I'm guessing you're from a privileged background. So that makes you middle class at the very least. Though you're very self-assured – and I mean that in a nice way – so I'd put money on you being upper middle class. Public school, even. You don't jump every time the door opens, so that means you were generally relaxed as a child. And that leads me to think your parents were and still are happily married. You're very laid-back in the company of women, and you don't mind making the tea and handing out the biscuits, so I'd say you have at least three sisters. And your shabby trainers suggest you just want a simple life, which is why you're working in a charity shop when everything about you indicates a good solid education and that you really ought to be working in a much better place than this. I know you said you were helping Sylvia out for a while, but I think you enjoy being here. You could probably have paid a carpenter to put up the shelves, after all.'

'That's amazing,' Dylan breathed slowly. 'It's all true. I have three sisters. My parents are dairy farmers with a bit of land around Appleton. My surname is Shawcross, by the way. And I still play rugby back home with the village team. I'm the skipper. Anyway, you're very clever.'

'Thank you,' Emily said, taking a little bow. 'I told you we were a nosy bunch in Northern Ireland. I also feel duty-bound to tell you I was baptized a Catholic, but I'm not religious any more. And I have no interest in politics – they're all as bad as each other in my book.'

'Okay,' he laughed. 'And I'm C of E. And I did once vote Tory, but only because the local candidate promised to save our village post office.'

'And did he?'

'Yes, he did, to give the guy his dues. But then there was an armed robbery. The owner of the post office had a nervous breakdown and moved to Cyprus. And now the post office is a branch of Cath Kidston.'

'Ah well, at least you'll never be stuck for a floral tea towel. Listen, I hope you don't think I'm neurotic mentioning religion like that? I just don't care for labels, you see. And I like to get all that sort of thing over and done with, when I meet a new person. Otherwise I'll only worry about saying the wrong thing. Or they might worry about saying the wrong thing to me. I'm pretty okay with most people – unless they're about to stab me.'

'Same here. So tell me about your family. Are you from a big Irish clan? Are there ten more of you back home – all girls, and all as gorgeous as you?'

'I'm very flattered, but how dare you suggest I have ten siblings,' Emily said mock-indignantly. 'There haven't been any really big Irish families since the 1940s. Believe it or not, we have heard of family planning these days. All those stories about cutting up flour sacks to make sheets were not an urban myth. I'm an only child, as it happens.'

'Are you, really? How unusual. I don't think I know very many only children.'

'Well, that's the situation. And I can't do anything about it now, I'm afraid.'

'It would have been nice to know there were some more girls like you in the world,' he said gallantly. 'You know, a few spares.'

'Very funny,' Emily said dryly. 'They certainly are getting their money's worth from whatever charm school they sent you to.'

'I'm joking,' Dylan laughed. 'So what do your parents do for a living?'

'They're retired,' Emily said quickly, helping herself to another broken biscuit.

'I'm sorry. Did I speak out of turn?' Dylan asked at once.

'No, please don't worry about it.'

'Only they must be far too young to be retired, surely? You're only, what, twenty-five?'

'I wish I was twenty-five. I'm thirty!'

'Well, you only look twenty-five to me. I'm thirty-two. It's just that I really like you, Emily. And I'm just dying to know everything about you. I take it you went home to Belfast for the holidays?'

Both Dylan and Emily were blushing furiously now. Dylan was wondering if he was coming on too strong to a girl he had just met. And how could Emily possibly tell Dylan she had spent Christmas Day on her own watching television, eating ready meals from M&S, and making ten phone calls to her parents that went unanswered?

'Look, my parents are a bit eccentric, that's all. Even by Belfast standards. And believe me, the acceptable standard for eccentricity is quite high over there.'

'So tell me about them. Please?'

'My mum left school at sixteen and worked in a sweet shop until she married my father when she was twenty. My dad worked for a bookmaker for a number of years, and after that he was a professional gambler. I don't think either of them ever felt particularly fulfilled. But then again, Belfast isn't exactly a career opportunity hotspot. And we're not very big on self-help and soul-searching either. That's it, really.'

'But you said they were eccentric. That all sounds reasonably normal to me, especially your mother being a full-time housewife.'

Emily bit her lip. How much could she sugar-coat the facts? she wondered. 'The truth is, my mum shops rather a lot.'

'A lot?' he said, puzzled. 'Like, more than the average woman?'

'Yes, much more than the average woman. An awful lot more.'

'Is she in actual fact a shoplifter?'

'No, she's not a thief. Thank the Lord!'

'Sorry for even thinking it. Do you mean she's a shopaholic?'

'Maybe I do.'

'Is she really a shopaholic?'

'Yes, she is.'

'I was only joking. Aren't all women shopaholics?' Dylan laughed.

'Not like my mum. She can spend an entire day browsing for one little thing – one candle or one packet of soup. She only comes home again when the shops are closing, and sometimes not even then. She window-shops until it gets dark.'

'Wow.'

'Yes, big wow. She's also a heavy smoker. And she likes a drink. That's pretty much my mother for you. Always shopping or smoking or having a wee sip.'

'You sound very sad when you talk about your mother.'

'We're not close,' Emily admitted. 'I was more or less reared on Kellogg's Corn Flakes, with the telly for company.' She laughed then, but the laughter didn't quite reach her eyes.

'What sort of things does your mum buy?'

'Do you really want to know?' Emily said.

'Yes, I'm totally into retail psychology. Can't you tell?' he laughed, indicating the shabby shelves

59

dotted with equal amounts of trash and treasure.

'Well, let me see. Ashtrays mostly – nice ones and novelty ones. Cups and saucers – preferably discontinued lines of fine bone china. She's very fond of leather belts and shoes, leather handbags and purses; she thinks having real leather accessories is a sign of good breeding. She also collects soap dishes, teapots, plant pots, egg cups, coasters, place mats and cutlery. And linen napkins and glass cruet sets. And small kitchen appliances...'

'Does she like giving dinner parties?' Dylan said.

'No, she's very antisocial,' Emily said matter-of-factly. 'She never cooks either. I have no idea why I'm telling you all this. It's sure to put you off me.'

'No, I think it sounds fascinating.'

Emily didn't tell Dylan that her mother had opted to visit a new department store in Belfast on the day that Emily had graduated from university. Or that she'd queued for seven hours to get into a big sale in Brown Thomas in Dublin on the day Emily was due to get married to Alex. Or that she owned over a hundred ashtrays but not a single picture frame with a photograph of Emily in it. Or that she'd been hospitalized three times during Emily's childhood when her drinking had spiralled out of control. No, there was no point in telling Dylan any of that, she decided, even if he did seem like the easiest person in the whole world to talk to. It was too soon to go making the big revelations. However, she did feel something in her heart wake up and begin to enjoy the attention that Dylan was paying her.

And she felt a sort of sadness too. For she knew now, in her innermost heart of hearts, that her mother would never change. She would never be the sort of devoted, clucking mother that Emily had always wanted her to be.

'How did you come to work for the magazine?' Dylan asked next.

'What? Sorry, I was miles away.'

'The magazine, how did you end up working there?'

'That was kind of a strange thing too, now you mention it. I was on the checkout in Marks & Spencer, and Arabella – that's my boss – was chatting on her mobile phone and she dropped her basket of shopping. Beetroot slices and red wine splattered all over her shoes! She was mortified, as well as reeking of vinegar and Merlot! And by the time I'd helped her pick everything up, and dried her off a bit, we'd got chatting. And it turns out she was looking for a new assistant. And we sort of clicked, so she gave me the job. And I've worked my way up from general dogsbody to chief features writer. So that's my story. My degree is in English.'

'Good for you. It must be great fun working on a magazine.'

'It's okay.'

'Oh, it must be really exciting sometimes.'

'Not *really* exciting. I meet the odd celebrity – "odd" being the operative word – but I love the work, it suits me. It's steady and predictable and I don't have all that much to worry about – just praying the car doesn't conk out when I'm ten miles down some tiny lane in Dorset. I'm a simple girl with simple tastes.'

'I don't believe that for one second.'

'I am.'

'Let's wait and see, shall we?'

For Dylan suspected there was a lot more to Emily than met the eye.

At that moment the door swung open. An old man wearing a tweed jacket came shuffling into the shop and wanted to know if they had any cloth caps for sale. His head was freezing, he told them, since he'd left his old cap on the bus by accident.

'It's your lucky day, sir.'

Dylan was able to show him a small selection from a drawer beneath the counter.

'Nice and clean they look,' the man said.

'These caps have all been dry-cleaned,' Dylan assured him. 'My sister is the owner manager here and she runs a tight ship, let me tell you.'

The man chose a cap and paid for it, delighted at the low price. 'Great job,' he said, putting the cap on and shuffling out again. 'I shall tell my mates about this place.'

'And another satisfied customer,' Dylan said happily.

'You're good at this retail lark,' Emily said, smiling at him. 'You make it feel like it's a real shop. I mean, not like a charity shop. There's no air of melancholy in here – you know, the way there is in most charity shops?'

'Thanks, Emily. I know the place isn't much to look at now, but one day soon it'll be a great attraction. That's what Sylvia reckons. She wants to focus mainly on vintage clothes eventually.

Obviously we need anything and everything right now to get started up, but then she's going to gradually phase out the bric-a-brac and sell only the good stuff.'

'Sounds amazing,' Emily said.

'Yes, amazing is the word I was thinking of too,' he said, looking very intently at Emily's face.

Emily had the strangest feeling Dylan was going to kiss her. He was gazing at her lips and she had a lovely, woozy feeling. Her eyes were almost closing in anticipation. He leaned in towards her and his breathing slowed right down. Emily's breathing, on the other hand, speeded up to such an extent she thought she was going to hyperventilate. His breath smelt of minty tooth-paste and chocolate biscuits. But just then Sylvia came bustling in through the door with another box of donated goods that she'd managed to collect from friends and family, and the romantic spell was broken.

'Hi there, you sweet little pair of lovebirds,' she teased.

'Don't worry, I am still on duty,' Dylan said, standing up and making a salute.

'Yes, he just sold a cloth cap,' Emily added in a weak voice.

'A cloth cap, you say? Ha, we're in the money at last,' Sylvia grinned.

Dylan went to help Sylvia carry her booty through to the storeroom. And Emily felt her lovely, woozy feeling slowly evaporate.

'I'd better be getting back,' Emily said, getting up and reaching for her coat. 'Thanks for the tea, Dylan.'

Sylvia smiled at them and then surveyed the two mismatched mugs and half-eaten packet of biscuits on the counter.

'Chocolate biscuits, I see? Broken biscuits – but they taste just as good, I suppose. He's very domesticated, isn't he?' Sylvia said proudly.

'I'm not the worst,' Dylan said at once.

'I never said you were,' Sylvia replied. 'I'm very impressed, actually.'

'May I call you tomorrow?' Dylan asked Emily.

'That would be lovely,' she smiled, then waved goodbye to her new friends.

On the way back to her car Emily wondered why she'd as good as told Dylan her own mother was mentally ill. Did she really have to mention the cruet sets? she wondered. Or state she was a non-practising Catholic? She must have sounded as if she were giving evidence in a court of law. She was an idiot! Why on earth was she such a rambling fool at times?

'I must really like him,' she said to herself. And at least she hadn't told him about her father, she thought sadly. Not yet, anyway. She drove home to her attic flat, feeling a mixture of euphoria and dread.

'I'm trying to act like a normal person,' she said firmly. 'I'm not exactly storming it, but at least I'm trying. He was going to kiss me, remember! He must have liked me!'

That night Emily opened the wardrobe door fully, and carefully took every item pertaining to her childhood out of it. Her tiny baptism gown, her Holy Communion dress and lace veil, her old

64

school blazer and ties, her tennis racket, 7 Barbie dolls, 3 teddy bears, 4 pairs of leather school shoes, 25 storybooks and a plastic carry-case containing 63 pop cassettes. All things her parents had bought for her, yes, but bought very reluctantly. Bless them, but they had found parenthood a bit of an ordeal, she thought sadly. Maybe the vast majority of parents found parenthood a bit of an ordeal, but they were smart enough never to admit it? Well, it was over now and high time she stopped blaming her parents and herself for not being the perfect family. That was all in the past now, and she had to look to the future. She packed all the things into the boot of her car and vowed to deliver them to the shop the following Monday, which was Dylan's day off. She wanted to help the shop get up and running, but she didn't want Dylan to think she was a cold person giving away her childhood things. It was just that she needed to give them away so that she could become ... well, unstuck.

She got into bed, leaving the curtains wide open, and spent ages just gazing out of the window. It was snowing again and the flakes were big and uneven, scurrying past her bedroom window as if they were all rushing to catch a bus. The wind howled through tiny gaps in the old wooden frames and made eerie moaning noises. Emily thought about Dylan and what he might be doing at that exact moment. She wondered, was he lying awake and thinking about her? She had forgotten to ask him where he lived, she realized. Perhaps he shared a house with some mates? She thought of her parents too, and shed a few guilty tears that she hadn't gone home for Christmas again this year. She could easily have forced herself to give them a couple of days of her time, just to cook a small turkey and put up a few decorations. It wouldn't have killed her, would it? No, it wouldn't have killed her. But she couldn't risk them pulling her back to Belfast with their hopelessness and their neediness, she told herself firmly. She didn't want to spend the next thirty years of her life acting as carer, cleaner and referee for the two of them. They didn't need a carer, but they'd soon get used to having one – that was Emily's worry. And that's exactly what might happen if she allowed herself to feel guilty, even for forty-eight hours. They were so useless, the pair of them. Sitting there watching the television for hours every night in the middle of a bizarre little nest of useless things, surrounded by the blue haze of her mother's cigarette smoke and a general air of under-achievement. Emily felt sick just thinking about the little house in west Belfast – especially when she compared it with all the gorgeous homes she got to photograph for the magazine.

'I know it's not fair to compare them with the millionaires of Mayfair. I know it's not fair to compare them with Dylan's parents. I know I'm a shallow, selfish, snobbish, mean and cruel cow,' she said to herself.

Then she thought of the little sliver of empty space at the top of her wardrobe, and it did feel as if she could breathe more easily. She felt that her heart was relaxing a little bit – it didn't feel quite so squashed any more.

Maybe there really was something Zen and em-powering about the simple act of de-cluttering? Maybe it was good for the soul to say goodbye to the past? Maybe it was a good thing to know you could give away the trappings of your past and still survive without them? Maybe you really could wipe the slate clean and start all over again?

And this time you'd be in charge – not your mad parents or your callous ex-boyfriend.

Emily snuggled down under the duvet and closed her eyes.

5. Bosoms and Buttons

Emily brought the tray of coffees over to Arabella's corner of the office and handed them out to the small group of freelance contributors and in-house staff. The office was stiflingly warm, but if they were to open a window now they might all expire of acute hypothermia within minutes. It seemed as if the snow would never stop falling.

'I'm sure Arabella will be here any minute,' Emily said briskly. 'She's probably stuck in a traffic jam somewhere. The traffic is a nightmare these days. Can I get anybody a biscuit?' she added, thinking briefly of Dylan and his Chocolate Digestives.

'Any decent ones, have you?' Jane asked, yawning. 'Don't trouble yourself if it's just a Rich Tea, mind – I won't bother with the calories.'

Jane Maxwell could be a right diva when she put her mind to it, but Emily decided to humour her today, just to make the wait for Arabella less stressful than it already was. There was hardly a month went by that Arabella didn't dream of firing Jane but, really and truly, she didn't think she could justify it. And something about Jane told Emily and Arabella that Jane wouldn't go quietly if she did get fired. She'd probably make it her life's work to ruin the magazine in the courts.

'She's quite clearly sex-starved,' Arabella would say, after every editorial run-in with Miss Maxwell. 'What that girl needs is the love of a good man.'

And then Emily and Arabella would have a secret giggle at such an outrageously sexist pronouncement.

'Just so happens I have some lovely biscuits, yes, Jane. One moment, please.'

Emily duly fetched the secret stash of butter shortbread from her desk, and set it on the round table where Arabella held their monthly meetings.

'Only shortbread ones?' Jane said, yawning again. 'I thought you said you had something lovely?'

Jane ate one anyway, Emily noticed. Then she ate another five, licking her fingers loudly. Everyone else flicked politely through the pages of rival magazines. After thirty minutes of fidgeting and clock-watching, mostly by Jane, the mood in the room was distinctly icy – almost as icy as the wind that whipped up and down the street outside. Jane kept saying she had seriously important things to do and that if Arabella was going to be so late today she should have let them know.

'I'll just call her,' Emily said, stepping into the corridor and flicking her mobile phone open. 'Maybe she's wedged in a snowdrift somewhere,' she said to herself as she selected her boss's private number.

Arabella answered on the first ring.

'David? David, is that you?' she said.

'Arabella, it's Emily here.'

'Oh, of course it is – I forgot to look at the caller ID.'

'Thank heaven you had your phone switched on. Where are you?'

'I'm still at home, my darling.'

There was a muffled sound as Arabella blew her nose and then sniffed loudly.

'Are you crying, Arabella?'

'Yes, I am. Listen, Emily, you've got to take over the meeting for me.'

'What? I can't do that. They'll take no notice of me.'

'Make them take notice of you, then. You're not exactly an intern.'

'Okay, okay, I'll try.'

'Yes, do try! I should have made you deputy editor years ago.'

'Do you really mean that?'

'Yes,' Arabella sniffed.

'Are you poorly?' Emily asked.

'No, I'm not poorly. I'm distraught. My toad of a husband, Mr David Harrington, the king of the toads, has just left me,' Arabella said after a short pause. 'The man is a big fat prize specimen! I'm all over the place, if you must know.'

'What did you say? He's left you? David's left you?'

'Yes, indeed. We had a massive fight last night and another one this morning. And I nearly trashed the house, I was so damn angry with him. He wouldn't even look at me, Emily. I said some silly things to him, but I was beyond livid. So he walked out and told me he wasn't coming back – not ever. And now I've cut my arm quite badly on a broken vase. Accidentally, I might add. That impossible man isn't worth my committing suicide

70

over. You'll have to hold the meeting for me, Emily.'

'Right, okay, I can see that. But do you need to go to A&E for stitches?'

'Look, don't worry about me. The bleeding is slowing down. I've put a nice clean towel on it. It's not even sore; I think my adrenaline is still working overtime.'

'Arabella, this is awful. You should get your doctor to have a look at you. How big is the cut?'

'Emily, there isn't time for this conversation. Just hold the meeting, choose next month's cover, and send flowers to our main advertisers in lieu of a lunch with me later on today. And don't take any nonsense from Jane, by the way. She's a great stylist but a cheeky madam sometimes – and given half a chance she'd take over the entire magazine. I'll call you later. Actually, could you come over here as soon as you can and help me tidy up? Could you, sweetheart? I wouldn't ask, if I hadn't cut my arm.'

'Okay, yes, of course I'll come over. Just you rest, yeah? And if the bleeding doesn't stop, will you please go to the hospital?'

But Arabella had already hung up.

'Well, here goes,' Emily said as she took a deep breath and pushed open the heavy glass door to the office. 'It seems Arabella has been delayed,' she said in her bravest voice. 'She won't be coming in today. And we can't postpone this meeting until tomorrow, so I've been asked to conduct the meeting and select the next cover. So let's begin with that, shall we?'

Everyone glanced briefly round the table, as if

waiting for an objection. When none came they began to place their cover submissions in front of Emily.

'Wait a minute. Is nobody else going to say anything?' Jane was glaring at Emily.

'Arabella just asked me to do this,' Emily said.

'Are you kidding us?' Jane said angrily, a seventh shortbread finger halfway to her open mouth. 'You're actually in charge here? You're choosing the cover?'

'Well, yes – I am. You see, the thing is, we have to let the printer have the cover layout by lunchtime today. So let's see what we've got, yes?' Emily smiled at them all, even though her heart was racing like a train going downhill without any brakes.

'Now, look here. If Arabella isn't coming in today then I'm the most senior person present,' Jane began. 'I should chair the meeting and make any major decisions that have to be made.'

But Emily bravely ignored her and started flicking through the photographs. She knew only too well that Arabella wasn't overly keen on Jane's fondness for modern interiors and typefaces.

'There are two front runners,' she said briskly. 'Personally I prefer the button-maker's cottage. It's like something from a fairytale, with all those hundreds of jars of buttons stacked up on every flat surface – though we should also give some consideration to the Daisy Churchill feature, of course.'

Emily didn't intend for one second to put Daisy on the cover, but she knew Jane would throw a hissy fit if her pet project was ignored completely. However, Jane was even more belligerent than

72

usual that morning.

'Consideration, did you say? Daisy is only the country's leading celebrity model,' Jane snapped. 'There's no question about who is going to be on the cover.'

'Daisy is a celebrity *glamour* model,' Emily corrected her carefully. 'And she's very lovely, and so on. But our typical reader is more concerned with buttons than bosoms, wouldn't you say? That's why they read our magazine, Jane – to get away from bosoms. From implants that resemble ostrich eggs. I don't know about you, but every time I see a cover featuring that woman I can almost hear the little chicks cheeping away inside her bra.'

There were some barely stifled giggles around the table. Jane wasn't all that well liked, and there wasn't anyone present who wouldn't mind seeing her precious feature bumped to the back pages. They didn't much care for Daisy either, after she'd dumped her normal boyfriend for a wealthy businessman the year before.

'Daisy Churchill is a multimillionaire model and fashion icon. She's the biggest star in the UK right now. She lives in a stunning mansion, and I styled that shoot personally,' Jane said frostily. 'It took over eight hours and was very tastefully done.'

'Yes, I'm sure it was, Jane. But this shot of Daisy lying on a white rug on the sitting-room floor, in a white fur bikini?' Emily said quietly. 'It's got the wow factor and everything, of course. But I'm not sure it fits our demographic. Is this really the sort of vibe we're aiming for?'

Emily didn't dare look up from the photographs spread across the table. She knew that Jane would be staring back at her, as if she were nothing but an annoying little upstart from the back of beyond, which she supposed she was. But Arabella needed her to be strong now and, really, Emily didn't think a white fur bikini was the right image for the cover of *Stylish Living*. Usually they had a shabby-chic patchwork quilt and some embroidered cushions, or an antique lemonade bottle with wild flowers in it, or a nice friendly-looking couple sitting on a willow bench in their garden.

'It was a winter wonderland theme,' Jane said slowly, as if Emily were a complete idiot. 'I used a white fur bikini because it was a winter theme.'

Petra Dunwoody, one of the more senior freelancers, could stand the tension no longer. She burst out laughing. Everybody else bit their lip nervously and looked out of the window. Really, that suggestive pose of Daisy's was as far away from a winter wonderland theme as anyone sane could possibly imagine. More like a cheesy roller disco in the 1960s, if anything, Petra thought suddenly.

'Jane, I admire you for getting the gig,' Petra spluttered. 'And Daisy probably is the most recognized face in the UK right now. But you've got to be sensible, darling. This is *Stylish Living*, yeah? Not *Nuts* magazine. Daisy hasn't got the right sort of image for us at all. So I think Emily is quite right. Let's go for the button-maker on the front cover. Look at those gorgeous little lavender bags hanging on the Shaker drawers behind her. It's so appropriate for this new era of make-do-and-mend. We could do a little cut-out-and-keep pattern for making lavender bags, to run alongside? I've got something like that on file. We could drop it into the feature.'

'Lavender bags, did you say? Screw the lavender bags. Arabella will be absolutely furious if you turn down a world-famous celebrity in favour of a two-room shack with exposed pipes and a six-socket plugboard in the background,' Jane almost shouted. 'I spent weeks negotiating that shoot so that we could get it without paying Daisy a massive fee. This is grossly unfair to me. Not to mention a right slap in the face for Daisy Churchill.'

There were more giggles then as everyone suddenly remembered Daisy had been bitch-slapped the week before by some super-possessive WAG outside a bar in Liverpool, after she'd posed for pictures with a group of Premier League footballers.

'I'm really sorry, Jane, but you do know that our last six covers have been very successful? And they've all had an old-fashioned feel to them. It is an antiques-based magazine, you know. Our readers won't be expecting a glamour model with a pout on her like two slugs mating in a bowl of jelly.'

Jane looked as if she might be about to thump Emily.

'Arabella did say the Daisy feature would have to suit the magazine's profile, didn't she? If you went ahead with it, that is. You know that Arabella wanted pictures of Daisy without her

75

heavy make-up on – just sitting in her kitchen, drinking tea.'

Emily did her best to sound sympathetic, but sometimes she wondered why Jane didn't just decamp to the gossip titles and be done with it. She clearly had no interest in antiques – or even in ordinary people.

'Slugs for lips! Well, that takes the biscuit. I'm going to phone Arabella right this minute for a second opinion,' Jane said defiantly.

'You can't do that. Arabella's busy today, she's got things to do,' Emily said quickly.

'What are you – her mother?' Jane said.

'Please, Jane, I just want to get the cover sorted,' Emily said firmly.

'Let's do it the old-fashioned way,' Petra interjected. 'Show of hands, please? All those in favour of the button-maker for the front cover, please put your hands up.'

Slowly everyone raised their hands – except Jane, who was so angry her lips had disappeared into a tight knot of suppressed rage.

'Actually, the Daisy feature is very lengthy. So it won't fit into this issue, anyway,' Petra added.

'Good point, Petra. Do you know, I think the Daisy feature might suit next month's bathroom supplement better?' Emily said, trying to be fair. 'We still have twelve pages to fill there – and all the bikini shots might be more appropriate in a bathroom setting. Hasn't she got a massive loofah, by the way?'

There was another round of sniggers.

'Forget about it. Don't bother doing me any special favours,' Jane said bitterly.

She left her other submissions in a neat pile in front of Emily, made her excuses and left the office. For a few seconds after she'd gone there was an uncomfortable silence. Then the meeting exploded into peals of laughter, and lots of derision was expressed for Daisy's white fur bikini.

'Good for you, Emily,' said Petra, clapping her hands loudly. 'Daisy Churchill is a shameless self-publicist who has no more interest in interiors and antiques than I have in nuclear physics. Dozy trollop! The truth is, every other magazine in the country is sick of the sight of her. There's not a single thing left to say about the personal life of that silly woman. So she's now targeting the niche magazines such as ours. It'll be the fishing quarterlies next: *Daisy Churchill Likes A Big Rod!* And if anybody takes the biscuit, Jane does. Greedy cow scoffed half that tin of shortbread.'

More laughter filled the office.

'Thanks, Petra,' Emily said gratefully.

'It's true. I mean, just look at these pictures. There's hardly any background in them at all – just Daisy in a succession of her ludicrous lingerie. And look at the kitchen pictures. There's just a toaster and a kettle on the counter, nothing personal whatsoever. If I were you, I wouldn't put this feature in at all.'

'Well, let's see what Arabella says when she comes back tomorrow. And if there's enough room, maybe we could put Daisy in next month? But definitely not that shot of her in the rubber corset. I feel a bit ill just looking at it.'

They all burst out laughing again. Emily wasn't considered prudish, but the way she was cringing at the pictures of Daisy was truly hilarious.

And so the button-maker's cottage was selected for the cover, all other business was duly conducted, and the staff and various contributors were very happy. Everyone had something of theirs included in the next issue. And Emily had selected two of Jane's other shoots for upcoming editions. Unfortunately for Daisy Churchill, though, her feature didn't even make the grade for the bathroom supplement. Petra was right: they simply couldn't hand Daisy twelve pages of free publicity when she hadn't even gone to the trouble of buying a second-hand teaspoon to fit in with the image of the magazine. They would be a laughing stock in the magazine industry if they used her.

'Thanks, everyone. Thanks so much for bearing with me today. I think Arabella will love what we've done,' Emily said gratefully when the meeting ended. Then she rushed straight to her phone. The printing company was given the necessary instructions just minutes before the cover deadline.

Meanwhile, the other pages were digitally composed and finalized by the layout team on the floor below. Emily phoned around to cancel the advertisers' lunch, sent flowers to their offices, and finally dashed over to Arabella's house to check that she hadn't bled to death.

'Come in, dear Emily; it's so good to see a friendly face,' Arabella chirped gratefully. She was still clutching the bloody towel to her arm.

'You didn't kill him, did you? He's not buried under the patio?' Emily asked when she saw the

78

state of the place.

Every vase and ornament in the house had been thrown, broken or smashed to pieces. At least one window pane was cracked. Arabella was all cried out, with big dark circles beneath her twinkling brown eyes. And her perfect bob was tousled and greasy.

The two women stood facing each other beside the fireplace.

'You poor love. It'll be okay,' Emily said uselessly.

'No, it's all over,' Arabella wept.

She did look terrible. Emily guessed Arabella had been up all night, drinking wine and venting her anger on the furniture.

'He'll come back again,' Emily soothed, giving her friend a hug.

'No, he won't come back. I know it. We said some awful things to one another, Emily – unforgivable things. Well, mostly it was me saying the unforgivable things. But he didn't look all that bothered. I think he doesn't care about me any more, one way or the other. That's worse than hating me, isn't it?'

Emily shrugged. She supposed that it was. But what could she say? 'You're a strong lady, you'll get over him,' she said.

'No, I've ruined everything,' Arabella sobbed quietly.

'Right, you go and get tidied up,' Emily told her friend gently.

'What for? What's the point of being glamorous, anyway?' Arabella asked dramatically. 'Nobody cares how I look.'

'Nonsense; we all admire your style in the office. Anyway, it's for yourself, for your own self-esteem,' Emily said firmly.

'Sensible Emily to the rescue once again,' Arabella laughed sadly. 'If I knew how to make a trumpet noise – like in those films where the cavalry appears on the horizon – I'd make one right now.'

'I'm serious. You'll feel so much better after you've had a hot shower and brushed your teeth and put on fresh clothes,' Emily said kindly.

'Will you make me some tea first? I'm parched,' Arabella said, flopping on to the sofa. 'All that wine has left me really dehydrated.'

'Yes, of course I will.'

'And a nice tomato sandwich with salad cream?'

'Yes, surely, if that's what you want.'

'And will you take me out somewhere later and get me blitzed?'

'No, I will not,' Emily said. 'You need to rest your arm.'

'Never mind my arm. I want to get so drunk I fall over in the street,' Arabella said darkly. 'I want some young hunk to take advantage of me.'

'And what good would that do? Better to phone a divorce lawyer, or whatever they're called, and ask for some advice,' Emily said gently.

'What do you mean – a divorce lawyer?' Arabella gasped.

'I mean, only if you're serious about it all being over. You said that David said that he wasn't coming back,' Emily reminded her patiently.

'Yes, that's right. I did say that.'

'Well, then. Better to be organized.'

'I'm sure he didn't mean it, though,' Arabella said in a panicky voice.

'You just told me he did mean it.'

'I wanted you to disagree with me,' Arabella sobbed.

'Has he said this before? Has he ever said he'd leave you?'

'No, he's never said that before – no matter how bad the rows were.'

'There you are, then.'

'Do you think he's really left me?' Arabella whispered, looking fearfully at the walls, as if the room might be bugged by MI5.

'Look, I don't know if he meant it. I haven't really met him, have I? Or really talked to him – he never comes to the magazine get-togethers. But there's no harm in finding out where you stand, that's all I'm saying.'

'So you think I should divorce David before he divorces me?'

'I said that I think you should get some advice. Why don't you get tidied up first, yes? And eat something afterwards?' Emily said slowly, shooing her boss up the stairs and then going towards the kitchen to fix her a snack.

Emily usually tried not to become involved in the personal lives of other people, because she was always so tempted to take over the *responsibility* for everything. And she also didn't like it when people wanted her to agree with their viewpoint, in case they blamed her later on if things went pear-shaped. So she was definitely letting the lawyers advise Arabella on this one.

'Thanks for standing in for me at work today,'

Arabella called down the stairs. 'And I know it's a bit of a mess around here. I'd leave it for the cleaning lady, but if she saw this lot she'd march straight out of here and never come back. She's very temperamental. And if my cleaning lady deserts me as well, I think I really will lose the will to live.'

'It's okay,' Emily called back. 'I think I can handle it.'

But the kitchen was even worse than the sitting room.

'Oh, Arabella, what have you done?' Emily said when she saw the scene of devastation in the airy basement kitchen. A large pan of spaghetti sauce had been emptied into David's open briefcase. Some of the sauce had spilt on to the floor and across the stone tiles, where it was now hardening nicely. The spaghetti itself was stuck to the kitchen window in a great, glistening lump. There were broken wine bottles and spilt red wine all over the floor. Emily counted the remains of about ten bottles before she gave up. Most of the bottle labels appeared to be vintage and expensive.

Maybe Arabella's husband really had meant it when he said he was never coming back?

'I think the poor man got out just in time,' she said under her breath. 'Arabella must have been in a murderous mood to have done this.'

Emily's stomach did a small somersault then. She suddenly had a premonition that something very bad was going to happen – something much worse than Arabella vandalizing her own lovely kitchen in this way. But then she told herself to stop being so silly, that she wasn't a psychic.

'Okay,' Emily said, reaching for the dustpan and brush and a whole roll of paper towels. 'Time for my Kim and Aggie routine; whoever said a career in magazine publishing would be all about meeting celebrities, and non-stop glamour?'

Then she thought of her little attic in Twickenham and how peaceful it was there, and suddenly she didn't feel quite so sorry for herself any more.

And then she thought about Dylan – and wondered if she was doing the right thing in letting a relatively normal man into her not-quite-normal existence.

6. Arabella's Husband

It was February now and Arabella felt heart-broken every time she saw a display of Valentine cards in a gift store window, or red roses in a florist's window, or one of those ribbon-and-cellophane affairs with a cuddly rabbit inside on the petrol station counter. She'd tried chatting to the handsome hunk in the red T-shirt, but he'd looked right through her, as if she were invisible. So presumably there wasn't much hope of the two of them conceiving a baby in the flower bed out the front any time soon. Arabella felt her age more than ever when she was sitting in the queue for unleaded petrol one day, and she saw the hunk of her dreams kissing his teenage girlfriend on the station forecourt. The girlfriend was wearing low-slung jeans revealing a tattoo of a rose on her lower back. She also had a diamond stud in her nose and super-long acrylic fingernails. Arabella's mating-in-the-marigolds fantasy keeled over and died instantly, for how could she compete with a rose tattoo and a nose-stud? She turned to look out of the passenger window and then switched on the radio for company. There was a play on BBC Radio 4. It was something to do with a tea plantation in India in Victorian times.

'*I am leaving for England tomorrow,*' a man said, '*but I will never forget you.*'

'For pity's sake,' Arabella said sadly. 'This is

84

getting ridiculous.' She felt loneliness trying to pull her down into its murky depths, like an octopus with super-sticky tentacles. Some days she was so tense and scared she could barely concentrate on her work. David had still not moved back in, and he was also refusing to answer his mobile phone. She'd been emailing and texting him obsessively for weeks, but she'd not received a single reply. Her letters to his office went unanswered, and she'd even been stopped at reception in the steel-and-glass building where David worked and been asked to leave by the security guard. That had been a bit embarrassing, actually, as the guard had told her to stop being so silly and hysterical and just leave quietly. Or he would have to call the police. He'd put one hand on her back, as if she were a psychiatric patient, and steered her out of the door and right down the mobility ramp on to the footpath. Talk about disgraceful. Was that any way to treat the good lady wife of one of their key workers?

'I'm telling you, Emily,' Arabella said now, lighting another cigarette on the fire escape at the magazine's offices. 'There's something crazy going on with David.'

There was a rare spell of sunshine that day, so they were having lunch outdoors on two fold-down chairs. Emily had a plain cheese sandwich from home while Arabella was picking half-heartedly over an M&S salad.

'Do you know, there's something about chilled orange segments that makes me feel quite melancholy,' she said.

'Stop buying that particular dish, then,' Emily

suggested. 'Get a nice bagel instead.'

'Yes, I suppose I should, but a salad always looks so healthy, doesn't it?' Arabella said, pushing the remains of her lunch to one side and lighting a cigarette.

'Listen, I don't mean to sound completely heartless, but I know there's something going on with David, Arabella. I'm so sorry, and I know it must hurt dreadfully, but it'd seem that he's left you.'

'Well, yes, I am painfully aware that my husband no longer appears to be living in the marital home with me. But there's something else going on – he wouldn't just walk out on me like this unless he had somewhere else to go, unless he had a Plan B. He doesn't like staying in hotels no matter how swanky they are. And he's got a slight germ phobia about using hotel showers.'

Arabella's ashtray on the fire escape was overflowing. She was now throwing her lipstick-covered butts into Emily's empty shortbread tin.

'What do you mean?' Emily said carefully. 'Do you think he's got another place to live? Like he's renting a city-centre apartment or something?'

'Yes, that's exactly it! I'm starting to think he's been planning to leave me for some time. It was the way he looked at me the last time we were arguing, his eyes were just so cold,' Arabella said forlornly. 'I got a feeling that day that he really hated me – you know, when I poured the pasta sauce into his briefcase?'

'You shouldn't have done that, I dare say.'

'Big deal – his briefcase was empty, anyway.'

'Arabella, look, please don't take this the wrong way,' Emily said carefully. 'But don't you think that maybe, just maybe, things had come to a natural end with you and David?'

'No. Not at all; we were madly in love.'

'But you just said he hated you.'

'I said I had a feeling he hated me *that day*. That was just my perception at the time, though. And it was only that particular day. Remember that; it wasn't all the time.'

'Why is it okay if he only hates you sometimes?' Emily said slowly.

'Look, he was mad at me because I told him he was rubbish in bed, okay?' Arabella said with a flash of guilt that turned her neck tomato red. 'Actually, I told him he was the worst lover I'd ever had ... and his feet were a bit yellow ... and he had bad breath.'

'Well, you know what men are like about that sort of thing. They have very fragile egos – no wonder he stormed off in a giant huff,' Emily said, shaking her head sadly.

'I didn't mean it, Emily. Well, he does have yellowish feet. But he doesn't have bad breath, and he wasn't my worst lover. But I was just so upset because I wasn't pregnant,' Arabella cried.

'Okay, okay, so he's a good lover, then? Maybe you should tell him that. He might come back again.'

'He's not always good in bed. Well, he's okay, I suppose,' Arabella said. She inhaled deeply, coughed loudly and threw her salad back into the carrier bag in disgust

'To sum up,' Emily said, taking a deep breath, 'David has yellow feet, isn't exactly the best in bed, sometimes hates you, and has ignored you completely for over a month?'

'Yes. That's about the height of it.'

'So why on earth do you want him back, if you don't mind me asking?'

'I want him back because I love him to bits. *Obviously.*'

Emily closed her eyes. She knew that she mustn't tell Arabella she was one deluded wife. Ideally Arabella would work it out for herself – and come to the conclusion that she would be better off without David.

'Why do you love him again?' she said.

'He's my husband, Emily. I took my wedding vows seriously.'

'And that's the only reason you love him? You took wedding vows?'

'No,' Arabella shook her head. 'I love him because he's my husband.'

'So you'd automatically love any husband? Even have an arranged marriage?'

'No, of course not, Emily, don't be silly. Though I do understand that most arranged marriages are designed to bring together two people who are well suited. They are not designed to fail, my darling.'

'Well, fair enough. Let's not get bogged down in a discussion about arranged marriage.'

'You started it.'

'Yes, I did... Give me another reason why you love him, then. Why did you fall in love with him in the first place?'

'He was rich and successful.'

'Apart from that,' Emily said.

'He can change a tyre really quickly.'

88

'So marry a mechanic next time,' Emily said, packing away her lunch box.

'Emily, don't be flippant. I meant that David is a resourceful man. That he doesn't just give up if he doesn't get what he wants right away. He's clever, you know? And I loved him for it. I'm totally devastated here.'

'I'm sorry. I know you didn't only love him because he could change a tyre. I know you didn't mean it that way.'

'It's okay. I know you understand.'

'Sometimes these things just come to a natural end. Nobody is to blame. The feelings just go away of their own accord.'

'Is that what happened with you and Alex?' Arabella said gently.

'Yes, our relationship came to a natural end all right. A grinding halt, more like. Pity he didn't tell me until the day of our wedding. Oh, don't get me started on all that business; it makes me feel like such a loser. But anyway, I don't think Alex and me actually got it right to begin with,' Emily said. 'It was a massive, all-consuming teenage crush; and then it became a habit and a crutch. It was never true love.'

'I'm sorry for bringing him up,' Arabella said guiltily.

'It's okay.'

Arabella opened a fresh packet of cigarettes. Emily briefly thought of suggesting that Arabella might have a better chance of conceiving if she gave up smoking and took some gentle exercise instead. And found another man to be the father, of course. But she didn't want to become a bossyboots. Emily had always found bossy people very tiresome herself. Also, all the magazine articles she had ever read advised strongly against taking *ownership* of someone else's problems. You could console and listen and hug and support and sympathize endlessly, but you should never try to take over.

'Emily?' Arabella said quietly.

'Yes?'

'What would you do if you were me?'

'Please don't ask me that.'

'No, really – would you beg David to come home?'

'I don't know.'

'Or would you send him flowers?'

'Really, I don't know.'

'Or would you have a crazy, unsuitable affair? Get your confidence back by seducing another man?'

'I doubt it. That would only complicate everything. What if you ended up having feelings for both of them?'

'No, only men say that! Would you go to a lawyer and tell him to hang David out to dry?'

'Arabella, please don't ask my advice. This is serious. It's not a magazine quiz.'

'Or would you look for a sperm donor?'

'Um...'

'One-night stand or clinic...?'

'I really wouldn't know where to start.'

'Or would you do something else entirely?'

'I really don't know, Arabella. It depends on what you want – and what he wants – doesn't it?'

'Would you be aloof and mysterious? Yes, you'd

play hard to get, wouldn't you? Do nothing at all for a year and see if he comes crawling back to you. Trouble is, I don't really have a year to spare.'

'Listen, Arabella, is that the time? I'll think about this later, but I have to dash now. I'm meeting a reader this afternoon over on the other side of the city. I'll call you this evening. Don't do anything silly. Promise me now?'

'I promise,' Arabella said, smiling at Emily through a fog of cigarette smoke. But it was already too late to promise not to do anything silly because she *was* going to do something silly that very evening.

When Emily had gone Arabella went to the bathroom and locked the door behind her so nobody else could barge in. She took a long blonde wig out of her large handbag and combed it with shaking hands. She tried the wig on. The effect was pretty natural. Then she tried on a short denim jacket, a long white T-shirt and a pair of lurid purple leggings. A pair of bug-eyed sunglasses and a pair of flimsy flat pumps completed the look. In two minutes flat she'd gone from Wealthy-Socialite-About-Town to Lowly-Cleaning-Lady. She was average height and average weight. David wouldn't recognize her in a million years. Nor would any of their friends and colleagues. Quickly she put her own clothes on again and folded the other things back into her bag.

Now all she had to do was hang around the office until five o'clock. Then she'd go and change into her disguise in the big bathroom on the ground floor, where nobody would take any notice of her.

91

At six o'clock precisely David came out of his office wearing a buttoned-up overcoat and smart brogues, looked right and left and then hurried towards the nearest Tube station. And Arabella was only ten paces behind him. She'd been sitting on a bench for over an hour, pretending to read *Heat* magazine. David walked very quickly. But Arabella was able to keep up quite easily in her comfy pumps – she was practically skipping along the footpath. Someone from a building site whistled loudly at her, but she barely had time to smile and wave back at them before she remembered she was supposed to be following her husband home from work. David got on a train going in the other direction from where they lived, sat down and took a novel out of his new briefcase. Arabella got on too, and sat a few seats away from him.

She watched David out of the corner of her eye. He looked happy, she thought. The worry lines around his ice-blue eyes had faded slightly and he was a few pounds heavier. So he must be eating well – wherever he was – she decided. His hair was nicely cut in a new style. Actually, he looked a bit sexy now. The hunted look had gone from his face. Arabella felt a bit sick again. David clearly hadn't been pining for her the way she had been pining for him.

Twenty minutes passed without anything out of the ordinary happening. But then David suddenly closed his novel, jumped up and sprang out of the train just as the doors were closing. Arabella dropped her bag in her hurry to get off

92

the train. By the time she'd retrieved it, the doors had closed again and she was swept on towards the next station. She cursed David under her breath all the way back to her own stop. Next time she'd be ready, she vowed.

And so the following week, she did it again. She was still disguised as a humble cleaning lady, but this time she wore a garish red headscarf, a baggy trench coat with no belt on it, and black leggings. She stood right by the door so that when David left the train, she did too. She followed him all the way along several suburban streets until he came to a row of expensive-looking houses near the river. There were eight homes in the development, all with a garage at ground level and a big sitting-room window on the first floor. Each window opened out on to a small balcony. The lights in David's house were on already and the curtains were drawn. Perhaps he had set the lights on a timer, she thought to herself. David took a key from his pocket, glanced right and left again and then went quickly inside. Arabella punched the air triumphantly. So she had discovered her husband's secret bachelor pad. Result! But what could she do now? she wondered. Should she ring the bell and confront him? As Arabella stood in the dimly lit street, trying to make up her mind, she heard the swishing sound of a sliding door opening. She looked up. David was standing on the balcony, sipping a small glass of wine. He'd taken off his coat and was wearing a heavy-knit cardigan. Arabella crept towards a nearby tree and stood there as quietly as she could, trying to look as if she were waiting for a lift or something. With any luck he wouldn't look down and discover her.

A minute later, a woman joined David on the balcony – a tall, beautiful woman who couldn't have been more than twenty-five years of age. And by the looks of it she was six months pregnant. Her pregnancy bump was neat and round and comfortable-looking. She was wearing a floaty black dress, black opaque tights and flat-heeled biker boots. Her skin was radiant and glowing. Her hair was a long rippling sheet of raven black. She looked like a goddess. She couldn't be with David, could she? This couldn't be happening. Arabella held her breath.

The couple on the balcony kissed tenderly.

'I must be dreaming,' Arabella whispered.

Somehow, against all the odds, Arabella's bad-tempered, workaholic husband had managed to secure the affections of a much younger woman and move with her into this trendy glass box of a house. Was it even his house? she wondered. Or did it belong to the young woman? Was this interloper someone incredibly well paid, to be able to afford such a house? Was she a songwriter or a stockbroker? Was she a best-selling writer or perhaps an heiress? Had David forgotten he was still legally married to another woman? What would he say if he knew his rightful wife was standing in this very street, wearing a blonde wig and chain-store pumps? Arabella's stomach jack-knifed and she almost threw up on the pavement – but she hadn't eaten all day, so luckily there was nothing to ride the wave of nausea that came rushing up her throat. She could barely contain her emotions, she felt so jealous and hurt.

Arabella strained to hear what the couple were saying.

'Is the wine okay?' the woman asked. 'It's only cheap plonk. But I saw some gorgeous baby clothes today and I only had a fiver left by the time I got to the supermarket.'

'It's lovely. Anyway, I feel bad drinking wine when you can't have any.' He put his hand on her bump and caressed it tenderly.

'Don't be silly,' she laughed. 'I don't care all that much for booze. And you deserve a glass when you work so hard all day. How did the Sharkey meeting go?'

'They dropped their price by two million.'

'Ha! I knew they would cave in if you flagged up their IT shortcomings. Good for you, my darling, I'm so pleased for you.'

They embraced again, holding each other in a languid, relaxed way before melting into a long and loving kiss that lasted for well over a minute.

Arabella's knees could no longer hold her up. She slid down and ended up slumped on the ground. An elderly couple came along and crossed the road to avoid her. Clearly they thought she was an alcoholic or homeless or mad – or all three. Arabella did get sick then. It was only a drop of acidic yellow bile, but she was glad of the distraction. Her nausea was mainly silent, but she didn't think David and his new love would have noticed if she'd keeled over and died right there on the pavement.

Soon afterwards she made her way home, sobbing loudly and not caring who saw her.

'You okay, love?' a policeman asked when she

95

was almost on her own doorstep.

'Yes, thank you,' Arabella said. 'My husband has left me, or so it seems.'

'He's not worth it,' the policeman said, nodding and walking on without breaking stride. 'Plenty more fish in the sea, and so on. Isn't that right?'

Arabella said nothing.

She let herself in, went up to the bathroom in a trance, peeled off her disguise and put everything in the bin. She stood under a hot shower for twenty minutes, sobbing her heart out. Then she was sick again. She cleaned the house from top to bottom and tried to eat some dry toast, but her throat kept closing over with disgust. David had been cheating on her for months. No wonder he'd run out of patience with her going baby crazy. He just didn't care any more – because he had already made a baby with somebody else. The nerve of the man! Why was she even surprised? Didn't David always get what he wanted in the end? At midnight Arabella rang Emily and asked her to come over and bring a few bottles of wine with her.

'I'll come over, but I've no wine left in the flat,' Emily said.

'Can't you buy some somewhere? Just any old Italian white will do.'

'It's very late, but I suppose I could make a detour to the all-night Tesco. It'll take about forty minutes, okay?'

'Look, never mind the wine. Just come over right away, Emily, please?'

'Are you okay, Arabella?'

'Not really, no.'

'Has something happened?' Emily said.

96

'Yes,' Arabella replied.

'Tell me?'

'Well, you won't believe it.'

'What *happened?*'

'It's David. I followed him home from work today.'

'You didn't, did you?'

'I did. I was disguised as a cleaner. Emily, I know where he lives.'

'Where's that?'

Arabella told her.

'Sounds very upmarket. Can he afford two mortgages?'

'I don't know. Maybe ... but there's something else,' Arabella said sadly.

'What else?'

'He's met someone else.'

'No!'

'Yes. So it could be her house they're living in. Maybe she's rich? She certainly sounded intelligent. He adores her. And she's having his baby.'

'What did you say?'

'It's true. There's no mistake. They were practically having sex on the balcony. She looked six months pregnant. She's young and gorgeous. I nearly died, Emily. I was sick on my pumps a little bit.'

'Pumps, did you say? I'll be right over,' Emily said, slamming down the phone.

Arabella only ever wore the highest heels. Victoria Beckham was her style icon.

Emily pulled on jeans and a sweatshirt, grabbed her handbag and boots from the bedroom floor, and rushed out of the door.

7. Love Triangle Inferno

April arrived in a burst of glorious sunshine. The Siberian-style weather departed, snowdrops appeared in gardens everywhere, and the May issue of the magazine was a resounding success. But despite all these good things Arabella had been very quiet at work for the last few weeks. Everybody in the office noticed it, though only Jane Maxwell had remarked on Arabella's sudden change in mood. There were no passionate debates and no slamming of doors over the selection of features, the securing of advertising revenue or the improvement in sales figures. Arabella simply looked through all the ideas and submissions without speaking or showing any emotion at all, and then she either accepted or rejected them. She went out alone to the fire escape for an occasional cigarette, and she never seemed to eat lunch any more.

Emily was the only person she had time for.

'What's up with Arabella?' Jane asked Emily one day when they were alone together in the kitchenette.

Jane was pouring a Diet Coke for herself, and Emily was making a round of teas and coffees for everybody else.

'Nothing's up, she's just concentrating on her work,' Emily said in a way that suggested Jane should do the same.

'Whatever,' Jane said, flouncing out of the kitchenette in a major sulk. It was coming to something when that little prig Emily was now Arabella's official gatekeeper.

Jane was still absolutely fuming about her Daisy Churchill feature being panned, but Arabella wouldn't have noticed if Jane had stripped naked and paraded up and down the office with a waste-paper basket on her head. Meanwhile, Daisy Churchill's agent was emailing Jane on a daily basis to ask if and when the feature was going to appear. Jane just kept saying that no date had been confirmed yet, that they were snowed under with submissions, or that they were waiting for the right moment. Daisy had promised to invite her round for dinner, but so far no invite had been issued. It was all Jane's own fault, of course, for not telling Daisy's agent in advance that Arabella had the final approval on all features and front covers. In truth, Jane had portrayed herself as a Deputy Editor who didn't need to consult Arabella on every little thing. But the damage was done now, and she knew she'd made an idiot of herself over it. Most of her colleagues were trying to avoid her – no doubt they didn't want to get a reputation for hanging around with a troublemaker.

For very little Jane would have handed in her resignation at *Stylish Homes* and applied to work at one of the tabloid magazines instead. But then again, despite her secretive ways and infuriating dedication to the image of the magazine, Arabella was a reliable boss. And she wasn't prone to sacking people on the spur of the moment. So Jane kept her mouth shut and her eyes open.

She'd get her revenge on Arabella someday – and on that arch suck-up Emily too.

One sunny morning in mid-April, Arabella finally took Emily's advice and went to see a divorce solicitor. The solicitor said he would contact David and ask him for confirmation that he had left his marriage and was now in a new relationship, and also for details of his current financial status. Arabella kept up a brave front at work, but she cried herself to sleep every night. Under no circumstances was she allowed to contact her husband, the solicitor had said. He would be handling everything from now on. He advised Arabella to seek counselling, and so did Emily. But Arabella knew that if she ever told a counsellor what she wanted to do to her faithless husband's genitals, they would lock her in a padded cell and throw away the key. She didn't go near alcohol either – for if she got drunk now there was no telling what she might do. Shoot David, possibly, for putting off starting a family until it was too late. And then deciding he did want to be a father, after all – but just not with her. It was a good job she didn't have a gun handy.

Seeing Arabella in such a mess reminded Emily of the devastation that a man could bring to a woman's life. It reminded her of Alex and their doomed wedding. And it left her convinced that she wasn't ready to get her heart broken again. But Dylan had been the perfect boyfriend so far. To be fair to him, he hadn't put a foot wrong. They'd been on some lovely dates to the local skating rink, the London Eye and a Florence and the Machine concert. They'd had dinner together three times and they'd been to the Twickenham Arms half a dozen times. They didn't go to Dylan's house, because he shared the house with five other guys and, apparently, it was a bit of a tip. Emily had joked that Dylan had a wife and kids tucked away there and that was why he didn't ask her round. So then he took a picture of the kitchen on his mobile phone and showed it to her. And Emily was quite satisfied that she didn't want to spend an evening at Dylan's house. It looked more like a recycling centre than a house – Dylan said they could never remember to put out the recycling on a Wednesday night. And each evening after their date, Dylan had walked Emily back to her front door and kissed her goodnight on the doorstep. He was a delicious kisser – just the right balance between passion and restraint – and she suspected that as a lover he would take her breath away. And they were almost at that stage now. They just needed to find a quiet weekend when they had no other commitments – when Dylan didn't have rugby practice and Emily wasn't round at Arabella's house, keeping her company while she waited to hear from the solicitor.

Mostly all Dylan and Emily had time for were quick cups of tea in the shop. Emily would admire the new shelving taking shape, or help Sylvia decide on a colour scheme for the walls. Emily didn't tell Dylan the full story of what was going on with Arabella. She was the very soul of discretion. Arabella didn't want anyone in the magazine industry to find out she had been dumped for a younger woman. Just in case the air of general failure permeated through to her career as well. So she'd made Emily promise to tell nobody about the baby. Nobody at all – not even Dylan. But Emily hoped that with the passing of time everything would begin to cool down a little. David's baby would be born soon, and then the solicitor would press him for a divorce plan and a financial settlement for Arabella. Until the baby was born the solicitor had recommended they all remain as calm as possible, so as not to cause any upset to the expectant mother and her child. And even though she loathed her ex and his new love with all her heart, Arabella had no desire to upset the innocent child at the centre of it all.

But unfortunately for Arabella the knife was about to be twisted once more. For one bright and breezy day at the end of April, Jane submitted a feature idea to Arabella and went off for lunch with a friend from another floor in the building. Arabella casually opened Jane's folder and there, right in front of her, was a photograph of a luxury nursery in Kensington with a delicate, hand-painted mural of fairies on the wall. A pink muslin canopy was draped over the white wicker crib and an antique rocking chair was filled with cuddly toys. Arabella wasn't sure if Jane had submitted the feature specifically to annoy her. She wondered if perhaps Jane had overheard her and Emily discussing the disastrous IVF appointment all those months ago. Could Jane really be that callous towards her? she wondered. Or had she just photographed this nursery because of the lovely antique rocking chair? Perhaps it was all just an unfortunate coincidence? But whatever the reason for it, the damage was done now, and Arabella's wounded heart finally constricted to the size of an apple pip.

She closed the folder and went out on to the fire escape for a sulk and a cigarette.

'Emily, are you sure you want to go on seeing me?' Dylan asked gently.

'Yes, I'm having a lovely time,' Emily replied, smiling up at him.

They were having lunch in the shop again – Brie and tomato sandwiches from the deli on the next street. Emily was sitting at the counter, sipping her coffee. Dylan was up a ladder, fixing one of the ceiling lights. Sylvia had gone back to the stables to care for a lame horse, so Dylan was in charge of the shop for another few days. He was hardly ever away from it these days, even though the initial agreement had only been for a couple of days a week – and, of course, the new shelving.

'You're very good at fixing things,' Emily said approvingly as the new light flashed into life. An entire wall of shoes and belts began to sparkle under its starry glow.

'Ah well, you pick up the odd little trick as you go along,' Dylan said modestly. 'In my younger days I once spent a summer as an electrician's apprentice. And then during another summer I worked with a carpenter friend of my dad's.'

'What a useful man you are.'

'I suppose I have my talents,' he laughed. 'Now, regarding my previous question, are you okay with things as they are? We haven't been out much this last fortnight,' he added.

'That's okay, I've been so busy at work,' she smiled.

'Yes, me too. But is everything really okay?' he persisted.

'Yes, of course it is. I do love the peacock-blue walls in here, by the way. They really show off the clothes beautifully, and the shoes too. It does feel just like a boutique.'

Clearly Emily wanted to change the subject, but Dylan needed to make sure things were fine between him and Emily before he could let it go.

'Emily, can I ask you something personal?' he said tenderly, getting down from the ladder and throwing the broken spotlight in the bin.

'Sure. Fire away.'

'Is there something else on your mind apart from us?'

'No.'

'Only I'm getting a feeling there's something bothering you.'

'No, really.'

'Look, I'll just say it straight out. Do you remember those things you donated a while back – the baptism gown and all the children's books? Well, Sylvia showed them to me. She's a bit concerned about you giving away such personal things. Were they your things when you were a little girl?'

'Yes, they were. Have you sold them yet?'

'No, they're still in the storeroom. Are you sure you don't want to keep them?'

'No, it's fine. I've really no room in the flat for a lot of stuff.'

'But surely you could make room for a small box of books and keepsakes?'

'I don't want them any more,' she said, still smiling firmly.

'Tell me why?' Dylan asked, sitting down and holding Emily's hand gently. 'Why don't you want to keep precious things like that?'

Emily looked out of the window at the traffic going by. Two young girls came walking down the street, wearing woolly hats and scarves over their denim jackets and embroidered jeans. They looked like sisters; they were laughing at some private joke. Emily wondered if she'd be a completely different person now if she'd had a happy childhood. If she'd be a carefree person now, like those two girls seemed to be. Or was there always an upper limit to each person's personal happiness level, predetermined at birth? Nature or nurture; who knew which one was the most important?

'The truth is, I don't want to keep those things because it upsets me to look at them. They hold me back. It wasn't a very happy childhood, that's all,' Emily said, looking down at the floor.

'Okay,' he said. 'I won't press you for details, but I'll wait another while before I put your things out on sale – just in case you ever want them back.'

'But you must deal with this sort of thing every day in the shop,' she said.

'Yes, of course we do. But mostly the donations come from people we've never met before. So Sylvia and I don't know the stories attached to everything. A pair of shoes is just a pair of shoes to us. We have no idea if the owner simply got fed up with them, or if somebody died of a heart attack.'

'I see what you mean, yes,' she said.

A sort of uneasy silence descended between them. Dylan pulled his chair closer to Emily's and looked at her intensely. She had beautiful eyes, he thought to himself. He was definitely falling in love with her. He hoped that she was falling in love with him too. But recently he'd been sure she would ask him to stay the night at her flat, and then she hadn't. When they were kissing on the doorstep he was sure she was longing for him the way he was longing for her. But always, at the last minute, she would pull away from him and say goodnight and run up the stairs alone. He wouldn't have minded if they were younger, but he felt that at their ages they should be able to talk about it. She'd told him she wasn't religious, so that couldn't be the reason she didn't want to sleep with him. It must be a commitment thing, he decided – which was why he couldn't help wondering if Emily was getting cold feet.

'My mother never really wanted me; that's it in a nutshell,' Emily said then, amazing both Dylan and herself with her honesty.

'What are you talking about? Of course she wanted you.'

'You don't know her, Dylan. She never wanted me. She said she never wanted a child. That she never had a career because of me.'

'She didn't mean that, surely?' Dylan was incredulous. His mother doted on her own four children.

'She did mean it, Dylan. She only ever worked in a sweet shop on the Crumlin Road for four years, but to listen to my mother sometimes you'd think she was the MD of Cadbury's.'

'I'm sure your mum was just having a bad day when she told you she never wanted you,' he persisted.

'She must have had a lot of bad days, then, for she said it more times than I care to remember. My birthdays were the worst. She said she nearly died having me, and that she would never get over the pain and embarrassment of that day. And that she should be getting the cake and the presents instead of me.'

'Well, okay, I'm sure childbirth is no picnic. But it was hardly your fault, was it? I'm so sorry for bringing this up today.'

'Don't be. We were never close, not ever. There were no big scenes or anything, no massive fights. Just lack of interest on her part and eighteen years of sulking on mine – until I left home to go to university. And Dad wasn't much better. He stayed out of the house, mostly. He's very good at ducking out of the way when there's any hint of a row brewing. I basically brought myself up. And now it's over. I know they love me in their own way, and I love them, but as a family it just never worked.'

'Okay. I see.'

'And that's why I don't go home to Belfast any more. I didn't go over at Christmas, by the way. Because somehow it's worse at Christmas, when you know your family unit just doesn't *work*. I sat in the flat, watching telly. And they didn't even answer the phone when I rang them.'

'Oh, Emily...'

'I don't want to see Mum at the minute – either of them, really. I mean, it's all in the past and I don't think I need to talk about it. Yes, I'm over it, Dylan. I've moved on. I just feel afraid sometimes, that's all. I feel afraid that you'll get bored of me the way they did. And then I get annoyed with myself for projecting all the time, because I know I should just stop worrying and let things happen. But it's so hard for me to let go of my self-doubt. It feels like jumping out of an aeroplane, every time.'

'Oh, Emily,' Dylan said again, wrapping his big strong arms around her.

Then he kissed her softly on the lips. It was a serious-about-you sort of kiss. Emily's eyes were moist with tears.

'I don't think you have moved on,' he said softly. 'Not yet.'

'Well, I want to move on,' she said defiantly.

'And I want you,' he replied.

Arabella phoned her solicitor for the sixth time that week to see if there had been any developments in her case.

'There is nothing to report as yet. We said we would let you know if anything happened, Mrs Harrington,' the solicitor told her patiently.

'So he hasn't been in touch? Really, not even an email? I can't believe he hasn't been in touch yet,' Arabella said.

'After the baby is born, maybe?'

'But he'll be even busier then.'

'I think we should give it another while. I'll turn up the heat in May or June.'

'I can't believe he hasn't called you. It's like he's trying to deny I exist,' Arabella said darkly.

'People sometimes react like that, by going into denial until they're ready to deal with the issues.'

'But I forward all his personal mail to the office, so he can't have forgotten me completely. He's still paying the mortgage on our house.'

'Yes, and that's all good news. It shows that he's aware of his responsibilities.'

'What about his responsibility to me? This is ludicrously unfair.'

'Mrs Harrington, please don't concern yourself any further. We'll discuss a divorce just as soon as the baby is born and your husband can concentrate on other matters.'

Other matters, Arabella thought to herself.

That's all she was to David nowadays: other matters.

At the beginning of June Arabella's solicitor finally summoned her to his office, and told her that David had agreed to a divorce. Arabella was very upset – even when she was informed that David was signing over his share of the equity in their home to her, along with a very generous cash settlement. It would be enough to pay off the mortgage. David had told the solicitor he wanted a clean break with no protracted negotiations, and that he wished to have no further communication with Arabella.

'All you have to do is sign these papers,' the solicitor said, sliding them across the desk towards her and offering her a pen.

'I still feel kind of short-changed,' Arabella said, looking over the papers and accepting a cup of tea. 'I just wish I knew why he left me.'

'Do you want me to give you some details about David's situation?'

'Might as well.'

'We had a civilized little chat, actually. David said he was very sorry to have hurt you the way he did, but he had fallen in love with a woman called Mary Barone. And he didn't feel able to tell you about it.'

'That figures; I'd have stabbed him.'

'Quite... He said he hadn't planned to have an affair, but when it began he could do nothing to prevent it,' the solicitor added.

'Bully for him,' Arabella said.

'And there's more. David and Mary are now the proud parents of twin girls named Venice and Paris.'

'They had twins? Venice and Paris ... oh, my word ... what silly names, actually...'

'And so David and Mary want to get married just as soon as they are legally free to do so. And then they are moving to Italy to live.'

Arabella just nodded. Barone was an Italian name, and that would explain the woman's good looks.

'Mary is Italian – she wants to bring up the children there.'

'Yes, I see. I figured that.'

'The glass house by the river is a rental. They are currently on a month's holiday in Cornwall.'

'There was no mention of how long the affair

had been going on before the pregnancy happened?' Arabella asked.

'No mention of that, no. Mary was one of the secretaries where David worked.'

'Was?'

'She's a full-time mum now.'

'I see,' Arabella said again.

But considering the settlement David was offering, the solicitor advised Arabella to accept the terms right away. She had no children to support and a very good career of her own, so getting the house in Twickenham was a very good outcome indeed.

'Fifteen years together,' Arabella whispered. 'Fifteen years together. And suddenly he doesn't wish to communicate further. Fancy that.'

'I'm sorry, Mrs Harrington. I'd advise you to accept this deal now, as Mr Harrington may not be feeling quite so generous in the years to come. I hear it's not as cheap as it used to be, living in Europe. We're expecting a rush of expats wanting to return to the UK and chucking out their sitting tenants before the leases are even up.'

Arabella signed the divorce papers, and then left the solicitor's office without speaking another word. Outside the sun was shining brightly and the streets were full of people enjoying the weather. Arabella felt as if she had left her own body and was floating six feet above the footpath. She felt as if she would never be happy again. She caught the Tube and walked along the river to David's rented house. She went round the back of the house, broke in using a brick she found lying beside the garden shed, and stood in the middle of the sitting room, wondering what to do next. And while she was thinking about it, she got out her cigarettes and lighter. The house was quite untidy and smelt of garlic, red wine and baby powder.

It was a very happy sort of house – and Arabella couldn't bear it.

Dylan and Emily were relaxing on the sofa in Emily's flat. It was late at night and the television was switched off. The only light came from some scented candles flickering on the coffee table. They were sharing half a bottle of Chenin Blanc.

'I think I love you, Emily,' he said suddenly.

Emily's heart skipped a beat.

'I bet you say that to all the girls,' she said quietly.

'I do not say it to all the girls. I'm not like that; you must know it by now. I'm no Casanova. I mean it, Emily.'

'Do you really mean it?' she asked, noticing a definite surge in hormones somewhere near her stomach.

'Yes, I never say things I don't mean,' he said gently. 'I've never felt like this before; I've never cared about anyone this much before.'

Then he kissed her tenderly. And somehow, despite his general gorgeousness and her general feelings of self-doubt, Emily believed him.

'Have you ever been in love before?' she asked him nervously.

'Yes, I have,' he said, gazing up at the ceiling. 'But it didn't last.'

'Why not, if you don't mind me asking...?'

'Rachel was her name. We got on really well. But she wanted more from life – a better career for me in banking, a better address for us both, and that sort of thing.'

'And you loved her?'

'Yes, I did, very much.'

'Then why didn't you stay in banking and give her the life she wanted?'

'Because I hated every minute of it, that's why. It was driving me round the twist, just making money like a robot – more and more and more money. Never enough money, though. No matter how many hours of overtime you'd put in, it was never enough for them. Endless meetings and endless phone calls, endless back-slapping and endless talk of bonuses; it gets very dull after a while, believe me. Not a thought to the morality of it all, Emily. Not a worry for the savers and investors who might lose out, or a care for the workers being paid a rubbish wage in other countries. I knew the whole thing would come crashing down eventually, it couldn't go on the way it was... So I told Rachel I was getting out. And she told me she was leaving me; it was as simple as that. We did part as friends, though.'

'Okay.'

'And no, I am not still secretly in love with her.'

'Ha! Fair enough, I've always found managing money very boring myself. It does seem to be a rather stressful occupation. Arabella's husband, David, was a stockbroker. I mean, he *is* a stockbroker. I mean, her *ex*-husband is a stockbroker and he's very clever and very wealthy. But she hardly saw him in recent years, because he spent so much time at the office.'

'Did you say her ex-husband?'

'Yes. Look, it's still a big secret at work, but they've split up. David and Arabella are living apart, and that's why I've been so busy at work lately. He's met another girl and she's having his baby. I've been covering for Arabella when she's been at home crying all day.'

'Poor Arabella...'

'Yes, poor Arabella! Now, remember – tell nobody about this, in case you tell somebody who knows somebody at *Stylish Living*. Because Arabella would die if this got out. She would honestly die.'

'She can't pretend she's married for the next fifty years.'

'She can. Trust me.'

'Right, okay, I won't say anything if we bump into each other.'

'Thanks. I'll be relieved when this is all over. David didn't give her a reason for leaving her, you see.'

'Wow.'

'Yes, wow. So Arabella can't analyse what went wrong with their marriage – because she didn't change over the years, and neither did David. She's stuck in a kind of limbo. Maybe when they divorce she'll start to get over him. I don't know anyone who's happily married,' Emily said.

'My parents are very happy,' Dylan said at once. 'Still like moonstruck teenagers, they are. Cuddling all the time; it's ridiculous.'

'What's their secret? I wonder.'

'Being nice to each other, Dad says. They're

114

just nice to each other.'

'Ah, that's lovely,' Emily said.

'Your parents are still together too? Not ideal parents to you, possibly, but they're still together?' Dylan said.

'Yes, but I think that's only because they can't be bothered filling out the forms to ask for another council house,' Emily said dryly. 'And Mum would never get around to packing up all her stuff, and Dad doesn't know how to open a can of beans.'

Dylan decided to leave it there for the time being.

'You know, I really think we've got something special going here, Emily. I've never felt this way about anyone before, I promise you. I know that's such an awful old cliché to say to a girl, but in my case it is true. I've fallen for you in a big, big way.'

'You say the nicest things.'

'Have you ever been in love before? Like, really madly in love?' he asked.

'No, I haven't,' she told him. 'Not even close.'

She snuggled up to him then and closed her eyes, breathing in the delicious scent of his peppery aftershave. As if on cue Emily's mobile phone began to ring.

'I'd better answer that,' she said. 'It might be Arabella. Oh, it is her.'

'I'll give you some privacy,' Dylan said, going into the kitchen to wash their empty wine glasses.

'Hello, Arabella?' Emily said.

'Emily, sweetheart, I know it's really late. But can you do me a massive favour?'

'Of course I can. Where are you? Are you in a

bar somewhere? How did the meeting go today at the solicitor's? Do you need a lift or something?'

'I'm fine, I don't need a lift. The thing is, I need to get away for a few days,' Arabella said.

'Well, okay. But why?' Emily said.

'I just need some time out, that's all. And that's why I need you to get into the office nice and early tomorrow morning.'

'Why?'

'Why do you think? Can you take over for me until I get back? I'm giving you full authority, Emily, and you can fire Jane Maxwell if she gives you any nonsense. No need to call me for advice, and so on. I'll be in touch. Bye.'

'Arabella, wait a minute,' Emily said. But Arabella was gone. 'For pity's sake, what's going on now?' Emily said loudly.

She tossed her mobile into her handbag and sat with her face in her hands.

'What's happened?' Dylan said, coming back and kneeling down on the floor beside Emily.

'Arabella's going away somewhere. She didn't say where. And I'm to take over for a while. And that'll be a complete laugh, because Jane Maxwell is no fan of mine,' Emily said crossly.

Then she burst into noisy tears. Dylan held Emily gently in his arms until she had stopped crying.

'What's the problem, Emily? Arabella's promoting you.'

'Yes, I know that. But this is so weird, because Arabella just lives for her job. It's so unlike her to go away like this. And let me take over the magazine? Or let *anyone* take over the magazine?

116

She's usually such a control freak. It's just so strange. I know I held that one meeting, but this seems open-ended.'

'It'll be okay,' he said tenderly. 'Arabella will be okay. Anybody can act a little strange from time to time. It happens to the best of us. There's no law against it.'

'I know,' Emily said. 'I'm fully aware of that. But I'm not a major fan of strange. That's why I came to London in the first place, do you see? To get away from strange. Oh no, I hope Arabella isn't going to go and attack David or something.'

'Don't be daft, she'd never do that,' Dylan smiled.

'She might.'

'She wouldn't.'

'You don't know Arabella the way I do,' Emily said darkly.

8. In the Mood

Dylan didn't set out to seduce Emily that night, and she didn't intend to seduce him either. But within minutes of Arabella's unsettling, late-night phone call they were tearing each other's clothes off and making love furiously on the sitting-room floor.

It all happened very suddenly. Emily was getting up to repair her make-up, after her crying had made her mascara run again, when she tripped over Dylan's ankles, landing on top of him quite heavily. In the resulting tangle of arms and cushions, Emily's T-shirt rode right up and Dylan caught a glimpse of her polka-dot balcony bra. Emily realized at once that he'd seen it, and that he was very turned on. And seeing just how much he fancied her did something magical for Emily's libido in return. They were alone, it was late, they were both consenting adults, and for once in her life Emily decided to be spontaneous. The poor guy had waited long enough to see her without her clothes on – almost six months. Nowadays if a nice man was prepared to wait for six months before making love to his girlfriend, it was so romantic it was almost newsworthy.

'Are you in the mood, by any chance?' she asked him, biting her lip with anticipation.

'I'm always in the mood when you're around,' he said hoarsely.

118

'Well, then. What are you waiting for?' she said playfully. 'I'm all yours.'

Five seconds later, they were undoing each other's jeans. Emily was so glad she'd worn her most expensive lingerie that evening. It had come from a designer boutique, the result of a recent gift voucher from Arabella. Good old Arabella – her gifts weren't all unwieldy kitchen gadgets, Emily thought happily. And when it came right down to it, wasn't modelling balcony bras and French knickers a far better way to spend one's time than winding endless lengths of pasta through a mini-mangle?

But soon the very expensive designer lingerie had been discarded by Dylan, as if it had just come from the bargain bin at Primark. He didn't even notice the labels as he peeled the delicate items from Emily's trembling body and dropped them on to the wooden floor. Then he pulled off his plain black shorts, and Emily could see he definitely wasn't lying about always being in the mood. As for Dylan's naked body – well, Emily was incredibly impressed. All his recent extra sports training certainly hadn't gone to waste.

'You're gorgeous,' she said before she could stop herself.

'Ha, thanks! But guys can't be gorgeous in the way that women are – the way you are,' he replied gallantly.

'Yes, they can.'

She kissed him softly on the lips as he eased the ponytail out of her hair.

'I've never slept with an editor before,' Dylan said mischievously.

'So you're only with me for the power?' she laughed.

'Not just the power,' he replied in a serious voice, 'but also for a free ticket to the next Ideal Home Show.'

'You can have all the free tickets you want,' Emily said, laughing again as Dylan pulled her down on top of him and lovingly caressed her body all over.

She began to have tingly feelings in places she'd never had them before. Even in the backs of her knees. And for once she wasn't embarrassed by her modest cleavage. For once she felt truly sexy and attractive and comfortable with what was going on. Even when she'd been with Alex, she'd never felt this sexy – or, indeed, this happy.

Then Dylan flinched with pain as his heel came down sharply on the plug from Emily's mobile phone charger.

'Usually I prefer to do this kind of thing in a bed; it's a lot safer,' he said.

'Come on,' she said, pulling him up and leading him into her bedroom. 'It's always cold in this flat, even in summer.'

They fell into bed, kissing again, and Emily thought she would die if they didn't make love in the next five minutes.

'Have you got a thingy?' she asked breathlessly.

'Whatever do you mean?' He laughed.

'You know what I mean. Protection...'

'Just so happens I have,' he laughed, racing back to his jeans pocket to retrieve one.

Emily watched his perfect bum as he went. It was so firm it didn't even wobble. She was tempted to nip out of bed herself and put on some more mascara and perfume, but there wasn't time. And since Dylan hadn't stopped to admire the lingerie, he probably wouldn't notice a little bit of mascara or perfume either. She lay down and tried to relax. And tried not to faint when she saw him coming back to bed; he was truly gorgeous from top to toe.

He kissed her again, all over, and Emily just gave herself up to the moment. She let Dylan lead the way and prayed that the retired couple in the flat below were already in a deep sleep and unlikely to hear her various expressions of ecstasy.

'Just tell me when you're ready,' Dylan said, exploring every inch of her with his fingertips and his kisses.

'I'm ready, I'm ready,' she gasped.

'Emily, I do love you.'

'Yes, yes, same here,' she whispered. 'Oh yes … oh yes … oh yes!'

Afterwards they tidied up the crumpled bedclothes, plumped up the pillows and lay comfortably together in each other's arms. The flat was indeed quite cold and they were happy to relax in a warm bed and just talk for a while before going to sleep.

They both had a lovely, light feeling – as if they had found something that had been missing for a long time.

'That was amazing,' Dylan said.

'Yes, it was rather special,' she replied, kissing his shoulder.

'I love you, Emily.'

'I think you do.'

'Do you love me?'

'Yes, I definitely do.'

'Say it, then?'

'Okay, I love you,' she said.

They kissed again.

'I hope you don't think I'm putting any pressure on you?' he said.

'Not at all,' she laughed.

'Because I just want to be sure; I just want you to know I'm serious about us.'

'I understand. It's all or nothing with me too,' she said as he kissed her hand softly. 'I think you know that by now. I've never been the ditsy type.'

'Is that a fact?'

'Yes, very funny... I know I'm a little on the serious side. But I can't help it, and I'm probably too set in my ways to change now.'

'I don't want you to change. I knew you were special the day I met you,' he said. 'I could feel something crackling in the air between us, couldn't you?'

'Yes, but I thought it was all the polyester blouses in the shop,' she teased him.

'Ha! I asked for that one.'

'No, I did feel something,' she admitted.

'I'm so glad, because if it doesn't feel exactly right, well, there's no point, is there?'

'Not really, no. I didn't think I'd mind if this turned out to be just a passing thing. I remember giving myself a little pep talk the night you rang to ask me out. I remember telling myself that I should go along to the shop for a cup of tea and a chat, and see what happened, and keep it all very simple and casual. And if we didn't click,

122

then that was that and no harm done. I mean, I'm not the sort of girl who hankers after an engagement ring after only two weeks. But I'm also not the sort of girl who can just have one-night stands without getting emotionally involved, if you know what I mean? But we shouldn't say it's something more if it really isn't, Dylan. I mean, it's okay if you need more time. Maybe we shouldn't use the L word just yet?'

'Wow, you're certainly a cautious one. We've both said the L word now, haven't we? So there's no going back! And I meant what I said earlier. I am in love with you, Emily. This isn't going to be like *Sex and the City*, so I'm sorry if you like the melodrama of an on-off thing. This relationship is *not* going to be terribly complicated. At least, I won't be making it complicated. There won't be endless break-ups and make-ups and tripping around Paris with you in a vintage prom dress, and us missing each other by seconds.'

'I'm not a big one for melodrama,' Emily said. 'I imagine that sort of personality could become quite tiring to live with, for me and you both. Hey, you sound pretty familiar with the storylines in *Sex and the City*,' she added.

'We might have caught a few episodes over the years, me and the lads. You know, when we were all too plastered to find the remote control?'

'Or maybe you just fancied one of the girls and were hoping to see her naked?'

'Yeah, you're very good,' he said. 'You could make a living at this.'

He turned to face Emily then and they kissed again.

123

'I'll let you go to sleep now,' Emily said dreamily. 'I think you've earned it.'

'Okay. Goodnight, Emily. Love you.'

Emily closed her eyes and drifted off into the most relaxing sleep she'd had for years. Dylan lay awake for a long time, just looking at Emily's face in the moonlight. Wondering what happy twist of fate had brought them together and also hoping she wouldn't change her mind about him in the cold light of day. English girls were complicated enough, he thought. He hoped that Irish girls weren't even more complicated. Life was a series of simple choices to Dylan Shawcross: he *didn't* want to be a banker and he *did* want to be with Emily. He was happy to help Sylvia at the shop until his savings ran out. Then he might set up a small business of his own. He wanted to live with Emily and wondered if it was too soon to bring the subject up with her. Would Emily be pleased if he suggested they live together? Or would she think he was a bit too intense?

He liked the navy walls in this bedroom, he thought to himself as Emily slept peacefully beside him. That antique wardrobe was a bit on the big side, but it was nice enough too, and the white carpet was pretty – he'd have to be careful not to walk dirt into it. He would be happy living here, he thought. Though he'd be more than willing to go house-hunting, if that's what Emily wanted. They could look for something really unusual and fix it up – an old warehouse in Shoreditch or an airy loft in Soho would be lovely. It would depend on what they could afford, obviously. Or maybe Emily would like a more traditional house? Perhaps a

Georgian terrace or a modern semi way out in the suburbs? He'd like to have a go at fitting his own kitchen, or at least a home office. Eventually, his head full of half-formed plans, he snuggled down under the duvet, kissed Emily on the cheek and fell asleep.

Several miles away, ten exhausted firefighters stood looking at the charred and mangled ruins of a serious house fire. The open-plan design of the modern building had made it impossible for them to contain the flames. The entire property was gutted, and all the contents within had been destroyed. Luckily there were no occupants in the building that night. They'd found the blackened remains of two pink cots in one of the bedrooms, but a neighbour had confirmed that the couple currently living there had gone away on holiday to Cornwall.

There was nothing left to do now but wait for a carpenter to come and start boarding the place up.

Arabella was putting the finishing touches to her make-up as the sun came up over London. She hadn't slept all night, but she wasn't remotely tired. She poured herself another cup of tea and switched on the television to see if there was anything about the fire on the breakfast news. There wasn't. Luckily the main story that day was yet another MP's expenses scandal. With an election due the TV companies didn't want to miss a single snippet of gossip. Both of the main parties were running scared. Some people were even betting on a victory for the Liberal Democrats.

'That was quite a night,' Arabella told her reflection in the sitting-room mirror as she savoured a cup of PG Tips. Her hair and clothes were immaculate, as was the entire house. Arabella had been very busy in the last few hours. However, her eyes were glassy and cold-looking, and her mouth was set in a hard, determined line. She looked guilty. She reminded herself of a police photofit. Arabella's heart began to race uncontrollably; she didn't think she'd like being in prison. But they'd never be able to prove it was her, would they? David would suspect her, but he'd never be able to prove anything. She stared at herself until her heartbeat slowed right down and she felt in control of her emotions once more.

'That's it; get a grip. I may have gone a *bit* over the top, but I think it was worth it,' Arabella said softly.

She felt purged and free, as if her heart had escaped from a locked metal box. She no longer wanted the traitorous David in her bed or in her life. She would erase all memory of his existence from her life, and she would go on to become a living legend in the magazine publishing world. People would look at her as she wafted around the room at trade events, and admire her for her dedication to the job and for her mysteriously single status. For one thing was certain now: Arabella never wanted a man to be close to her, ever again. Liars and cheats the lot of them. She would never get her heart broken again. She would revert to her maiden name as soon as it could be arranged. She would redecorate this

126

house entirely to her own taste; all in shades of silver and beige with zebra-print armchairs and fresh orchids. She might sleep with some handsome young man the next time she was on a foreign holiday, just to conceive her much-wanted baby. Or she might do it the official, safe way at a private clinic – just as long as there was no chance of the father turning up and wanting to be a part of her child's life. She would commit murder if that happened – some idiot man on the doorstep with a bag of toys in his hand. Men! They always played the Daddy card when they were bored with womanizing, or when they wanted somebody to cook and clean for them. Selfish creeps! She wanted no commitments now.

No, she was over all that silly, sentimental rubbish.

'It's just me, myself and I,' she said in a strangely hollow voice.

Arabella picked up the phone. She confirmed her reservation at the small but luxurious hotel in Scotland that she had spotted in a rival magazine. She had already booked a seat on an early flight. She called a taxi to take her to the airport. They said they would be there in ten minutes. Arabella always kept a small suitcase packed in case she had to go away for work at short notice. She went upstairs, took the case out of her wardrobe and laid it on the bed to check she had left nothing out: dressing gown, pyjamas, slippers, underwear, novels, chocolates, tea bags, bottle of red wine (hotel prices were extortionate), packet of Digestive biscuits. She'd stay in her hotel room, read a novel and have some early nights. She'd order

127

meals from room service to avoid any unwanted approaches in the dining room. Just a few days would see her right, and then she would get on with her life. Emily would be fine on her own at the magazine. Arabella was justifiably proud of her little protégée from Belfast. Emily had a good head on her shoulders when it came to the magazine.

'And she still has most of her slates on when it comes to relationships, hopefully. That new man of hers is super-hot, that's for sure,' Arabella said to nobody in particular.

She added some dresses and shoes, snapped the case shut and carried it to the front door. She checked that everything was switched off and returned to the sitting room to finish her tea.

'Yes, Emily is a wise one,' she said to her reflection. 'Not like some of us,' she added.

And then, in spite of herself, Arabella managed a watery sort of giggle. She went to light a cigarette as she waited for the taxi to come and then she realized she'd lost her cigarette lighter. Could she possibly have dropped it in David's house? Arabella's heart convulsed with fright; her initials were engraved on that lighter. And, even worse, David had given it to her for their wedding anniversary just a couple of years earlier. He'd recognize it straight away.

Arabella felt like fainting with fear.

The taxi arrived, so she grabbed her bag and case instead, and went running down the front steps, slamming the door behind her.

At that exact moment David Harrington was answering a phone call from his local police station, telling him that his rented home in London had been virtually destroyed in an apparent arson attack. They'd found a cigarette lighter in the debris, they said. It bore the initials A.H. Did that mean anything to him?

David was too stunned to reply at first.

'Arson?' he stuttered.

They thought it was arson because the back door had been quite badly damaged, so clearly someone had gone to great trouble to gain access to the house. But they could find no real signs of ransacking. Was there a safe in the house?

'No, there wasn't.'

Did anyone know he'd be away from home for a month?

'Only the landlord, our neighbour and my team at work.'

When asked if he had any idea who might target him in such a way, David didn't have to think for very long. He wouldn't have believed it possible that Arabella could turn arsonist like this, but the lighter was proof of it; there could be no doubt whatsoever.

The policeman noted his hesitation and urged him again to name names, but David couldn't bear to put Arabella through any more pain and anguish. He had simply stopped loving her, and they hadn't been able to have a baby together – and that was punishment enough. He didn't want to have to come back to London from Italy every few weeks for some long-drawn-out court case. He'd much rather leave all the financial and rebuilding headaches for his landlord's insurer.

129

Well, David did have the soul of a stockbroker when all was said and done.

'Look, I'm sorry I'm no help to you. But I really have no idea what could have happened; it must have been a burglary gone terribly wrong,' David said eventually, kissing Mary's hand tenderly and thanking his lucky star their beloved daughters were safe and sound. They'd go to Italy early now – just as soon as he could make the arrangements. They could stay in a hotel until their new home was ready.

'You can't think of anything, sir?'

'Nothing. The burglars must have got angry when they found there was nothing worth stealing, and just vandalized the place instead. You know what these hoodies are like; they think every nice house in London must be chock-full of Picasso paintings and diamond rings. The idiots don't realize how much it costs just to rent a decent place these days. That's the comprehensive system for you. I don't know; they were probably high on drugs,' David added.

'Could be something like that, yes. There are lots of drugs about.'

'There you are, then – drugs and boredom. We ought to bring back National Service, I expect,' David said, hoping he wasn't laying it on too thick.

'National Service – you're kidding, mate. These young lads never get out of bed before four o'clock in the afternoon. A week in the army would finish off the lot of them.'

'Well, I'm just thankful we weren't all asleep in our beds when the fire started.'

'Yes, that's true enough.'

'And you definitely don't know who A.H. is?'

'No. Must be one of the burglars, I expect.'

The police mustn't have known that his wife was called Arabella. And David decided they wouldn't find out from him. If it ever came to light, he could say he was in shock at the time, and had forgotten all about Arabella. They couldn't prove a thing.

David didn't care about the fire. He just wanted to hold Mary in his arms and fall asleep with the fresh scent of her grapefruit shampoo in his nostrils. He wanted to kiss his daughters' tiny little starfish hands now, and then go back to sleep. He hoped this awful turn of events could be reduced and compacted into nothing more than a mild irritation. Arabella had always been too complicated for him. She was such a restless person – forever rushing about the place, never sitting down to have a chat with him over a bit of supper. Never wanting to go for a simple, aimless walk…

He was glad he wouldn't be seeing her any more.

'Thank you for telling us about the fire, anyway,' he said.

'The property is being boarded up as we speak.'

'Okay, I'll keep my phone switched on just in case there's any more news. And we'll come back to London first thing tomorrow morning, of course. Thanks again, and good morning to you.'

'Good morning to you, sir.'

9. Wedding Dress, Never Worn

When Emily opened her eyes she saw Dylan standing by her wardrobe with one hand on the open door and the other hand scratching his head. He was topless and barefoot but had managed to put his jeans back on. The sun shone through Emily's tapestry curtains and made a mottled pattern on Dylan's bare back. She thought she'd like a photograph of him standing like that – to keep with her for ever.

'Hi there,' she said sleepily.

He turned to look at her.

'Hi there,' he smiled.

There was an endearingly confused expression on his face.

Emily suddenly remembered her wedding dress.

'Dylan, are you looking for something?' she said nervously.

'Oh, it's nothing,' he said, smiling at her again. 'I just thought you might have an old T-shirt or something that I could borrow? My top has red wine spilt on it. I wonder how that happened! Anyway, I was going to surprise you with breakfast in bed.'

'Hang on, I'll find you something to wear,' she said, leaning out of bed and flicking open a large wicker trunk. 'I keep my casual clothes in here. I never really use the wardrobe. It's mainly full of old stuff.'

She handed him the baggiest T-shirt she could find.

'Emily?' he said carefully.

'Yes?'

'Why have you got a wedding dress and other wedding things in the wardrobe?'

'You saw them, then?'

'I'm sorry, I couldn't help it.'

'That's okay.'

'I wasn't snooping, honestly. They were right there on the top of this great pile of things. There's an awful lot of wedding stuff. Is it all for a photo shoot or something?'

Emily briefly thought of lying to him, but she couldn't bring herself to do it.

'The truth is, I was due to get married a while back,' she said, slipping on her robe and a pair of socks. 'But the wedding was cancelled. I should have told you about it – but, anyway, there it is now. Do you just want a cup of tea for breakfast, or would you like cereal and toast as well?' she asked, leaving the room suddenly. Dylan followed her through to the tiny kitchen.

'Yes, please. Anything that's handy – I really don't mind. But, Emily, you said you'd never been in love before, when I asked you last night.'

Dylan looked at Emily patiently. He waited for her to fill the kettle, and then he folded her into his arms.

'You look gorgeous in the morning,' he said. 'Your hair is all mussed up. But listen, you don't have to tell me about it ... if you don't want to,' he added.

'No, it's okay; I'll tell you. There's no big secret

133

love in my past, Dylan. I have never been in love. I thought I was, once. But it wasn't true love, just an infatuation,' she admitted sadly. 'It was a bit of a disaster, really. I wasn't trying to hide it from you, Dylan. I just didn't feel ready to tell you about it.'

'So what happened? Why were you getting married if you weren't in love? And why didn't you mention this last night when I told you about my ex? You could have told me, you know. I would have understood.'

Emily slipped out of Dylan's embrace to fetch a bottle of milk from the fridge and put bread in the toaster.

'Yes, I know you would have been very sympathetic. But it was the most embarrassing day of my life, and I still find the experience very difficult to talk about. We were having such a lovely evening yesterday, I didn't want to go and ruin it all. Anyway, it means nothing; he means nothing, and it's all in the past now.'

'But is it in the past? I'm really sorry for asking,' Dylan said humbly, while still looking absolutely adorable but slightly ridiculous in Emily's glittery skull T-shirt from River Island.

'It's over; it was all over and done with eighteen months ago. My beloved stood me up, at the altar, if you must know,' Emily said, setting out cups and plates and avoiding Dylan's gaze. 'He stood me up on our wedding day.'

'You are joking?'

'No, I'm not joking. It doesn't just happen in romantic movies, you know. It happens in real life too, sometimes. I was there at the church,

134

doing the whole mental bride thing – biting my false nails and pacing up and down the path and asking everybody what time it was. And he just didn't show up.'

'Where was the wedding?' Dylan said, clearly horrified. Emily sat down on a kitchen chair and indicated to Dylan to do the same.

'It was in Belfast. The December before last, it was. A lovely old church right in the city centre! One hundred and fifty guests all present and correct – mostly extended family on my father's side. I had four bridesmaids, who were all cousins of mine, all with very expensive hairdos and make-up. A luxury reception booked and paid for by my sweet self – at Belfast Castle, no less. There were oysters and lobsters, five tiers of white cup-cakes with silver balls on the top instead of a wedding cake, a string quartet in the foyer and gallons of pink champagne. Oh well. They do say pride comes before a fall. And that was a pretty spectacular fall, I can tell you.'

'And the guy actually did a runner?'

'Yes. He sent me a text, would you believe it? A tiny little text! He was thirty minutes late by that stage, and there was no sign of the best man either. I was imagining all sorts. I thought they'd done something terrible to him on the stag night; I thought he was in a booze-induced coma. Or maybe they'd had a car accident on the way to the church? So anyway, I'm freaking out and thinking I ought to start ringing round the hospitals ... and then I get a text from Prince Charming. And he says he doesn't want to be tied down when he's only thirty-three. And he's very sorry, but it's better to tell the truth now than to get married and regret it later. And as the final touch, he told me he'd met someone else a few days earlier and he thought she might be the one for him. Just a few days, and he'd found the one! We'd been together for over ten years, off and on.'

'The absolute scumbag! What was his name?'

'Alex. I'm not telling you his surname – in case you go and beat the hell out of him.'

'Didn't your father beat the hell out of him at the time?' Dylan wanted to know.

'No, of course not. My poor father weighs nine stone at the very most. He couldn't beat the hell out of a wet paper bag.'

'Still and all...'

'Dad was quite nice about it, really. He said Alex didn't deserve me and I was better off without him. It was the nicest thing my father's ever said to me, actually. I was so moved when he said that. We had a nice little moment where we held hands by the church door, and he really seemed like a picture-book father. Then he disappeared off to the greyhound track.'

'Why?'

'He was too mortified to face the guests. He said a flutter on the dogs would calm his nerves. Frankly, I didn't blame him one bit.'

'Fair enough, I think. And what did your mother say?'

'She didn't say much at the time – because she wasn't there.'

'Where was she?'

'She was shopping in Dublin.'

'She went shopping on your wedding day?'

Dylan gasped.

'Yes, I told you she was very fond of shopping.'

'I can't believe it,' he said.

'I think Mum was too nervous to be at the wedding, really. You know how the mother of the bride gets almost as much attention as the bride herself? Well, my mum doesn't like wearing posh hats – and she doesn't care much for my father's relatives either. She says they're very pushy and nosy types. Mind you, with all the drama, nobody noticed she wasn't in the church. I don't think they ever found out that the mother of the bride was wandering round Dublin with half a dozen carrier bags on each arm.'

'Oh, Emily, I'm so sorry.'

'Afterwards she said, what did I expect? She said Alex was a big-shot and a smooth playboy – and that he was well out of my league, anyway. And that I was, and always had been, a day-dreamer with ideas above my station.'

'She did not say that, did she? What an un-forgivable thing to say to your own daughter.'

'Listen, it makes no difference what my mother says to me or anybody else. She's always been a bit odd, Dylan. Actually, I should tell you ... that she's ... an alcoholic. She's a bad-tempered, painfully shy, bitter and resentful inverted snob ... and a desperate, incurable, unapologetic alcoholic.'

'Come here,' he said, pulling Emily into his arms.

He kissed the top of her head as she wept silent tears.

'Thanks for being so kind,' she said eventually. 'I know it isn't my fault, or Mum's either, but I've been carrying the shame of her alcoholism around with me all these years. I think that's part of the reason Alex broke up with me; he didn't want the hassle of living with an alcoholic mother-in-law. He was very conscious of his reputation and, as I said before, Belfast is a very small town. Everybody knows everything about everybody else in their social circle. So there was that – and the fact we have no money.'

'But that must have been so awful for you. What did you do? I mean, when this Alex *loser* didn't turn up at the church?'

'I thought I was coping okay, but after Dad left I had a full-blown panic attack in the porch, gasping on my hands and knees in a cloud of white tulle. A real fairytale wedding all right! I was shaking so much, I dropped my phone in the holy water font. The priest was very nice about it; he got me calmed down again and gave me a paper bag to breathe into. I thought I'd die of shame and hurt and rage. But we had a little chat out in the gardens, me and the priest, and he told me there must be something better in line for me. Or someone better. So I told the guests to go ahead and have the meal – the poor loves were all dressed up with nowhere to go. The priest made the announcement on my behalf. After all, I'd already paid twelve thousand pounds for the reception.'

'Ouch!'

'And I went back to my parents' house in the wedding car, changed into my ordinary clothes and rang for a taxi to the airport. Needless to say, I never want to show my face in Belfast again. It's not that they'd laugh at me or anything. I just don't want their sympathy. Something like that will never be forgotten – not ever. They have long memories in Belfast, very long memories. Fifty years after I'm dead they'll still be describing me as *the poor critter that got left at the altar.*'

'Why did you keep the wedding dress?'

'It cost me a fortune. And it looked beautiful on me. And also, I wanted a reminder of my madness.'

'It wasn't madness, Emily. Alex was totally cruel to do that to you. He should have gone through with the wedding, just to save face on the day. And then maybe you could have split up later, in private. You could have split up the following day and asked for an annulment. But he shouldn't have done that to you. That was unforgivable.'

'You're so thoughtful and sweet,' she said, putting on fresh toast and throwing the cold slices of bread in the bin.

She boiled the kettle again and filled the teapot.

'Well, I don't know about thoughtful and sweet, but I would never stand a girl up on her wedding day.'

'I know you wouldn't.'

'What happened to this Alex chap in the end?'

'He's engaged to another girl now. The one he met a few days before he left me. She comes from old money; she's a lawyer. Alex is a lawyer too. Did I mention that?'

'He's nothing but a grubby little gold-digger. You had a lucky escape, Emily.'

'Ha! Thanks.'

'He was only after her money, Emily. You know

139

it's true.'

'Maybe he was. But anyway, my dear old mother was right all along.'

'Huh! With a mother like yours, who needs enemies?'

'She's a depressive, Dylan. To her, life has always been a crushing disappointment. And everything that goes wrong simply confirms her belief that life will always be a crushing disappointment. I don't think she knows how to deal with happiness. It's very sad for her, really. I'm the lucky one, because I got away from Belfast and made something of myself. Would you like some toast?'

'Yes, thanks.'

Emily set a plate of toast on the breakfast bar and calmly poured two cups of tea.

'I don't agree with that assessment, Emily. There's simply no excuse for treating you like that. She ought to be ashamed of herself. What she said to you was even worse than that idiot standing you up on your wedding day. Parents should always be on the side of their kids – no matter what they're going through themselves.'

'It's okay, I'm used to it. She can't help the way her brain works, I suppose. I should just be grateful I've found something to be interested in. I love my work, even though it's true that it isn't very exciting. But the interiors business never disappoints either, do you see? That's why I love all those perfect rooms – empty of people, empty of emotional baggage and the untidiness of human affairs.'

'I can understand that, yes.'

'Arabella was brilliant about it all too. She

couldn't make it to the wedding, because her father was very ill at the time. But she was so supportive for weeks and weeks afterwards. I feel I've let her down very badly over her husband's recent behaviour, you know. She did beg me for advice, but I wasn't able to give her any. I wish I knew where she was now. I wish I knew why she just took off like that. I wish I could do something to help her.'

'I'm sure Arabella knows you care about her very much. Listen, you should give that dress away to a friend – or sell it. Get rid of the memories.'

'Yes, I'll donate the dress and all the accessories to the shop this very day. I'm sure Sylvia will be pleased. Or will she think you're going out with a flake? She might as well know about Alex now – in case she finds out later on down the line and thinks I'm hiding a whole bunch of other things.'

There were one or two other secrets lurking in Emily's wardrobe, as it happened. But Alex's desertion was the main one – the big one. Emily decided that would be enough information for Dylan for one day.

'Sylvia likes you, Emily. She says you're very real.'

'That's nice, I like being real,' Emily smiled.

'Yes, it wouldn't be much fun living life as a hologram, would it?' Dylan said, munching toast.

The walls of Emily's small kitchen were painted a zingy lime green, and she'd bought tea canisters and tea towels to match. A row of cup hooks held six green and white floral patterned mugs.

Dylan complimented her on the decor.

'Thanks,' she said happily. 'I do try to live

141

stylishly on a very small budget.'

'Don't they pay you well enough at the magazine?'

'Yes, the salary is quite good. But the rent here is pretty high, and also I'm still paying off my wedding debts.'

'Did your father not pay for some of it?'

'No – he'd like to, but my parents live on benefits, Dylan. I have to send them money from time to time, dear love them.'

'Of course, look, I'm such an idiot sometimes. I had no right to ask you about any of this.'

'No, I'm glad to be able to tell you,' she smiled. 'It feels less surreal now it's out in the open. It's hard keeping secrets. Nobody here knows about this. I mean, apart from Arabella; she knows pretty much everything.'

'Does anyone else at your work know?' Dylan asked gently.

'No, it's just Arabella. The others are lovely too. I'm sure even Jane Maxwell wouldn't say anything mean if she found out.'

'Jane Maxwell?'

'Long story... But I'm trying to portray a nicer image of Belfast, do you see? So I like to keep the most embarrassing things hidden under the carpet. Even though, if that carpet was real, it would look like Mount Everest. Would you like more tea?'

'Yes, please. So you're truly over this Alex chap, then?' Dylan asked gently.

'Yes, of course I'm over him. Haven't you got it? What we had together was *nothing*. And compared to last night, well, we weren't even all that compatible. That makes me sound terribly bitchy, but it's true. Just so you know.'

'Well, it was quite a night.'

'Alex honestly doesn't matter any more. I was a romantic fool, that's all. Alex is from a wealthy family and I grew up in one of the poorest neighbourhoods in the city. We went to the same grammar school, though. And I was young and foolish, so I kidded myself that material things didn't matter.'

'They don't matter, Emily.'

'Oh they do, I'm afraid. Anyway, we were teenage sweethearts and I guess he was a schoolgirl crush that I just never got over. He was my first love and my first lover. We broke up lots of times over the years. It's obvious in hindsight that it was never going to work, because we never even lived together. I think he liked the idea of breezing in and out of my life, keeping me in reserve until he found somebody better.'

'That's an awful way to treat anybody.'

'And he proposed to me when we were on holiday in Australia two years ago, both of us wasted on cheap cocktails. You see, even the proposal was an indication that all was not well. But I got all carried away, became a total wedding fiend and planned this great big fancy wedding. Borrowed a fortune and blew it all on daft things like vintage cars to the church, and fresh flowers on all the pews. I mean, it was silly. I'm not even religious... And Alex said he'd move to London permanently instead of flying back and forth from Belfast all the time. Then he met this other girl on the plane one day about a week before the wedding and realized he'd found the one.'

'So you said… Still, he fairly picked his moment to break up with you,' Dylan said, shaking his head with disapproval.

'I can see it from his point of view now,' Emily said. 'I mean, he is a lawyer. So he knew how foolish it would have been to go ahead with the wedding.'

'You're a bit weird, Emily.'

'Yes, I know,' she laughed.

'You're infuriatingly practical sometimes.'

'Yes, I know – but I have to be. When and if you meet my parents you'll understand why I cultivate my practical side as much as I can. People who live entirely by their emotions can end up in an awful muddle. Tell you what; I'll pack up all the wedding things and my honeymoon clothes and I'll give the lot of it to the shop. You can bring it in with you today, and then you'll see that I'm genuinely over Alex and not in love with him any more. Will that do you?'

'Sure, but only if you want to,' Dylan said.

'I do want to. It's a Zen thing. I made up this Zen theory one day to stop Arabella coming round to the flat and finding out that most of her gifts to me were on their way to your shop. But, you know, I'm really starting to believe in the power of de-cluttering – one memory at a time.'

Emily leapt off her chair and went striding into the bedroom. Pulling a large carrier bag out of her wicker trunk, she opened the wardrobe door and lifted out her wedding dress, silk posy, lace veil and satin shoes. She laid them gently in the carrier bag and then added four bridesmaid dresses, several summery outfits, three brand-new bikinis, two pairs of leather sandals, two woven clutch bags and four silk scarves.

'There,' she said to Dylan, who was leaning on the door frame, sipping his tea and blowing her a kiss. 'All done – I'm truly over it. Now, I've got to hurry up and get dressed. Remember, I'm the new editor until further notice.'

Dylan looked at Emily and fell in love with her all over again. But he didn't complicate the moment by saying anything. He just hoped he never met Alex in the street, for he couldn't promise not to punch him in the face.

How could any man not love Emily? he wondered. How could any man think he was too good for her?

10. Charity Begins at Home

It was late July and Sylvia had deserted her post yet again, but with very good reason: the stables were taking in a batch of nine elderly ponies that had been found half starved at the side of the road in Cumbria. The poor creatures had been left tethered to a gate, so they couldn't even graze or drink while they waited for their callous owners to come back. Sylvia had rearranged the entire stables to fit them all in, booked a day-long visit by the vet, and was working out if they could afford more heating oil. She was also planning to invite the local press to come along and take pictures in a bid to raise fresh funds.

And so Dylan was once more running the charity shop single-handedly. He didn't mind at all, he said, for it gave him more time to think. And it gave him a little more time to decide what he wanted to do with the rest of his life. On the final Saturday in July, Emily decided to spend the day with him at the shop, sorting out the new stock and maybe changing some of the wall displays. She bought a few fashion magazines from a near-by shop, so she could study current trends and maybe attempt something eye-catching in the window. Now that the new decor was complete, Sylvia felt it was time to begin the transformation from shabby-chic to style boutique. Consequently she had given Emily her blessing to tinker with the shop displays to her heart's content.

'I think I'll begin with clearing the back wall,' Emily said, after a while spent flicking through her magazines. 'And then I'll put some summery tea dresses and straw hats up.'

'Sounds fine,' Dylan agreed. 'Tell me if you need the ladder.'

'Shall I put my wedding dress in the window?' Emily asked Dylan suddenly. 'It is the height of summer, after all. We might attract the attention of a passing bride-to-be. You never know.'

'Look, are you sure you want to do this?' Dylan asked gently. We could always give it all to another charity shop, so you don't have to look at it.'

'No, I'm ready. I think it would be lovely if my dress had a happy ending. You know, to restore some good karma to the whole thing? And if you price the gown and all the accessories very reasonably, you'll get some much-needed money for the shop too. I know I paid thousands for it, but Sylvia needs all the funds she can get – what with the poor starving ponies and everything.'

'You're being infuriatingly practical again.'

'I know. But that's no bad thing. We have animals to feed.'

'Well, do you want me to move anything out of the window for you? We don't have any nice mannequins or anything, though. Sylvia thought of buying couple, but you wouldn't believe the price of them.'

'Um, good point... I know, there's a nice little wardrobe in the storeroom, isn't there? That pretty, painted one? I think Sylvia brought it in

147

from her house, to keep the spare stock in. But it's far too pretty for mere storage. Could we maybe set that in the window, towards one side so it doesn't block out the light too much? And then I'll just iron the dress, slip it on a hanger and hang it on the wardrobe door? It'll look lovely there, I think. It'll look as if it's hanging on the wardrobe door ready for the bride to put it on and step straight into the wedding car.'

'Okay. Listen, I'll fetch the wardrobe and you can start ironing. But, Emily ... if you change your mind about selling the dress in here, will you please tell me? I can't imagine what you must have gone through that day. I know you said you were over Alex, but you don't have to put on a brave face with me – honestly. I know how important weddings are to girls. I never thought weddings were just about the frills and the flowers.'

'Yes, you're very perceptive for a bloke, aren't you?'

'I try to be. When I want to be; but I don't always get it right.'

'Ah, you're doing all right so far. I admit, I did think I'd lose my sanity before that day was over. My thoughts were racing for hours, and I felt panicky and weird. As the minutes crawled by, it was like an out-of-body experience.'

'No wonder.'

'And yes, I did cry until my face looked like a crumpled-up crisp packet. If it weren't for Arabella, I might have jacked in my job altogether and gone on antidepressants.'

'But you didn't.'

148

'No, I didn't. Because eventually I realized that Alex wasn't the right man for me. We had nothing at all in common. Alex was ultra-ambitious – he was into extreme sports, and his idea of romance was asking his secretary to send me flowers on my birthday.'

'What an idiot.'

'I was crazy to think we were going to live happily ever after – together for fifty years. He didn't even want to live in London. And I must have told him a hundred times I was never going to settle down in Belfast. I think that he thought I'd just come home like a good girl when the wedding was over.'

'But you must have loved him to agree to marry him?' Dylan said gently. 'You must have loved him a bit?'

'I did love him, yes. But I loved the *memory* of Alex when he was a nineteen-year-old; when he was fun and always making me laugh and playing practical jokes on everyone. I was in love with our student days and that lovely, light feeling you get with your first love. Snogging in the park beside the ice-cream vans, and running all the way home in the pouring rain... But by the time Alex was thirty-three, all of those nice things had been replaced by an all-consuming desire to make money.'

'Yes?'

'Yes. He was a completely different person, Dylan. All he ever talked about was his career path, and the expensive cars and houses he liked, and who he ought to be playing golf with. He was an insufferable bore, if I'm honest about it. If I'd met him for the first time when he was thirty-three, I would have thought he was an annoying little social climber. I wouldn't have given him the time of day. And he was terribly ashamed of my parents. I mean, I was ashamed of them too. Well, I've a right to be ashamed of them. But they were no reflection on him, surely? No, I was just as guilty as he was. It was me who should've put the brakes on it all.'

'You mustn't blame yourself, Emily.'

'I know. But we're all responsible for how we deal with life's little setbacks, aren't we? I shouldn't have let myself get blinded by all the trappings.'

'It wasn't your fault.'

'But it was my fault, Dylan. I should have known better. I don't like it when people refuse to accept any blame for their own troubles. That's the one thing that really, really frustrates me about my mother, you know? She blames everyone but herself for her alcoholism.'

'What do you mean?' Dylan said, carrying the small wardrobe carefully out of the storeroom and setting it down in the space that Emily had just made by the window.

'She says it isn't her fault that alcohol is so addictive and so cheap, and the government should have more rehab facilities. And the school she went to was useless and gave her no preparation for the world of work. And my father should have done better for himself, and should have given her a nicer lifestyle. He should have been a more romantic husband, and he should have made her happier. And then I held her back from entering

150

the job market properly, and that's why she drank so much – because she was so bored of sitting at home with me all the time.'

'Did she not think of leaving you in a nursery, if she was all that unhappy?'

'I think nurseries are a relatively new phenomenon back home. She was only earning buttons, anyway. Would you listen to me rambling on again? I hope I'm not boring the pants off you. Let's not talk about my parents any more today, or Alex. That's supposed to be the point of all my de-cluttering. I'm trying to stop thinking about all the times I messed up.'

'You didn't mess up.'

'Okay, all the times when life let me down.'

'Fair enough, let's change the subject.'

Dylan put his hands up in a gesture of surrender and went off to boil the kettle.

Then Emily fetched her wedding gown from under the counter and gave it a careful pressing on the wonky old ironing board. She hung it carefully on the inside of the wardrobe door, which she left standing wide open. Then she draped her lace veil over the padded hanger too, and set her satin shoes on the floor beside her pink beaded posy. The bridesmaid dresses she hung inside the wardrobe. Luckily they were made of crushed silk and didn't need to be ironed. There was a pretty ribbon garter, which she tucked into the bodice of the dress; it would make a nice little surprise for whoever eventually decided to buy it.

'I had four pairs of the sweetest pink patent pumps to go with these dresses, but I think the girls forgot to give them back to me,' she said.

151

'Never mind; it's a lovely display, Emily,' Dylan said, hugging her tightly. 'There's the kettle boiled now, so. I'll brew up.'

'Okay, and I'll vacuum the carpet. There are beads from the posy scattered all over it.'

But before they had even finished their tea, an excited young woman with bright red hair came teetering across the road in blue platform sling-backs and almost ran straight through the door of the shop without opening it first.

'Watch yourself there,' Dylan said, springing to his feet as the door crashed open with an almighty wobble.

'Sorry, sorry. But I really want the wedding dress. I'll take everything in the window,' she said breathlessly. 'It is a Vera Wang, isn't it?'

'Yes, it is,' Emily said, amazed at what was happening.

'How much do you want for everything in the window, and the posy too? I just love it all.'

'Don't you need to know the dress sizes?' Emily said, struggling to overcome her shock at such a swift expression of interest.

'Oh yes. Please tell me the sizes – but they look just right to me.'

'The wedding dress, is a size 12, regular. The shoes are a nine. And the bridesmaid dresses are all a size 10.'

'Perfect ... except for the bridal shoes,' the woman said, picking up Emily's satin shoes, making a disappointed face and then setting, them back down again on the pale blue carpet. 'I'm a six, so there's no point in taking these shoes. What a shame ... they are utterly gorgeous. And two of my bridesmaids are size 8, but I can take their dresses in. I'm pretty handy with a sewing machine. Yes, okay, I'll have the lot, please ... except for the bridal shoes. They'd only fit a bride with feet the size of boats, wouldn't they?'

Dylan and Emily exchanged mischievous glances, and Emily had to bite her bottom lip to stop from laughing out loud. They hadn't had time to put individual price tags on Emily's wedding things, so Dylan suggested an overall price and the woman readily agreed. She set her handbag on the counter, and delved inside it for her chequebook.

'I can't believe my luck,' she said, giddy with happiness. 'We're getting married on a shoestring budget,' she explained. 'We're trying to do everything for two thousand pounds, including the buffet and the honeymoon. It's a new trend; I'm sure you've heard of it? Debt-free weddings; it's all the rage. I mean, why line the pockets of those rotten greedy banks when you can have a perfectly nice wedding without spending a fortune?'

'Why indeed,' Dylan said dryly.

'Yes, I've heard of that trend,' Emily said, sighing with regret. She'd borrowed thousands of pounds to pay for her wedding – she'd be paying off the debt for years. And all because she'd been trying to impress Alex's posh parents. She wondered if they ever thought of her nowadays.

'I'll see what we've got by way of a box,' Dylan said.

He hoped Emily wouldn't collapse in a puddle of tears when she realized what she was doing.

'I must tell my fiancé,' the woman said, taking

out her mobile phone and sending a quick text.

Emily began to fold up the dresses, amazed that her lovely display had only lasted for fifteen minutes altogether. Dylan managed to find a large, clean cardboard box and lined it with some crisp sheets of white tissue paper. Then Emily folded in the yards and yards of immaculate white tulle and crushed pink silk, and laid her lace veil and small posy lovingly on the top. The woman handed over her cheque and showed her ID card to reassure them she was genuine, and within seconds she was gone. The last Emily saw of her precious wedding gown was the delighted woman hailing a taxi at the end of the street, tightly clutching the large cardboard box to her chest.

'I can't believe what just happened here,' Dylan said, placing the cheque gently in the cash register. 'Can you believe we just made five hundred pounds in one sale? It's not a fraction of what you paid, I know, but Sylvia will be absolutely delighted. That should cover the rest of the vet's bill this month. Are you feeling okay, Emily? You look a bit flushed.'

'What? Oh yes, don't worry about me. I'm not going to have another panic attack. Not over Alex, anyway – he's so not worth it. It's a huge relief, to be honest. I feel a great wave of sheer relief washing over me. It's only a dress, isn't it? Letting go of it doesn't mean anything significant, not any more.'

'You can buy an even nicer dress for the next time,' Dylan said. And then he realised how dismissive that sounded. 'I didn't mean that in a casual way,' he said quickly.

'I know you didn't,' she smiled.

'I mean, the next time you are getting married – to somebody who is actually worthy of you – you can buy the dress of your dreams.'

'No, I don't want a big white wedding, thanks,' Emily said, picking up the satin shoes and setting them underneath the counter. 'I'm done with making grand statements. And like the girl said, why line the pockets of the banks just to feed and entertain a lot of people you haven't seen in years, and won't be seeing again in a hurry? No offence about banks, by the way.'

'And none taken. Don't worry about it.'

'Big weddings are a form of madness, when you think about it. All that stress for one day. Arabella's got friends who spent even more than I did. One of them fainted on her way up the aisle. And another one had to get married in a hospital ward, because the groom broke his leg on the stag weekend.'

'Why didn't they wait until his leg got better?'

'They wanted to get married before they went on the honeymoon. And the honeymoon was a six-week cruise that cost over ten thousand pounds, so they couldn't afford to miss it.'

'Okay, a six-week cruise sounds very nice.'

'Yes. Now, speaking of cruises, let's keep my boat-shoes safe in case our transvestite friend comes back,' Emily said. 'And if he does come back, you can tell him you've got something he might be interested in. Maybe he'll get married himself some day – in these very shoes? Wouldn't that be a lovely thought?'

'You're a very special girl, Emily,' Dylan said,

hugging her again. 'If any of my sisters had been stood up like that, they'd have committed murder. And I wouldn't have blamed them.'

'Do you know, I feel different now? I feel sort of free,' Emily said, snuggling in to Dylan and closing her eyes. 'I thought I'd cry my heart out when that dress finally went out of my life. I loved it so much; it was my fairy-tale dress. But I don't feel sad any more. And I hope that girl looks lovely in it. I really do. I loved her red hair, didn't you? Very Florence and the Machine, wasn't she?'

'Yeah, she was. So did you mean it when you said you never wanted to get married?'

'I'm not sure about never getting married. But if I do get married, it'll be a very small, very intimate and very private affair. No vanishing parents, no obligatory relations, no coterie of bridesmaids, no overpriced flowers, no showy cars, no hassle with bank loans...'

'Right, I get it. What sort of a wedding would you like?'

'I'd like a five-minute service at my local registry office with just two witnesses, and then we'd go straight to the nearest airport for a lovely holiday somewhere really peaceful.'

'Sun or snow, do you think?' Dylan asked.

'I don't mind – as long as it's not too crowded. Maybe it'd be nice to have a lovely winter wedding and then a really sunny honeymoon on the other side of the globe, to get the best of both worlds?'

'Okay.'

'That is not a hint, by the way,' she said, going

156

through to the storeroom to heat her tea up in the microwave.

'I know it isn't,' Dylan smiled, but he looked very happy.

'We might as well put something new in the window now,' Emily said briskly. 'Seeing as you went to all the trouble of putting that cute wardrobe there. Shall I have a look at the stock and see if anything jumps out? And I'll put the display of summer dresses out too, now that I've got the ironing board up.'

'Okay, and thanks, Emily. You've been a great help to the shop.'

'Don't mention it,' she smiled. 'It feels good to know I'm doing something useful with my day off.'

And the mood was light and blissfully relaxed for the rest of the afternoon.

That night Dylan stayed over at Emily's flat, and they shared an Indian curry and a bottle of red wine. Then they kissed for a long time on the teacup-embroidered cushions.

Dylan didn't ask if he could stay the night, because he felt that Emily mightn't be in the mood after seeing another woman make off with her wedding finery.

And Emily didn't like to ask Dylan if be wanted to stay over, because she felt that she'd appear overly dismissive of her cancelled wedding.

In the end they both fell asleep on the sofa, arms entwined, as the candles burned down to a tiny blob of melted wax and then softly went out, one by one.

11. Sins of the Father

October came, the weather turned colder, and Emily still hadn't heard from her parents much since the previous Christmas. She'd tried to call them countless times, but their house phone was rarely answered and they didn't have mobiles. Emily had therefore assumed they were simply sulking over her decision to stay in London for Christmas, and were just trying to avoid her. Her parents had no real sense of the time passing, so ten months would mean nothing to them. But, although she tried hard not to, she couldn't help thinking about them. She imagined all sorts of awful things involving illegal vodka, pantomime-villain loan sharks and chip-pan fires. She could almost hear an ambulance in the background every time the phone rang.

She didn't like to say anything to Arabella about her parents, because Arabella wasn't always feeling very well herself these days. Her hair and make-up were as impeccable as ever, but Emily could see beyond that to the loneliness and hurt in her eyes. And she didn't like to mention it to Dylan, because they were having such a lovely time together. Their days had fallen into a smooth routine where they'd work hard all week and then spend their weekends in bed together. Occasionally they'd venture out to see a show, or have a nice meal, but their favourite way to while away

158

the time was simply to make love, sleep, talk for hours, and drink wine or tea by candlelight.

Then one quiet Sunday morning, when Emily and Dylan were having a cooked breakfast in the zingy green kitchen, Emily's mobile phone began to ring. Without even looking at the screen she knew it was her parents.

'Hello?'

'Emily, love?'

'Hi, Dad. How are you?'

'Not so bad, love. Not so bad. Mind you, we've been better.'

'Dad, just tell me if there's anything wrong,' Emily said quietly.

'I'm only ringing to say hello,' he said. 'We didn't see you at all last Christmas, Emily. We didn't see you all year. And I'm just being civil now and keeping in touch.'

'Okay, but I did phone you lots of times, Dad. There was never anybody home, or maybe you didn't hear the telephone out in the hall. But I was always thinking of you, and that's the truth. Where were you both? Or were you just ignoring me – because I didn't come home for Christmas?'

'Well, now. I can hear you're very upset, so I suppose I'll have to tell you what happened.'

'Oh, Dad, did something happen? What happened?'

'It's your mother. She ... um ... she hasn't been feeling so good lately. She's been overdoing things in the drink department, that's the bottom line. And her doctor said he'd take her in for a few weeks – just for observation, like. A bit of a rest for

159

her, you know?'

'Has Mum been sectioned again, Dad?'

Dylan looked up sharply from his plate. Emily turned away from him, shaking her head.

'I wouldn't call it that, love. They're just feeding her up a bit, and so on. You know how these young doctors fuss and worry? Maybe they had a bed free and they wanted to fill it up to keep their funding? So anyway, the few weeks she was in hospital turned into a few months. And I didn't answer the phone, because I didn't want to worry you.'

'Oh, Dad, you should have told me. Mum could have died.'

'Died; not a bit of her. Sure, your mother has been doing her own thing for a long time now and she's never died on us yet.'

'Dad, I wouldn't call it *doing her own thing*. She's a chronic alcoholic.'

'Chronic be damned. Emily, listen to me – there's no need for you and me to go over all this old ground again. You know she won't give up the drink, and that's all there is to it. I visit her every couple of days, and she's doing fine. She's getting out next week. I didn't phone you today for an argument.'

'Okay, I'm sorry. What did you phone me for, Dad? Are you well enough yourself? You sound very tired. Is there something else wrong? Look, I'll come home today and go with you to visit Mum. I'll look up some flights right away and then get back to you, yes?'

'Ah, love, that would be grand. I'd love to see you again, surely. And so would your mother.

160

That would cheer her up no end, thanks very much. The other thing is … well, I'm in a bit of bother. Yes, a little bit of trouble.'

'Is it money, Dad? You can tell me. Do you owe money to somebody? Have you had your electric cut off again?'

'It's something like that, yes. But it's not the electric.'

'How much do you need, Dad?'

'A lot, I'm afraid,' he said.

'Is it more than I can afford to give you, do you think? Is it more than five hundred pounds?'

There was a lengthy silence at the other end. Emily thought she could hear her father cursing himself softly. Her heart turned over with worry.

'Dad, just say the amount. I need to know before I can help you.'

'Five thousand pounds would cover it, I dare say,' he said wearily.

'What? Five thousand pounds! Are you serious? I haven't got that sort of money, Dad. What did you do? How did you get into that much trouble? Was it poker?'

'Maybe it was,' he said in a doom-laden voice.

Emily had a feeling she wasn't hearing the full story.

'Dad, are you sure it's only five thousand pounds? Or is it more than that? Please tell me the truth. We might as well get to the bottom of it here and now.'

'It's ten thousand – are you happy now? Ten thousand. And I promise that's the truth. I have to pay the money tomorrow or this guy I played poker with will sort me out. He already gave me a bit of a push and a shove in the pub last week, if you know what I mean?'

Emily closed her eyes and took a deep breath.

'Ten grand, okay, I'll tell you what I'll do. I'll try to get the money today, though it is an awful lot, Dad. A flight at short notice won't be cheap either. I wonder, is there any other way of getting the money to you? And that way we could save a couple of hundred pounds? No, on second thoughts I'd better come home and see for myself just what's going on. I'll phone you back in a while. Stay close to the phone, yes?'

'Right, Emily, I'll stay right here. And thanks, love. I'm sorry I had to bother you with all this old nonsense. I wouldn't have called you if I had anybody else to turn to, I swear to you.'

'That's okay, Dad. But you've got to promise me faithfully that you won't play poker again. I mean it, Dad. If I give you this money now, it'll take me two or three years to pay it back. So I can't do it again in a hurry. Do you understand me, Dad? Even if you do get threats, I can't give you any more money – because I can't afford the repayments on any extra loan above ten thousand. And this is really going to make life hard for me; I'll be economizing for years to come. Is that clear?'

'Yes, it is, love.'

'Well, you bear that in mind. Because I've rent to pay here and a car to run and the wedding debts to pay off. So I mean it when I say it'll be years before I can help you like this again – and maybe never, if I get a mortgage.'

'I'll never ask you for a penny, Emily, love.

Never again.'

'I love both of you, Dad. I always have and I always will. But I know I'm not able to force you to give up gambling. And I can't force Mum to give up drinking. And if I go on sending money to you both, then I'll be a part of the problem. Do you know what I mean?'

'Surely, I know what you mean. All I ask is this one favour, that's all. And it'll be the last time. I'll pay you back, Emily. Every penny of it; I promise you now.'

Emily knew there was more chance of her mother marrying Johnny Depp than her father paying her back all the money she'd given them over the years. But she didn't want to rub it in. Her father sounded desperately scared. As long as she could make him understand she wasn't made of money, that would have to do for now.

'Dad, can you make yourself some breakfast there? Have a cup of tea, yes, and a bit of toast and try to stop worrying? I'll get back to you as soon as I can. And you'd better be at home when I get back to Belfast today. So please, please don't go out anywhere, do you hear me? And don't you dare go and try to win that money back. Do you hear me, Daddy? You might end up in even more trouble. And I won't be able to give you twenty thousand, right? If that happens, you are definitely on your own.'

'I understand, Emily. I understand, love.'

'Okay, Dad. I'll be in touch, then. And I'll give you a ring when my plane lands in Belfast, just to let you know I'm on my way.'

'Right, okay. Bye.'

Emily clicked off her phone, went into the sitting room and sat down gently on the sofa. Dylan came after her with two mugs of fresh tea and set them on the coffee table. He gave Emily a brief hug and looked at her with love in his eyes.

'I heard that,' he said, 'or most of it.'

'So now you know,' she said. 'My poor father is a gambling man.'

'That's got to be pretty tough on you,' he said, shaking his head.

'It is tough, yes. I thought I was used to it by now. I mean, Dad's had a gambling problem for as long as I remember. Betting on horses mostly, but poker too when he gets really bad. It's tragic enough when you have one addict in the family, but when you have *two* addicts it gets a bit over-whelming. I feel terribly guilty sometimes. I should have stayed at home when I was eighteen and looked after them.'

'Emily, I know I've said this before, but you mustn't blame yourself, please don't do that. You know that any addiction can only be cured by the addicts themselves. All the TLC in the world won't help people make the decision to quit. In some cases it only makes things worse, because then they become dependent on all the attention and kindness that their addiction inspires in other people. I know that for a fact, because one of my sisters does the odd spot of volunteer work at a drop-in centre for teenagers.'

'Does she? Wow, is there no end to the gener-osity of the Shawcross family?'

'I'll take that as a compliment,' Dylan said.

164

'Of course, I know about addiction. My mother's doctor told me years ago not to pamper her when she was very depressed, because she would enjoy it too much to attempt to get better. And I've told myself that a thousand times over the years. I mean, if I moved back to Belfast and took over the housework and all the household expenses for my parents, they would only end up spending even more money on their addictions. And they'd be home at six o'clock every night for their tea, and they'd be all excited about getting fish and chips and a slice of bread and butter. And we'd be sitting there pretending it was all very jolly and normal, with Mum sneaking vodka into her tea, and my dad keeping the racing pages hidden up his jumper. I think I'd go nuts myself if we ended up like that. It's hopeless really.'

'Well, look, if your dad owes some thug of a poker player ten thousand pounds, and your mum is drying out in hospital, then it does sound pretty bad, Emily. But we can't have you going nuts too, now can we? So I'm going to Belfast with you today,' he said firmly.

'Oh no, I couldn't let you do that, Dylan. Please don't say you'll do that. I want to go to Belfast on my own.'

'Emily, love, I can see you're in pieces. Now, I won't tell you not to borrow all that money and give it straight to a gambling addict. You know as well as I do that the experts always advise against making gestures like that. Your Dad will be relieved in the short term. He'll be on his knees with gratitude, I suppose. But then he'll do it again next week when the shock wears off.'

'Yes, he probably will.'

'So it's up to you. And I'll stay out of it. But I'm coming with you today, and that's final. I wouldn't be a decent boyfriend if I went home and put my feet up and let you try to cope with this all by yourself. I've still got some savings from my banking days. That's what I'm living on, actually. It's not enough to bail your father out, but I'll pay for the flights and we'll stay overnight and come back on Monday.'

'Dylan, I really don't want you getting mixed up in this.'

'Stop it, I won't take no for an answer, okay? It's happening. I'll sort out the flights and maybe a hotel, nip home and pack a bag. And you can decide what you're going to do regarding the money – though I wouldn't give a complete stranger a cheque, if I were you.'

'I know – I'll ask Arabella to lend me the money. She's very well off and possibly the only person I know who could lay their hands on that much cash at short notice. Though, obviously, I'll be mortified at having to ask her at all.'

'I wish I hadn't taken your donations now; we made over a thousand pounds on your stuff, including the kitchen gadgets and the designer shoes and the bridal wear.'

'No, I'm glad of all that. I've had no regrets about it, none at all.'

'Okay, can I have a look at your laptop?'

'It's in that cupboard over there,' Emily said, pointing to an Ikea desk in the corner of the sitting room. 'And, Dylan, thanks a million for not running out of the door the minute you found out about my father. And my mother! Not to mention Alex standing me up at the altar.'

'Hey, why would I run out of the door? None of those things reflect badly on you, Emily. You've just been incredibly unlucky so far, that's all.'

'I hope bad luck isn't catching,' she smiled sadly.

'You have to make your own luck in this life.'

'Yes, but it's got to be easier to make your own luck if you have sane parents and a boyfriend who isn't obsessed with social climbing.'

'I take it that's Alex you're referring to?'

'Of course it is.'

'Well, don't worry – because I'm your boyfriend now, and I have no interest in playing golf with a bunch of old men in pink pullovers.'

'Thanks, Dylan, I don't know where you get your wisdom from.'

'Hey, I'm no genius. But I've had my setbacks too, you know. I lost one friend in a climbing accident when we were both nineteen, and another good mate died when he crashed his car last year.'

'I'm so sorry. I didn't know you'd lost two friends.'

'Yeah, well, I used to have dozens of friends, so I suppose it was bound to happen eventually.'

'Used to have?'

'Yes, I don't socialize as much as I used to. I don't go climbing any more either. When I turned thirty I grew up a little bit, I guess. I used to get a thrill out of travelling, but when I gave up my banking career I couldn't afford to indulge. And I sort of lost touch with a lot of my London friends. We didn't fall out or anything.'

'Yes, I know what you mean,' Emily nodded.

'I've still got my rugby pals back in Appleton. Anyway, then Sylvia started rescuing horses and I said I'd help her until she was on her feet. And somehow six months has turned into a year.'

'You're very good to work for free,' she told him.

'It evens out, because I used to be disgustingly overpaid,' he laughed.

'Oh, I've just remembered – we were meant to be having a lovely breakfast,' Emily said, going back to the kitchen to find their plates of bacon and eggs all dried up and cold.

'Never mind,' Dylan said. 'I'm taking you out for breakfast. Come on, we'll go to that lovely café nearby. And then we'll go and sort out your silly old parents, shall we?'

'Okay,' she said, and gave him a long, lingering kiss as a reward. 'I never thought I'd say this, but I'm glad Alex got cold feet about the wedding. Because if I'd married him, I'd be stuck in Belfast now and I'd have to listen to him complaining about his in-laws embarrassing him, for the rest of my life.'

Quickly they got ready and went bounding down the stairs in the communal hall to face the world.

A few hours later, full of bacon and lattes and carrying a wad of donated cash from Arabella, Emily and Dylan boarded a flight to Belfast.

'Now, listen – you're, not to worry if you see any houses with cages over the windows,' Emily told Dylan nervously. 'My parents don't live in an

168

interface area as such, but they do live pretty close to one.'

'What's an interface area?' Dylan asked at once.

'It's where they've built a peace line.'

'What's a peace line?'

'It's a twenty-foot steel wall dividing two communities that don't like each other very much. And sometimes teenagers throw bricks over the wall – if they've got nothing else to do. And then the teenagers on the other side throw the bricks back again. That's the *interfacing* part of the equation. And that's why the windows near the peace lines have cages.'

'Can't these teenagers just go round the wall? Or break windows in other neighbourhoods?'

'No, they can't – because the police would see them walking along the main roads with bricks in their hands. Or maybe half-bricks, which we call halfers. Halfers are much easier to throw over a twenty-foot wall, do you see? But, anyway, they don't stray too far from home, because they like to be able to run back to their mammy when the riot police turn up with their shields and batons.'

'Oh, I see. So do they throw bricks at the police too?'

'Sometimes they do, yeah. That's why the police vehicles also have cages on their windows. It's not really the kids' fault, you know – usually it's just one or two hotheads leading them on. Some people seem to get their kicks by starting trouble.'

'Well, thanks for explaining all of that. I just hope I don't get shot,' Dylan joked as they fastened their seat belts.

Emily rolled her eyes, as if such a thing were unthinkable. But in her heart of hearts she was secretly terrified of bringing Dylan home to west Belfast. It wasn't the most scenic part of Belfast. What a pity her parents didn't live near the beautiful Mourne Mountains, just a few miles south of the city; the mountains were thought to have inspired the Narnia books by C.S. Lewis. What a pity they didn't live in a posh village – Holywood, Hillsborough or Helen's Bay. What a pity they didn't live in a gated mansion in north Down, or in a bungalow with sea views on the north coast, or on the super-posh Malone Road in south Belfast.

Northern Ireland was packed full of gorgeous scenery and fabulous houses. But trust Mr and Mrs Reilly to live on a bland concrete estate with stray dogs, vandalized trees, sectarian graffiti and empty cider bottles everywhere. She wondered if Dylan would run a mile when he saw the state of the place. Emily tried hard not to resent her parents. And then the guilt came flooding in again like a tsunami, and so the endless cycle of resentment and guilt continued.

It was almost a relief when a spot of turbulence over the Irish Sea temporarily took her mind off it all.

12. Woman in Chains

'I'll never be able to thank you enough,' Emily said to Arabella as she discreetly handed over a cheque for ten thousand pounds two weeks later. Her bank loan had been approved the day before so she could pay her friend back. 'My father might be dead in his grave by now, if it weren't for your generosity.'

'Thanks, sweetheart, don't mention it. What did you tell your bank you wanted the money for?'

'I said I needed a new car for work,' Emily grimaced, 'and some new furniture for my flat.'

She'd have loved a nicer car and a beautiful sleigh bed, but there was no point in thinking of those things now.

'Well, I just hope your poor father was grateful,' Arabella sniffed. She was disgusted with the male of the species these days. 'Imagine asking your only child to bail you out of your poker debts. The rascal! I wouldn't have done it, if I were in your shoes.'

'He was so grateful, though, really he was. He wept like a baby when we turned up on the doorstep; he was that glad to see us. Dylan went to the guy's house with Dad to hand over the money. He told him this was a one-off thing, and we would not be covering for Dad again. Wasn't that very masterful of him?'

'I suppose so,' Arabella admitted.

171

'Meanwhile, I gave the house a thorough clean. I filled two black bags with rubbish and got through two bottles of bleach. We had battered sausages from the local chip shop for tea. Then the three of us went to visit Mum in the loony bin.'

'Sounds like a dream weekend,' Arabella said dryly. 'Thugs, bin bags, bleach, battered sausages and a loony bin.'

'And I mean that in a nice way,' Emily added. 'Loony bin sounds less scary than saying my mother is receiving *acute psychiatric care*.'

'Poor woman, I hope I never end up in a place like that. It's a very thin line, isn't it? When David's *new love* had those twin girls, it was touch-and-go for my sanity, I can tell you.'

'Ah yes, Venice and Paris,' Emily said.

'What awful names.'

'Well...' Emily grimaced.

It was only then that Emily noticed Arabella hadn't been smoking for a few days. She wondered if Arabella had finally decided to kick the habit. She decided not to ask, just in case she triggered a craving in Arabella.

'How is your mum?' Arabella asked.

'Oh, I felt really sorry for her this time,' Emily said sadly. 'I thought she was looking terribly old. And she was as white as a sheet. Dylan was a complete honey, as usual. He bought her a box of chocolates and six magazines, and chatted away to her as if she were just in there having a sprained ankle looked at. I still can't get over how pale she was.'

'Yes, well... Booze and cigarettes can do that to

a person, my darling, and that's why I've given up both of them.'

'Have you really, Arabella?'

'Yes, I have. Last night I threw out my entire stash of cigarettes, all the wine in the house, and all the ready meals, biscuits and crisps. Everything went into the wheelie bin at midnight and then I went to M&S first thing this morning and stocked up on porridge, apples and salad. I'm going to be healthy, Emily. I should have done it years ago.'

'Well, good for you, Arabella. I'm very impressed.'

'Yes, I'm having porridge for breakfast, tuna salad for lunch, and chicken with a baked potato for dinner. All tea will be decaf, and my only snack will be a rice cake with a teaspoon of honey on it.'

'Steady on, woman; you'll be fading away on us,' Emily smiled.

'Oh, I could do with dropping a few pounds. Now, let's crack on, shall we? What have you got lined up for my perusal today? I feel really empowered, Emily; I sent the last of David's stuff to his old office yesterday and I didn't even cry. They can send it on to him. Needless to say, I haven't been told his new address in Italy.'

'Good for you.'

'Yes, this is the first day of the rest of my life,' Arabella laughed. 'I really feel as if things can only get better now.'

Just then, three men in dark suits and cheap shoes came into the office and asked for Arabella; Jane pointed them in the right direction. Arabella and Emily barely had time to look up from their desks before one of the men told Arabella he was a detective. He wanted Arabella to come with them for questioning; something to do with a house fire a little while ago, he said in a very discreet whisper. It was a good thing nobody, in the office could lip-read.

'Listen, I have no idea what you're talking about,' Arabella said at once. 'Please leave this office at once. I really have a lot of work to do.'

'It's not an invitation,' she was told.

'Am I being arrested?' Arabella said calmly.

'Yes, you are,' the man said quietly. 'We've found new CCTV evidence. So I can arrest you here in full view of your colleagues. Or you can come down to the station, and we'll arrest you a bit more discreetly.'

'There must be some mistake,' Emily said, aghast.

'The wig was clever, Mrs Harrington, but we've just found footage of you taking it off on a nearby street. Your ex-husband, David Harrington, has identified you via email. If it's any consolation, he was most reluctant to give us your name; most reluctant indeed. But there's a lot of money at stake here. The house that was burned down has to be completely rebuilt – and if we don't get a conviction then your ex-husband might have to stump up for the bill. The owner says he isn't going to let the matter drop until somebody pays for the rebuilding. His insurance company are keen to make sure it isn't them.'

'Arabella, tell them it isn't true,' Emily beseeched her. 'A house was set on fire? You didn't

174

do it. You didn't do it, surely?'

But Arabella just pursed her lips and switched off her computer.

'Oh no,' Emily gasped.

'Right, then, I suppose we'd better get this over with,' Arabella said. 'Emily, will you please phone my solicitor? The number is in my address book. And tell him where they have taken me. Oh, and you are in charge until I get back. Consider yourself the acting editor *again*.'

Arabella stood up slowly and gracefully, and slipped on her belted trench coat. She put her mobile phone into her glossy red handbag and draped it across her arm as if she were the Queen going to inspect the troops. Jane Maxwell's bottom jaw was scraping the carpet as Arabella left the office with her head held high, flanked by three detectives. The rest of the staff were utterly shocked, and one or two of them were even teary-eyed.

Emily's hands were shaking as she dialled the solicitor's number. After she'd given him a panicky explanation of what had just happened, she heard him sigh long and loud at the other end of the line.

'I'll go there right now,' he said.

'Will I come with you?' Emily said.

'If you like,' the solicitor said. 'But it could be a long night. I've got a bad feeling about this.'

175

13. Showdown in Suburbia

It was early November and Emily was having a quiet Saturday to herself. Her mother was out of hospital and recuperating at home. Her father had sworn off the gambling for a while, still pretty ruffled over his run-in with the darker side of illegal poker. Arabella had admitted to a charge of arson, pleading diminished responsibility. She wasn't being held on remand, but she had been told not to leave the country. David wasn't pressing charges, because he didn't want his move to Italy to be disrupted in any way. He was currently staying with Mary and the twins at an unnamed location in Rome while his new house was being completed. The owner of the fabulous glass house that had been reduced to a smoking shell had had a mild heart attack and was threatening to sue both David and Arabella for stress, and for the cost of rebuilding. The insurers said they wouldn't be paying out any time soon, given the circumstances.

Dylan had gone to France with a couple of his best friends to see a rugby match. He'd be back again soon, though, and was going to come straight round to see Emily.

And so Emily had an entire day to herself – a lovely, empty Saturday with nothing to do but idle round the shops for a while in the morning. Perhaps she'd go home in the afternoon and paint her nails, lie in the bath, have a takeaway for dinner and maybe watch a DVD on her portable telly. She was looking forward to spending a day just being on her own. And she had also promised herself she was not going to waste it dwelling on past events and future possibilities. So far she'd bought a bar of handmade soap that smelt of vanilla, a cute necklace made of chunky plastic strawberries, a packet of M&S chocolate biscuits, a pink mug, a skinny belt and a packet of Fairtrade coffee. Now she was dithering over whether to buy a new suede brush for her boots or a couple of glossy magazines. She hovered by the magazine stand in Tesco, trying to make up her mind. Daisy Churchill was on the cover of no fewer than nine of that week's offerings. Nine magazine covers! Apparently, she'd given up on her bid to break into the interior design sector and was instead garnering column inches by dating a high-profile TV producer from the United States. Emily gazed at the pictures of Daisy's surgically enhanced pout, and wondered if the model ever looked in the mirror, had a fleeting moment of self-awareness and asked herself what the heck she was doing.

'Hey you, what the heck do you think you're doing? I want a word with you,' said someone standing behind Emily.

And suddenly a very sharp object was digging into Emily's back. It felt like a fingernail. It was a fingernail. Emily spun round and gazed into the spidery eyelashes of Daisy Churchill herself. And the woman was even thinner and more orange in real life than she looked in her glamour pictures. Emily couldn't help glancing downwards at

Daisy's most famous assets. And yes, there they were, all hoisted up in a balcony bra and looking like a couple of ostrich eggs about to hatch. They even had the hairline cracks, which Emily supposed must be stretch marks. She looked incredibly angry too.

'I'm sorry, but I don't think we've met before,' Emily stuttered.

'We haven't met before, but I know who you are. I've seen your picture in *Stylish Living*. And let me tell you that nobody turns down Daisy Churchill.'

'I'm terribly sorry, but this isn't the time or the place,' Emily began, her face ablaze with embarrassment.

'How dare you turn me down – how dare you! You think you're better than everybody else? Who the hell are you, anyway?'

'I'm sorry, but I'm in a dreadful hurry,' Emily gasped. 'Excuse me, please.'

Emily began to walk briskly away from Daisy and the small crowd of shoppers who'd paused to enjoy the sideshow, but a group of housewives chatting near the escalator had blocked her path.

'Don't you dare walk away from me, you snob!' Daisy shouted.

'Excuse me, please,' Emily said again, slithering past the shoppers and stepping on to the escalator.

But Daisy Churchill wasn't that easy to evade. She abandoned her trolley (full of expensive champagne, fillet steak and imported strawberries, Emily noted – not exactly working-class foods) and followed Emily, shouting all the way down to the ground floor. Emily thought the escalator she was standing on was surely the slowest escalator in the whole wide world.

'Come on, come on, hurry up, hurry up,' she urged it.

She couldn't walk any faster, as her path was being blocked by a very large lady with not one, but two, overflowing shopping baskets.

'That's right, go on … and try to walk away from me, you nasty little *snob!* Toffee-nosed, stuck-up, butter-wouldn't-melt, snobby-knickers little cow,' Daisy roared again.

'Let's play cliché bingo,' Emily said under her breath.

She took a slouchy grey bobble hat out of her shoulder bag and deftly pulled it on. Then she lowered her gaze and pretended she had no idea who Daisy was shouting at. Some teenage girls saw Daisy and began to take pictures of her on their mobile phones. And Daisy, in spite of her white-hot rage at being snubbed by *Sylish Living*, took the time to pout her lips for the cameras. She blew air kisses and leaned over the edge of the escalator suggestively.

'That's right, girls,' Daisy cooed. 'It's me, Daisy Churchill. And I'm not too stuck up to do my own shopping in Tesco. Not like that one over there – that's Emily Reilly, right there, in the stupid grey hat. And according to her I'm not good enough to be in a posh magazine.'

Emily pulled her hat off again and stuffed it in her pocket. She thought she was going to faint, she was that mortified. The teenagers looked at Emily and giggled. They took some pictures of her as well. Mercifully the world's slowest escalator finally delivered Emily safely to the entrance porch, and she belted for the sanctuary of her car. But Daisy wasn't going to leave it there.

'This isn't the end of it,' she shouted as Emily hopped into her car and locked the door firmly behind her.

'You're on loads and loads of magazine covers this week,' Emily forced herself to shout back. 'Why can't you just leave us alone? We're just a harmless little magazine, minding our own business.'

'I spent all day working hard for that shoot. And time is money, in case you didn't know.'

'You call that work?' Emily was beyond furious now. 'People in this country are cleaning toilets for five quid an hour. That's hard work in my book. Where on earth did you get your sense of entitlement from? You don't deserve to be a millionaire, Daisy Churchill. And what's more, you're a terrible example to young girls everywhere. They can't all make a living blowing kisses to a camera. You're a disgrace to the sisterhood.'

'Bitch,' Daisy shouted.

And she threw her umbrella at Emily's car for good measure. The umbrella got tangled up in Emily's windscreen wipers and one of them broke off with a loud twang.

'Takes one to know one,' Emily cried, remembering the most popular retort from her Belfast childhood.

'Don't you mess with Daisy Churchill,' Daisy roared.

'Don't you mess with my magazine,' Emily

shouted back.

Emily reversed out of the car park and drove home, shaking with righteous anger.

Her lovely day off was ruined.

The following week, the pictures of Emily and Daisy having a ding-dong in Tesco were published in *Closer* magazine.

But thankfully Emily's face was almost hidden behind a sign advertising fifty per cent off Daz pomegranate-scented washing powder, so it wasn't the disaster it might have been. And the name of her magazine hadn't been mentioned either.

Probably they didn't want to give another publication a free plug, Emily thought to herself.

She decided to carry a pair of dark glasses around with her in future, just in case she ever ran into Daisy Churchill again.

14. A Surprise Visit

Emily was sitting at Arabella's desk, doing her best to avoid the resentful glances from Jane Maxwell and one or two others. It seemed that Emily's temporary promotion to the position of editor had really ticked off some of the staff, especially the ones who were older than Emily, or had been at the magazine longer than she had. There was talk of Emily being made deputy editor when Arabella came back to work. Even good old Petra Dunwoody seemed a little miffed; Emily thought Petra was rather overdoing the politeness in recent days. And no doubt Jane was doing her best to spread dissent within the camp, Emily thought dryly. Well, they were getting no extra information from her regarding Arabella's sudden absence. The official line was that Arabella was taking some time off to remodel her home; and the infamous arrest had been an unfortunate mistake. Nobody believed it for a second – but they still hadn't discovered David's infidelity, the twins or the house fire.

It was such a shame it had come to this, Emily thought sadly. She wished she could tell everyone the truth about Arabella getting divorced – but, of course, she could not. For any sign of weakness in an editor would be seized upon in the cut-throat world of magazine publishing. And Arabella might be tipped over the edge now, if her own story were to be emblazoned across one of the minor gossip rags.

Emily sent her boss a text every day to let her know that things were going okay. Arabella was having some privately funded therapy for her anger and rejection issues, and was also waiting to find out if she was going to stand trial for arson. In the meantime, she was resting (and crying a lot) at home and had told Emily she was to go ahead and do whatever she wanted at the magazine.

'I've given enough of my life to *Stylish Living*,' she'd said, the last time she'd spoken to Emily on the phone. 'Right now I need to put my own well-being first.'

And so Emily was putting together a major feature on de-cluttering. It was going to be a very glossy booklet for the January issue; a timely thing to do considering recent events all round. But this wasn't just the usual advice about putting cooking ingredients in a wooden trough to make wiping the larder shelves easier, or storing rolled-up bathroom towels in pretty wicker baskets. No, this was a radical feature on total de-cluttering – stripping rooms right back to the bare walls and starting all over again. This was nothing short of a lament on the modern disease of hoarding – a disease that particularly affected women, since they were the ones lumbered with the 'gathering' gene.

Emily had chosen a palette of soft greys and whites for her big idea, and she was busy sourcing coffee tables with built-in storage. She had photographed her own wardrobe for the cover, spending hours lighting it just so. She wanted women everywhere to share her new-found de-cluttering confidence. She wanted women everywhere to give their old things away, to say no to buying new clothes every weekend, or even every season. She wanted women everywhere to address their emotional needs, instead of just pottering up and down the High Street looking at clothes and trinkets, and feeling bored and unfulfilled and inadequate.

She was almost beginning to relax into the task when there was a phone call from the reception desk down in the foyer to say two people were asking for her.

'I wasn't expecting anyone today. What company are they from, please?' Emily asked absent-mindedly.

She picked up a photograph of a vintage-style peg bag, and placed it beside her other selections for the laundry room section. Then she put it aside again; she would have no floral peg bags in this feature. She'd have traditional wooden pegs in a thick glass jar – something that would never date and would never need to be replaced.

'They're not from a commercial company, Miss Reilly. This is a personal visit.'

'What's that you said? Who are they again?' Emily asked, flicking through her scrapbooks for a wooden peg supplier.

'They say they're your parents, Miss Reilly. They've come to London to surprise you.'

'What did you say?'

'Emily, love – surprise!' Emily heard her father call down the phone, and then she heard the receptionist asking him to please not take possession of the handset again.

'They have certainly succeeded in surprising me,' Emily said to herself as she closed her eyes and suppressed an urge to panic.

'A Mr and Mrs Reilly... Shall I send them up?' the receptionist said again.

'Just one second,' Emily gasped, snapping out of her self-pity.

Her heart was twanging like an elastic band. She stood up suddenly, and then sat down again. There was no way she could let the staff meet her parents. If that happened, she'd have to resign with immediate effect. Her parents were simply so loud and spirited and *Irish* that she'd never be able to live it down. She'd never be able to live them down.

'Miss Reilly, are you still there? Is there a problem?'

'Yes. I mean, no ... there's no problem. I'll come down immediately,' Emily said shakily, slamming the phone into its cradle and bolting out of the office.

She'd have to take them out somewhere – anywhere, as long as it was a long way away from the magazine. All she needed now was to give that vinegar-faced Jane Maxwell yet another excuse to look down on her. All she needed now was her poor father blathering on about politics. And her hiccupping mother, shuffling along behind him and looking bored rigid. Emily ignored the lifts and went galloping down the stairs. Her breathless rasping was echoing round the bare grey walls.

'This cannot be happening to me,' Emily said to herself. 'It just cannot be happening.'

She burst into the bright, airy communal lobby

185

(*Stylish Living* shared the building with several other publications) and glanced frantically around for her parents. Please let this be a practical joke of some kind, she pleaded silently. She didn't know who would play a stupid trick like this on her, but she still hoped it was a trick. But no, it was only too real. There they were, as large as life! Her father was chatting away merrily to the owner of the magazine. What rotten luck that Mr Carson was passing through the foyer at the same time Mr and Mrs Reilly bowled up looking for their beloved only daughter.

'I'll tell you what's at the heart of the problem back home,' her father was saying. His hands were outstretched like a plaster saint. 'It's a bunch of numbskulls in charge. The half of them never even finished secondary school, never mind gracing the corridors of a university. Now, I think you'll agree with me, you just can't let anybody off the street into power.'

'Well, now...' said Mr Carson nervously, looking left and right and up and down for some excuse to flee, '...many of our own MPs are very well educated, but they haven't always acted as they should... And I certainly, wouldn't be an expert on Irish politics, Mr Reilly.'

'That's *Northern* Irish politics, do you mean? Irish politics is that other crowd down in Dublin.'

'Daddy, is it really you? How lovely to see you,' Emily almost shouted. 'What a lovely surprise. Come on away from Mr Carson, now, and don't be keeping him back. He's a busy man, Daddy; you've no idea how busy. How did you all get introduced so quickly, anyway?'

'Ah, Emily, I overheard your father asking after you,' Mr. Carson explained, a bead of sweat on his upper lip.

It was a rare thing for the owner of the magazine to be lost for words, but this bedraggled couple had scared the living daylights out of him. The fact that Emily's parents looked like two extras in a Tim Burton film didn't help matters. Those clothes of theirs were years old. For all Mr Carson knew, one of them might have a cut-throat razor in their pocket.

'Emily, love, how are you?' Mr Reilly said.

Emily's father held out his arms to her, and his smile was as bright as sunshine. Emily was mortified to see he was wearing a pair of white leather golfing shoes with tassels on them, a shiny tan suit that must have been thirty years old, and an ancient, padded *yellow* anorak with at least six blue toggles swinging off it. His thick grey hair was combed into a steep quiff and worn long at the back. He gave the impression of a cheesy 1980s bingo caller about to climb Mount Everest.

'Hello, Dad. Hello, Mum,' Emily said, equally brightly.

How could she let Mr Carson witness her acute embarrassment? She wished she could snap her fingers and transform her parents into two tiny glass marbles that she could scoop up and drop into her pocket. Then she felt a wave of hot shame envelop her; it swept up and down her body like an electric shock. Would there ever be an end to this cycle of guilt and shame? she wondered.

'Hello, Emily,' Mrs Reilly said slowly. She raised one hand in greeting and then let it fall heavily, as if she were too weary to hold her hand up for another second. 'It's nice to see you.'

Emily thought her mother was slightly tipsy. Mrs Reilly was sitting on a black leather banquette near the reception desk. She was wearing a pink tweed coat and carrying a very large pink handbag. The effect was slightly marred, however, by a pair of dark brown woollen tights sagging over extremely spindly ankles. And yes, a pair of grey Converse trainers completed the ensemble. Emily's mother had always preferred comfortable footwear to what she called 'court shoes'. Her hair was also far too long for a woman of her age. With those untidy curls and awful brown tights she looked like a cross between Shirley Temple and a bag lady.

'What the hell...? I mean, what are you doing here?' Emily whispered as her father enfolded her in his arms.

Mr Carson saw his chance and sprinted towards one of the lifts. Emily saw him jabbing the lift button a dozen times before the doors finally began to open, and he immediately slithered through the chink. The doors closed again, and Mr Carson was swept away to blessed freedom.

'Well, now... What do you think we're doing here?' Mr Reilly began. 'We've come to London to see our only child. And to say thanks again for saving us from that little spot of bother we had with the poker club. And sure, we never go anywhere. So I thought I'd take your mother here on a bit of a holiday.'

'A holiday,' Emily croaked, wondering if they'd spent all their benefit money on the travel costs.

188

They'd be broke now for a fortnight, so she'd have to reimburse them when they went home again in a couple of days.

'Aye, a couple of weeks' holiday will do us the world of good. Get away from the old routine, you know? Get away from the same old streets and the endless rain, and the motor-mouths and gossips. And those cheeky hoods throwing beer bottles at our back door. The parents should be ashamed of themselves, letting their kids drink in a public place.'

'Two weeks, Dad? Where are you staying?' Emily asked weakly.

'We're staying in your house, Emily – where else would we stay? This is a budget holiday we're on, do you see? We haven't got the money to be checking into the Ritz.'

'I know that, yes, but I've not got a house. I've got a flat on the third floor of a house – and no spare room. And I've to go to work every day, Dad,' she said, but it was no use.

'We can sleep on the floor, love. We can throw the sofa cushions down and make a bed; don't be worrying about us. Just give us a key and go on to your work each morning. You work away, love, and we'll come and go as we please. Sure, we'll be out all day, anyway – looking at the sights. We'd hardly come all the way to London and then spend the whole visit sitting on our arses, would we?'

'Just how did you get here, Dad? Did you fly?'

'Aye, and now our arms are killing us, I can tell you,' he laughed. 'No, seriously, we got the ferry in Belfast, love. We just took a mad notion yes-

189

terday, do you see? And then we got a train from Liverpool, and then a nice man at the train station showed us what Tube to get on. And here we are.'

'Where are your bags, though?'

'What bags? We don't need any bags. Haven't you got soap and towels at your place? Your mother has our night things in her handbag, and we'll buy some odds and ends in the shops as we need them. We hadn't really time to pack a load of stuff – and we hadn't a nice suitcase, anyway.'

'Are you in trouble, Dad? Were you playing poker again?'

'I was not playing poker.'

'Were you, Dad?'

'No, I swear it.'

'Promise me.'

'I promise. Are you not going to hug your mother? She made a real effort to dress up for you, Emily. And you know that boats give her a bad stomach. I thought she was going to throw up when it got a bit rough halfway over. I'm telling you, her face was as green as grass.'

'Oh, Mum,' Emily said, remembering her mother's terrible nausea on boats. 'How are you feeling now?'

'I'm not so bad,' said her mother dully.

Mrs Reilly glanced around at the gleaming white walls and metallic grey ceiling. She seemed mildly disappointed by the foyer in Emily's building.

Perhaps she was expecting something grander, Emily thought crossly. Perhaps she was expecting a doorman in a green coat with gold epaulettes,

190

and a massive flower arrangement on a mahogany desk. Well, she'd just have to settle for a black leather couch and a glass desk with a vase of daffodils on it.

'You see an awful lot of scruffy types in London,' Mrs Reilly added. 'I've never seen anything like it. Even on the Falls Road itself you wouldn't see such poor raggedy people.'

Emily went over and sat down beside her mother. She sat deliberately facing away from her father, so that he had no choice but to leave the desk and come and join them. Otherwise he would have tried to involve the receptionist in their conversation. That was her father all over, Emily seethed – any amount of time for complete strangers, but hardly a minute for her. She had no idea what they were doing here in London, but no doubt she would find out soon enough.

'Raggedy people,' Mrs Reilly said, and then she yawned and closed her eyes.

'I expect they'll be the immigrants?' Emily's father said. 'You see them everywhere, wearing those big puffy coats. I expect they find it cold over here?'

'Hush, Dad, you mustn't say things like that. You mustn't say anything racist in London, not ever,' Emily told him. 'Mum, don't go to sleep here, please.'

'What's racist about asking if somebody is cold? I'm only saying they must be cold here. Why can we not talk about the foreigners, Emily? It's no shame to be a foreigner. Weren't the Irish always great ones for emigrating? It was Irish navvies that built America. And they built most of this country too. That's the great pity of it, really, because the Irish did most of the hard work years ago – and now there's nothing left for these foreign lads to do, except maybe for sweeping up and washing dishes.'

'Hush, Dad, please, I'm begging you. Will you stop talking about immigrants and politics? Nobody here wants to talk about those things, right? It's not polite. It's not *acceptable*. Mum, will you wake up!'

'Well, I'm sorry if we're an embarrassment to you,' her father said loudly.

'I told you she wouldn't be pleased to see us,' Mrs Reilly added sadly, blinking herself awake again.

'I am pleased to see you,' Emily soothed.

'You don't look too pleased,' her mother told her.

'Oh, Mum. You never change,' Emily snapped finally.

The three of them sat sulking silently on the banquette.

The security guard at the main door began to smirk, while the receptionist busied himself with sorting the mail into pigeonholes. Emily couldn't help being sorely irritated that her parents seemed to belong in the 1940s. For pity's sake, her father was only fifty-three and her mother was fifty. How had they managed to assume the beliefs of two old relics from a bygone era? Was it their insular lifestyle that had made them this way? They surely hadn't failed to spot that there were plenty of what they called 'foreigners' in the professional classes?

'What say you take the rest of the day off, and we'll go to Madame Tussauds, hey?' said Mr Reilly, trying to rescue the situation. 'And then we'll go to Buckingham Palace and give the Queen a shout?'

'Look, Dad, I'm really sorry. But I just can't take any time off work right now. I'm acting up for my boss.'

'What does that mean?'

'It means I'm the boss now,' Emily explained.

'You're the boss of the whole magazine?' her father asked, his eyes as wide as saucers.

'Just for a while,' Emily said, thinking that he'd assume she was a millionaire now.

Arabella hadn't actually discussed a pay rise for Emily, because she was hoping she'd be back at work within two or three months. And Emily was almost glad of that – she didn't want Jane to find out she was getting a pay rise and use the information to start a mutiny.

'The boss of the magazine, did you hear that? Well, that's just brilliant news altogether. The big boss at last, hey? I hope they're paying you top dollar, Emily?'

'Never mind that now. Dad, tell me, have you both eaten? I can take you round the corner for something to eat. And then maybe I could see you both back to my flat in a taxi. I am sorry, but I've got to work today. We've so much to do. And I've no assistant to help me, because I used to be Arabella's assistant. Do you understand?'

'Well, that's a crying shame,' Emily's mother said at once, suddenly coming out of her sleepy reverie. 'We come all the way to London to see you – we come to London for the first time ever – and it turns out you're too busy to show us around.'

'Mum, I'm working. You should have told me you were coming.'

'Ah well...' Emily's mother said heavily, then sniffed loudly.

She obviously had no concept of the nine-to-five. She obviously didn't know that a person with a proper career couldn't just take time off without applying for it days – or even weeks – in advance.

'It's only a magazine about houses,' Emily's mother muttered darkly. 'Aren't the shops all stuffed to the rafters with magazines about houses? I'm tripping over them every time I go to the doctor's. Speaking of which, it's not like you're a surgeon and there's somebody lying in the hospital waiting for a heart operation. Well, is it?'

Emily closed her eyes and swallowed down the urge to remind her mother that she'd never had a career of her own. And that she'd never had to pay her own rent either, or run a car. Her parents had probably been on benefits for so long, they'd forgotten where the benefit money came from in the first place – from time-poor taxpayers like Emily.

'Now, don't be making a big thing out of it, woman. Emily can't help it if she has to work, can she? She'll take us out tonight for a nice supper, won't you, Emily? And to one of them fancy shows in the West End maybe?'

'I'd love to, Dad, I really would. But meals out and theatre tickets are very expensive,' Emily said

194

quietly. She didn't want the security guard or the receptionist to know she was up to her neck in debt. 'I haven't much money to spare at the moment.'

'So much for being the boss,' Mrs Reilly sniffed.

'Excuse me?' Emily said.

'Oh aye, I forgot about that side of things,' her father said humbly. Then he bit his lip with embarrassment. 'Yes, indeed ... the lack of money is a real scourge, Emily, love. Nobody knows that better than me. Well, we can manage rightly on a bag of chips and a stroll by the Thames, hey?'

'Oh, Daddy...'

Emily wanted to hug her father there and then and tell him how much she loved him. She also wanted to strangle him for coming over to London without giving her a warning first, and for promising Emily's mother a lovely holiday when he must have known the three of them hadn't a spare penny between them.

'You both stay right here, okay?' she said. 'And I'll go up and get my coat and handbag, and tell the staff I'll be out of the office for an hour or so.'

'Yes, love,' he smiled.

'Don't be too long,' her mother added. 'I'm starving.'

Emily caught the lift back up to her floor and told Jane she'd be out of the office for an hour or so. Then she locked Arabella's desk, so Jane couldn't go for a sneaky rummage in it.

'Is it something to do with Arabella's arrest?' Jane said bluntly as Emily passed her desk on the way out again.

'No, it isn't. Don't be silly,' Emily replied.

Emily had told the staff that Arabella's recent arrest had been a simple case of mistaken identity. But Jane's gossip radar had gone into overdrive, and Emily knew it was only a matter of time before Jane resorted to going through Arabella's bins late at night looking for clues.

'Just get on with your work, everyone,' Emily said loudly. 'I'll be back before you know it. Petra, if anyone rings and asks for me, please take a message.'

Petra Dunwoody rolled her eyes.

'Yes, Miss Reilly,' she said. 'Of course, Miss Reilly...'

Jane giggled.

Emily left the office before Jane could think of some excuse to accompany her down to the foyer.

Ten minutes later, Emily and her parents were sitting in one of the purple velvet booths of a bohemian café nearby, having just ordered tea and sandwiches.

'Now, Mum and Dad, let's get one thing straight; I *am* very pleased to see you.'

'But what?' her mother asked suspiciously.

'But I'm afraid you'll have to do your best to have a nice time in London on a non-existent budget,' Emily told them firmly. 'I wish it was different, but that's the situation.'

'That's okay,' Mr Reilly said cheerfully. 'We've got enough for Tube fares. We can go and see things that are free. And just eat at your place.'

'Thanks, Dad, you're a great sport,' Emily said, patting him tenderly on the arm.

196

'Story of our lives,' Mrs Reilly muttered, and then she went off to the Ladies.

Emily resisted the urge to follow her mother – to check she wasn't hiding a half-bottle of vodka in her handbag.

'So how is Mum keeping?' Emily said as soon as her mother was out of earshot.

'She's doing great,' Mr Reilly said quickly. 'She's only drinking about half of what she used to. And she's eating better, and sleeping more.'

'That's something, I suppose. And how are you keeping, Dad? How's the gambling?'

'Emily, I haven't gone near the bookies since I last saw you,' he said.

'Please tell me the truth, Daddy.'

'I have a limit of two pounds a day,' he admitted.

'Is that all?'

'Okay, three pounds.'

'Is it five pounds?'

'Look, I spend five pounds a day, and that includes any winnings from the day before. I swear that's my limit. And I don't bet on Sundays.'

'Thirty pounds a week is still a lot of money,' Emily said carefully.

'I know it is.'

'You could paint a room a nice colour for that. Or buy six novels. Or buy enough groceries for a week's home cooking.'

'I know I could. But I'm not interested in painting rooms and reading books. And I'm not interested in cooking either,' Mr Reilly said stubbornly.

'You should find a new hobby, both of you, to

help take your mind off your addictions.'

'Poor Emily, you've been saying that to us all your life. When will you just accept we can't be like you, and just let us be who we are?'

'I'm sorry, Dad. I can't help it,' Emily said quietly.

'And neither can we,' he replied. 'On the bright side, I definitely won't be playing poker any more. For word is all over the city that my daughter isn't going to bail me out again, and now nobody will play poker with me.'

'Okay,' Emily smiled. 'That's very good news.'

Then the waiter brought their food, and Mrs Reilly returned from the Ladies with a sort of half-smile on her face and the merest whiff of vodka on her breath.

Emily poured the tea, handed round the sandwiches and paid the bill.

15. The First Snow of Winter

Emily checked that the wardrobe door was firmly locked, and then she slipped the little bronze key into her jeans pocket. She was giving her parents her bedroom during their stay in London, but she didn't want them trying to hang their coats up in her wardrobe. That scenario was just too difficult to cope with emotionally. Even the thought of her mother rummaging through her old things filled Emily with horror. The wardrobe was the keeper of Emily's emotional baggage, and she wasn't ready to share that space with anybody else – not just yet.

But Mrs Reilly had other things on her mind that day.

'Oh dear, I really don't like those old skylights,' she said when she came in to inspect the bedroom. 'If it rains at all, I can't get to sleep with the noise – it sounds like a marching band.'

'When were you ever in a room with skylights?' Emily asked.

'That's none of your business,' her mother replied defensively.

And Emily suddenly remembered that the hospital room her mother had stayed in had had skylights.

'I'm really sorry, Mum, but I can't do anything about them,' Emily said simply.

'Never mind... It probably won't rain now, it's

that cold outside. I bet it'll be snowing by bed-time,' Mrs Reilly said, peering up at the ceiling with a faraway expression on her deathly white face.

'Don't make a fuss, woman,' her husband told her firmly. 'You can't make a fuss when you're getting free accommodation.'

'I suppose that's true enough.'

Mr Reilly winked at Emily, and she winked back at him. 'I'll make us a nice curry for supper,' she said.

'I don't like curry,' her mother said. 'It gives me heartburn.'

'I'll make a frittata, then.'

'What's that?'

'It's an omelette with potatoes and cheese in it,' Emily said.

'Sounds okay to me,' Mr Reilly smiled.

'We've come a long way just to eat eggs and spuds,' Mrs Reilly said.

'This is fancy eggs and spuds, you'll love it,' Emily told her.

She went breezing into the kitchen while her mother went back to the sitting room, looking even more disappointed than usual.

'It's very cold in this flat, Emily,' she said, rubbing her arms. 'Could you maybe light the fire?'

'That's not a real fireplace, Mum. It's only a fake one.'

'Is it really?'

'Yes, it is.'

'It looks real enough. Who'd bother putting in a fake fireplace?' Mrs Reilly wondered.

'The landlord, I suppose,' Emily said, and the tears sprang into her eyes. She was beginning to feel a complete failure.

'What a waste of time, putting in a fireplace that doesn't work,' her mother said in a reedy voice. 'Oh dear, I'm really frozen here. I hope I don't catch a chill from sitting in such a cold room. There's nothing as nice as a real coal fire. I'm beginning to wish we'd stayed in Belfast.'

Emily began to understand why her father spent so much time in the relative peace and comfort of his local bookmaker's. She'd only been with her mother for a few hours, and already she was exhausted and longing to crawl under the duvet. And then she remembered with a sinking heart that she wouldn't have her beloved bedroom to herself for another two weeks. A flash of acute anxiety worked its way around her nervous system.

She wondered, should she give Dylan a call? And would he be able to think of anything she could do to entertain her parents for two whole weeks? Maybe she could take them down the road to Dylan's shop for a fashion makeover? He was bound to have something nice they could wear, she thought to herself. Something smart and relatively tasteful they could wear for their first ever holiday in London – or, indeed, outside of Ireland. She even thought briefly of asking the girls at the *Rock & Fairy* hair boutique if they needed a couple of models to practise new styles on. Her father could do with a decent trim, and her mother could do with losing about ten inches off her untidy mane. If she suggested a makeover, she knew her parents would be dreadfully offended. However, Dylan might be able to make it all sound like great fun.

At that exact moment the buzzer rang, and Emily just knew it was Dylan back from his rugby trip to France. She was exhilarated at the thought of seeing him, and a bit disappointed they wouldn't be able to go straight into the bedroom and make love.

'I think it's Dylan,' she said to her parents. 'Be nice to him, won't you?'

'Why wouldn't we be?' her father said.

'Because of the poker thing,' Emily explained. 'Because he told that thug to back off and leave you alone...'

'That wasn't his fault,' Mr Reilly said matter-of-factly. 'You told him to do it.'

'I'm still starving,' her mother complained. 'My stomach thinks my throat's been cut.'

'Oh boy,' Emily groaned.

As Dylan came bounding up the stairs, the three of them stood in a little huddle to greet him.

'Oh, hi there,' Dylan said when he reached Emily's door.

His face was flushed with the cold and his eyes were bluer than ever. Emily longed to kiss him passionately, but she made do with the briefest of hugs instead.

'I didn't know your parents were coming over.'

'Mum and Dad are staying with me for *two whole weeks*,' Emily said.

'Isn't that lovely?' Dylan said at once, shaking their hands warmly. 'I hope you have a great time

202

while you're here, Mr and Mrs Reilly.'

'Don't be so formal, lad. You've met us before. Call me Pat – and this is Annie, in case you've forgotten,' Mr Reilly said.

'Won't you stay for supper?' Emily asked him.

'He will, surely,' Mr Reilly said.

'It's only eggs,' Mrs Reilly pointed out.

'I love eggs,' Dylan nodded.

'It's a *frittata*,' Emily said, smiling determinedly at her mother.

'We're on a tight budget, money-wise,' Mr Reilly said, winking crookedly at Dylan.

'Half-rations; the story of our lives,' Mrs Reilly added.

'Mum and Dad, that'll do,' Emily warned.

'Well, look, we can't have you on half-rations your first night in London. I wonder, would you let me take the three of you out somewhere nice? There's a fantastic restaurant about a mile from here. They do a mean steak, and their toffee puddings are to die for.'

'There's really no need, Dylan,' Emily began.

'We'd be delighted,' Mr Reilly said at once. 'That's very generous of you, Dylan.'

'Have you got a car? Because I'm too tired to walk far,' Mrs Reilly said.

'Yes, I have my car right outside the door,' he smiled.

Soon the four of them were sitting in Dylan's old BMW with the heating turned up full blast.

'This is a nice car,' Mrs Reilly said approvingly.

'Thank you,' Dylan said, pulling out into the evening traffic.

'I hope you don't mind me sitting in the passenger seat, Dylan? Only I can't sit in the back or I'll get travel sickness,' Emily's mother explained.

'Don't worry about it,' Emily said. 'I was going to suggest you sit in the front, anyway.'

'Would the two of you like to see some horses in the country?' Dylan asked them.

'I love horses,' Emily's father said at once.

'He loves them far too much for his own good,' his wife added.

'My sister Sylvia rescues old ponies. The stables are about fifty miles from here. I could take you for a spin tomorrow, if you like? If you've nothing else planned? I can take the day off work tomorrow.'

'I'd love that,' Mr Reilly said.

'I'd like a spin in the car,' Mrs Reilly admitted.

'It's a date, then,' Dylan said.

Emily could have kissed him – except she couldn't kiss him, because she was sitting in the back seat beside her father.

'Will you come with us, Emily?' her mother asked.

'Emily can't come with us, because she's got a big important meeting with the printers tomorrow. Haven't you, Emily?' Dylan said, steering calmly down the heavily congested road.

'You remembered?' Emily said, feeling suddenly very moved.

'Of course I remembered,' he said. 'Emily's arranging for this handy little booklet on decluttering to be given away with the magazine,' he told her parents. 'I love it when people declutter, because it means we get more donations in the shop.'

'Well, we'll just have to manage without you, Emily,' her mother said kindly. 'Is this a nice restaurant we're going to, Dylan? Only I'm totally famished. I could eat a horse, I'm that hungry.'

'Don't say that to Sylvia,' Dylan joked.

They all laughed.

'It's a really lovely place,' Dylan told Mrs Reilly. 'I used to go there all the time when I was in my last job. Let's go mad, shall we? I don't know about you, but I'm going to have three courses – soup and a steak and a toffee pudding. I know the menu like the back of my hand, and everything they serve is absolutely delicious. And we'll even try a bottle of bubbly; just the one between us? That'll be okay, won't it, Emily?'

'Go on, then. Why not?'

'Yeah, let's live a little,' Dylan said brightly. 'We'll have a real family get-together.'

'I like this fellow of yours, Emily,' Mrs Reilly said after a minute's pause. 'That last one – Alex – was hard work. He wouldn't give you the time of day if he could help it, Dylan. I bet you any money his wallet had a moth living in it.'

'Mum, please don't start.'

'All the years you wasted on that man, and he never took us out to dinner once. Tight as two coats of paint, he was.'

'Mum, that's enough,' Emily said.

'I'm only telling Dylan the truth,' Mrs Reilly protested. 'Honestly, even at Christmas he'd get us some old cheap tin of biscuits from the supermarket. Though he didn't mind lavishing the money on himself, oh no. He only wore designer

205

clothes. Mind you, he still didn't look all that great in them. Bit of a tummy on him. And he had a massive car, though he couldn't even park the thing without denting it.'

'Thanks, Mum, but I'm quite sure Dylan doesn't want to hear another word about Alex,' Emily said loudly.

'Oh yes, I do,' Dylan laughed. 'Just as long as it's all bad.'

'He wasn't as handsome as you are either,' added Mrs Reilly.

'Mum, if you don't give over about Alex, I am getting out of this car and walking home,' Emily threatened. 'And you can have your swanky dinner without me.'

'She's a right bossy madam sometimes,' Emily's mother said to Dylan then, and she patted his knee in a sympathetic way. 'I do hope you know what you're getting yourself into?'

Laughing his head off, Dylan parked the car outside the restaurant, ushered them all up the steps and held the door open for Emily's mother. Then all four of them went breezing into the elegant interior in grand style. The waiter was a friend of Dylan's, and he gave them a table upstairs by the terrace with a great view of the city. They had a fabulous meal; every morsel was divine. The conversation never faltered for a moment. Mostly it consisted of Mrs Reilly regaling Dylan with funny tales from Emily's childhood and Dylan laughing heartily at every one. Emily was amazed her mother was able to remember so many details, as she'd seemed tipsy for most of it. Emily's father simply enjoyed the fine food – such

206

a change for him after a lifetime of battered sausages and fish suppers. He even decided not to ask the waiter for a bottle of tomato ketchup to go with his lemon sole.

As they were finishing off a perfect evening with a round of Irish coffees, it began to snow softly. The temperature outside plummeted, and within half an hour the road markings were hidden beneath a soft layer of white. It was tempting to stay in the delicious warmth of the restaurant for another half-hour, and to gaze out of the huge windows at the twinkling lights of London, but eventually they conceded it was time to go home.

'That was truly a lovely meal,' Dylan said, signalling for the waiter.

He decided to go and pay at the bar, because he didn't want Emily or her parents to see the bill. He didn't think there'd be much change left over from two hundred pounds. Their evening in the restaurant had been so enjoyable; he didn't want Emily to worry about the cost of it now.

'I told you it was going to snow today,' Mrs Reilly sniffed as they stood up and put on their coats. 'I could feel it in my bones. I wish we'd brought more clothes over from Belfast with us.'

'Oh, Mum,' Emily muttered, but she was too full of garlic chicken to be cross with her parents any more tonight.

By the time they stepped outside the snow was coming down in huge, feather-light tufts. One landed on Emily's nose, and Dylan brushed it away tenderly.

'Thanks for a lovely time,' Emily said happily.

'I'm going to die of cold,' Mrs Reilly said quietly.

'We just got some lovely stuff in at the shop,' Dylan said as they settled back into the car for the drive home. 'Vintage coats, lovely quality – we could take a look at them on our way to the stables tomorrow?'

'Well, that'd be great … if the snow doesn't leave us trapped in the house for days and days,' Mrs Reilly muttered.

'I'm sure it won't,' Emily said absent-mindedly.

She was already thinking of her meeting the following day. She needed to convince everyone it was worth spending the rest of their budget on the de-cluttering booklet. Emily didn't need their permission, of course, but she didn't want to alienate them any further either.

She was so engrossed in her thoughts, they were soon back at the flat and she hadn't heard one word of the in-car chat.

'What are you thinking about?' Dylan asked Emily as they lay whispering on the ancient sofa bed later that evening. Dylan had told Emily's parents he'd stay the night, so they could leave for the stables bright and early the following morning. And amazingly they hadn't displayed any signs of disapproval. Instead, they'd gone off to bed, all happy and contented, with two mugs of cocoa.

'I'm thinking that you're going to think I'm a liar,' Emily admitted.

'Why would I think that?' he said, kissing her shoulder hungrily.

'Oh no, don't do that,' she said, buttoning her pyjamas right up to the neck.

'We can be really quiet,' he whispered imploringly. 'Please?'

'No way, absolutely not.'

'Please?'

'No! When my parents are around I feel like I'm ten years old. Besides, you'd better take it easy for a while – you've eaten so much food.'

'Okay, okay. So why would I think you're a liar, then?'

'Because I told you they were always a bit difficult. Yet so far today they've been very nice to you,' she said crossly.

'Of course they were nice to me. I bought them a lovely dinner,' he said simply.

'And they were chatting away to you non-stop. Usually they can't wait to get away from me,' she complained. 'When I ring them they pretend there's a caller at the door, or the toast's on fire – any excuse to get me off the line. Once they even said there was a bomb-scare in their street, and they had to evacuate to the community centre.'

'I'm a new face. I'm a novelty,' Dylan said kindly.

'I guess so...' she said sadly.

'Yeah, I reckon they just find life a lot more difficult than the rest of us. They're a nervous little pair, aren't they?'

'You're a good man.'

'You're worth it.'

'No, you've a good heart,' she said generously.

'Ah, come on, it's easy for me to be kind to them, because they aren't my parents. I might be cross with them too, if they were my mum and dad. Just try thinking of them as endearingly hopeless rather than deliberately awkward, yes?'

'Okay, but I think tomorrow is going to be tough on you,' she added.

'No, it'll be fine; I'll take them to the shop for the day, if the roads are going to be a problem,' Dylan said. 'I can bring them to the stables another day. Yeah, I'll take them to the shop and let them have a good old smash-and-grab on the new donations.'

'I wonder, would they be offended, though?' she asked.

'I'll tell them it's a new sort of boutique, and not a charity shop as such. You know it looks great nowadays,' he said, undoing her buttons and kissing her shoulder again. He slid one leg across Emily's knees and pulled her closer to him. 'You look really sexy in those flowery pyjamas. All 1950s and so hot, hot, hot...'

'I do not look hot. Don't talk utter rubbish.'

'You're gorgeous; those pyjamas are doing things to me,' he whispered huskily.

'I told you, I cannot undress with them in the next room,' she hissed.

'Okay, then – we'll compromise,' he said.

'What on earth are you talking about?' she asked.

'I can be very discreet when I want to be,' Dylan said, slipping one hand inside Emily's pyjama bottoms. 'Just a little something to relax you, Miss Reilly, after the stressful day you've had today?'

'Don't you dare touch me,' she told him. 'Don't you dare touch me, I'm warning you.'

But she knew she'd die if he didn't. Then she couldn't protest further, because he was kissing

210

her tenderly on the lips – and she was discovering that Dylan could indeed be very discreet and incredibly sensual when he wanted to be. She had to put her own hands over her mouth so as not to make any sound...

'Goodnight, gorgeous,' he said five minutes later. 'See you in the morning. And don't worry about the meeting. It'll be fine.'

But Emily was already fast asleep.

Outside the snow continued to fall, and once again Londoners issued a collective groan as the gritters and snowploughs and salt depots geared up for another long and difficult winter. By midnight the city was fully blanketed in a thick layer of icy frost and glittery snow.

But Emily slept through it all, snuggled up to the lovely warmth of Dylan's body.

That night she dreamed of happy things: enjoying her work at the magazine, holding hands with Dylan as they watched TV on the sofa, and kissing him tenderly by candlelight. Not once did she dream of her boss committing arson, or a surprise visit from her parents.

When she opened her eyes in the morning she felt so happy, she didn't even care that the old sofa bed had almost crippled her back.

16. And the Award Goes to...

Emily stood on the doorstep of Arabella's smart Chelsea town house and rang the buzzer for a second time, then a third time. She had been sure Arabella was going to be at home that day. Her car was parked nearby, but there was no sign of her answering the door. Emily knelt down on the mat and peered through the shiny gold-coloured letter box. She thought she could smell cigarette smoke; Arabella must be back on them, she thought to herself.

'Arabella, are you there? It's me, Emily. I've got great news.'

After a minute, Arabella came trailing down the stairs in her dressing gown and unlocked the heavy wooden door. She was indeed smoking a cigarette. Emily didn't mention it, however.

'Hi there, sleepyhead,' Emily said, breezing into the cavernous hallway. 'Those tubs could do with a bit of water. Shall I sort them for you?'

She went to the cupboard under the sink, fetched and filled the watering can and gave the tubs a much-needed drink.

'What's the great news?' Arabella asked half-heartedly.

She was sitting on the bottom stair, looking quite desolate. Emily set down the watering can and took a deep breath.

'Oh, Arabella, you'll never believe it but we've

won an award! *Stylish Living* has been nominated for an award, and I've been told on the quiet that we've actually won it. So buy yourself a new dress, because you'll soon be posing on the red carpet. Isn't that brilliant news?'

'What's the award?' Arabella yawned. 'What do we have to do?'

'Okay, it's for you and one guest for a black-tie dinner at The Dorchester; it's the Women of the Year Awards held by *Good Housekeeping* magazine, and you've won the award for excellence in publishing. Thank heaven we didn't run that feature on Daisy Churchill in the end. It might have knocked us right out of the competition.'

'Well, that all sounds lovely. But I'm sorry, I can't go.'

'What?'

'I just can't go, Emily.'

'How do you know you can't go? I haven't told you the date yet.'

'Look, you can accept the award and take Dylan with you for the experience. I'm sure he'll look gorgeous in a tux with those broad shoulders of his. You deserve a night out, darling, for keeping things running so smoothly at the office. I owe you one, big time. And I'm *so* not in the mood for a red carpet do.'

'Arabella, are you feeling all right?' Emily asked, sitting down on the stairs beside her friend. 'You're very pale.'

'I'm okay. I just haven't slept all night. My solicitor was here yesterday,' Arabella said.

'Okay, and what did he say?' Emily patted Arabella's hand gently.

'Well, it's all very complicated, of course – lots of legal speak. But, in a nutshell, I have to pay for the rebuilding of the house I burned down.'

'Oh no, how much will it cost?'

'About half a million pounds. And it'll take six months to complete, so they're adding on the lost rental income – as if I care about another twelve thousand on top of half a million.'

'So you'll have to sell this house?'

'Yes, I'm afraid so.' Arabella said again, and then she began to cry fat, silent tears.

'Will you still have to go to court?' Emily asked.

'No, I won't, which is the only chink of light in the whole sorry saga.'

'Oh good, that's such a relief.'

'The solicitor – he's called Reginald Blakelock, by the way, what a great name! – he says I could still go to court and argue that I was in the middle of a nervous breakdown at the time of the fire. But if the judge rules against me, I could still end up liable for the damage. And I could go to prison, and my professional reputation would be ruined into the bargain. You can see how arson wouldn't look so good on the CV of an interiors expert. The owner won't press charges if I pay him in full within six weeks, which is very generous of him when you think about it. I mean, the guy did have a heart attack. So I either lose my home, or I go to court and run the risk of losing everything.'

'Oh, Arabella, I'm so very sorry. This is awful, just awful news.'

'Thanks, Emily, you've been the best friend to me always.'

'What has David said?'

'He said he can't possibly afford to bail me out now he has a new family to support.'

'I see.'

'I've only got myself to blame for this great big fat mess, Emily.'

'Well, I should have helped you more, to get over the shock of David's treachery.'

'Oh no, missy; I will not allow you to take the blame for any of this. I made this mess all by myself, and I won't have you shouldering *any* of the blame. Do you hear me? Boy, did your parents do a number on you, Emily. You're riddled with guilt. Speaking of which, where are they today?'

'They're going home tomorrow, so Dylan's taken them into town to do the tourist stuff – and no doubt he's paying for everything. He's been great about their visit; he's taken them somewhere nearly every day. Luckily Sylvia was around to keep the shop open! They were helping in the shop at the weekend, did I tell you? They got some new clothes there, and Dylan even treated them to new haircuts at the *Rock & Fairy*. My parents have had the same hairstyles for thirty years, but of course Dylan was able to talk them into trying something new. The man is a genius.'

'Wow, he certainly is.'

'I know,' Emily said, hugging her knees with happiness. 'I do love him for being so kind to my parents.'

'And I love this house,' Arabella said then.

'Yes, I know,' Emily agreed.

'I've pored over every inch of it. It's taken me

years to get it looking this good. I've decorated every room with care and consideration and, well, love. This house is worth much more than money to me.'

'Will there be anything left over, do you think? When the debt is settled, will you have enough to begin again with a little apartment or something?'

'Oh, there'll be something, yes. I might be able to buy a bedsit in Hackney. How long do you think my tubs will last around that neighbourhood?'

'I'm so sorry, sweetheart,' Emily said again.

'Not to worry; I've learned my lesson. Every cloud has a silver lining, and I'm a much wiser woman now. I did need a wake-up call – and, heck, did I ever get one. David and I ran out of steam about two years ago, but I couldn't admit it, not even to myself. I don't loathe him any more. I don't love him any more. And I won't contact him ever again, or send him emails or texts, or set fire to anything he owns. Ha, ha... Don't worry about me on that score.'

'Nobody at the office has any idea, you know. I promise you that. The fire hasn't been on the news. And they all think you've been lying low because you've had a major face lift or implants or liposuction.'

'Do they really think that? Do they really think I *need* a face lift or implants or liposuction?'

'No, they don't think you need anything, you silly mare! Petra told me that's what they've been saying, that's all. They don't think you need any work; they just can't think of any other reason for you to be away from the office like this.'

'How is Petra?' Arabella asked.

'She's fine – been a bit frosty towards me in recent weeks, but she's back to her old self again. We had a quiet cup of tea together yesterday, and she told me she was very upset when I was promoted instead of her. But then she realized she'd rather be a stylist than a manager. And that's when she confessed that everyone has decided you're in a Swiss clinic or something, being totally overhauled.'

'Good old Petra. She always did have a vivid imagination. And how has Jane been behaving herself?'

'Now, funny you should ask that, because there's definitely something weird going on there. Petra thinks Jane has a new boyfriend, a real catch of some sort. Jane's been getting her hair done every other day, and she's wearing nicer shoes to work. Killer heels! And she's got a new Tiffany bracelet that she rattles a lot and simpers over constantly. But she won't tell anyone what's going on; it's all a big secret.'

'She must be having an affair with a married man – or at least, a man who's already spoken for,' Arabella said, yawning again. 'Knowing Jane, there's bound to be some nonsense involved. Silly girl...'

'That could be it, you know. You're so clever, Arabella.'

'Not clever enough, dear Emily,' Arabella said, gazing around the hallway at her beautiful flower prints and limited-edition wallpaper. 'I actually feel sorry for Jane, if she's getting all lovesick over a married man,' Arabella added. 'Most of the available men out there aren't much to write home about. Useless, most of them... You'd need to be totally brain dead to get mixed up with a *married* man. I mean, talk about commitment issues, on both sides.'

'Yes, I expect so,' Emily agreed.

She couldn't really disagree. After all, Arabella's husband had been very much a married man when he'd met his current partner, Mary.

'What's happened to love, Emily?' Arabella asked suddenly. 'I mean, real, true, till-death-us-do-part love? Where has all the romance gone?'

'Dylan's rather romantic.'

'Fair point... You're a lucky duck. And you deserve it, petal. Nobody deserves it more, after all the time you wasted on that Alex chap. But nowadays it seems to be thousands of wannabe WAGs chasing a handful of overpaid footballers, and a bunch of stuffy old actors chasing after some naive young models. And then you've got your single mothers on benefits, your hopeless nerds playing computer games in their bedrooms, and your bitter old wrecks like me.'

'You are *so* not a wreck,' Emily said loyally.

'Bless you, my darling. But seriously, where have all the normal people gone? When was the last time you heard of two people just falling in love and getting married, with no regard to background or money or anything else? When did you last hear a simple, old-fashioned love story? Or were we always obsessed with status and money?'

'Well, you make a good point. I mean, I was dumped for a richer girl, wasn't I?' Emily finally admitted.

'What's this, a breakthrough moment? I thought you always claimed Alex left you because he didn't love you any more? Because you were an ugly loser and he was a golden prince!'

'With hindsight, I do think he left me because my father was skint and my mother was a boozer. In short, Alex left me because he was as shallow as a puddle.'

'I'm so pleased you have seen the light, my dear. Do you know, I think this calls for a celebration? Let's have a champagne breakfast. I've some bacon in the fridge; we'll have bacon butties and a glass of Moët. There's a bottle around here somewhere. I'm pretty sure one bottle survived my recent clear-out. Oh, and don't worry about the cigarette just now; I'm only having five a day.'

'Wouldn't you rather celebrate winning the award?'

'No. It's *much* more exciting that you've finally gotten over that awful man. I insist you take Dylan to The Dorchester and enjoy every minute of it.'

'Are you sure you don't want to go yourself? You and I could go together?' Emily offered.

'No, really, I'm quite sure. I can't wait to get back to work, though. Now that it's all over. I'm going to sell this house for as much money as I can get, buy a smaller place, and then come back to work all guns blazing – metaphorically speaking, of course. Thank you for being such a good and dear friend to me, Emily... Oh, and if you find out what that idiot Jane is up to, will you please tell me immediately? I could really use a good laugh right now.'

'Okay, well let's make those butties now, yeah? I could murder one – metaphorically speaking, of course.'

Laughing, they linked arms and went into the kitchen.

Two days later, Dylan collected his tuxedo from the rental shop and tried it on to show Emily.

Her parents had gone home – and it was just as well, because the bow tie was barely fastened around Dylan's neck before he was taking everything off again as quickly as he could.

'You are so *gorgeous* in that suit,' Emily panted, peeling off her own clothes and dropping them to the floor. 'I insist you make love to me right this instant.'

'My pleasure,' laughed Dylan as they tumbled into bed, almost breaking the bedsprings. 'You'd better not do this on the night of the awards, though; we don't want to be late and miss your moment of glory.'

'I've thought of that,' Emily said. 'You'll just have to wear the tux every night until the ceremony, so I can get desensitized to it.'

'Good plan,' Dylan said, and he kissed her hungrily.

On the night of the awards Emily wore a full-length, olive-green gown that brought out the colour of her eyes. Dylan looked magnificent in his tux, and they had a great time pretending to be celebrities on the red carpet.

Emily went up to receive the award on Arabella's behalf. She said a brief but amusing thank you that made her the darling of the night.

Daisy Churchill was also at the event, but thankfully they were seated at opposite ends of the room

As soon as the proceedings were over, Dylan and Emily made a beeline for the door ... and bed.

17. House to Let

On the first day of December the weather turned very cold again. But since the city had hardly warmed up from the winter before, nobody really lamented the dip in temperature. Emily brought out her Christmas decorations and made herself a hot chocolate. She hung up the various baubles while listening to the radio, and just enjoyed having some rare time to herself. She was starting to look forward to a wonderful Christmas with Dylan. Would they spend the day together here in London? she wondered. What would she buy him? What would he buy her? It was all so exciting. Emily's artificial tree didn't take long to put up, and the lights worked first time. She went round the flat, plumping cushions, dusting everything in her path and humming 'Silent Night'.

Around lunchtime, however, Emily's parents rang her up unexpectedly and asked her if she could possibly help them organize a move to London. Just out of the blue, they wanted to move to London. Emily could have passed out with shock. She looked at her mobile phone, as if she had never seen it before.

'Did you just say you wanted to move to London?'

'Yes, that's right.'

'Have you been drinking again, Mum?' Emily asked cautiously. 'You might want to start watering it down a little bit.'

'How dare you! I have not been near it for a few days, actually. Well, that's a nice thing to say to your mother on the first day of the Christmas season. And we do want to move to London. We fancy a change, that's all.'

'I'm sorry, Mum. I really didn't mean to hurt your feelings. It's just a bit of a surprise, that's all. Can you put Dad on the phone, please?' Emily said quietly.

'Hello, pet,' her father said brightly. 'How are you keeping?'

'Hello, Dad. I'm fine, but what's going on?'

'Nothing's going on. Honestly, pet, you do treat the pair of us as if we're mentally ill sometimes,' Emily's father scolded.

'I'm sorry, Daddy,' Emily said, genuinely contrite. 'Just tell me what's happened. Are you in any sort of trouble? Is there a loan shark after you? Have you insulted somebody with dodgy connections? Oh sorry, I shouldn't have said that. It's just that you never go anywhere.'

'Look, nothing dodgy has happened, okay? Why do you always think something has happened? It's just a notion of your mother's, that's all it is. We had such a lovely time in London when we were over, and it's been very quiet here since we got back. I'm barred from the poker games, and your mother's been cutting back on the old you-know-what and also on the shopping. And because of all that, we're a bit bored.'

'Well, that's understandable, Dad. But you do know that Dylan made a special effort to be nice to you when you were here before, don't you? He

223

wouldn't be able to take you out every day, if you came to London to live. He has the shop to run, and I have to go to work.'

'Yes, we know that, love. We thought we might get jobs too.'

'What sort of jobs?' Emily said, mystified.

Neither of her parents had worked in years. She heard a muffled struggle on the other end of the line as her parents fought over the handset.

'Emily dear, we'll get a couple of basic jobs; we're not completely stupid,' Emily's mother said, taking the phone back from her husband. 'We'll get jobs and we'll just see how we get on. Now, do you know of anybody that needs a couple of housekeepers or cleaners or something? And we can live in, or rent a room. Will you ask around, please?'

Suddenly Emily was overcome with love for her parents; bless them for trying to do something out of the ordinary, she thought to herself.

'Are you serious about this?' Emily asked, scratching her head.

'Yes, we are.'

'What about all your stuff there? All your nice things...' Emily asked, thinking of her mother's clutter.

'What about it? The stuff can sit here and wait for us.'

'Well, what if you like it here and you never want to go back to Belfast?'

'Ah, the Council can dump the lot of it. Sure, it's only rubbish, anyway,' Emily's mother said briskly.

'This is very sudden, Mum.'

'Aren't you happy we want to live in London? We thought you'd be pleased that we wanted to be near you. Or have you changed your mind about playing happy families?'

Emily was momentarily dumbstruck by her mother's direct and slightly hostile approach. Yes, she had always complained about their lack of a traditional family life. And she did often comment on how bad her parents were at remembering birthdays and anniversaries, and so on. Yet now they were offering to come and live near her, she could feel nothing but doubt.

'Listen, Mum. I'm really sorry, but I don't think I can help you,' she said lamely.

'No?'

'It's just that none of my friends could afford a live-in cleaner – and I don't know if an agency would take you either, given your employment history.'

'We don't need a fancy agency, for pity's sake. Emily, will you ask Dylan if he knows of anything that might suit us?' her mother said impatiently. 'Please try to see things from our point of view, Emily. We're just sitting here, day in and day out looking at the blessed wallpaper. I'll go mad, if I don't see a change of scenery very soon.'

'Yes, okay, I'll ask Dylan right now and I'll ring you back,' Emily said.

'Do you promise you'll really ask him? And not just tell us you asked him?'

'Yes, I promise.'

'Good, we'll be home all day as usual,' her mother said in a grim voice.

'Fingers crossed, Emily,' her father added.

'That'll do for now,' Emily heard her mother say. 'Hang up, will you?'

The line went dead. Emily immediately called Dylan at the shop before she could chicken out of it.

'Dylan, listen. This is utterly ridiculous, but I just told my parents I would ask if you know of anyone who needs a couple of live-in house-keepers. They want to move to London! Now, I know you don't know anybody who needs live-in housekeepers, and they couldn't *keep house* if their lives depended on it, but they seem so keen, I promised them I'd ask,' she said wearily.

'Cleaning houses, huh?'

'Yes. Honestly ... just when you think they can't get any dafter, they come up with a crazy plan like this. Cleaning houses? They clean their own house about once in a decade. I think they still have the first bottle of furniture polish they ever bought. I think they're actually trying to drive me mad.'

Dylan laughed loudly down the phone.

'You are such a diva,' he said affectionately. 'Bless the two of them; they're only bored to death since they cut back on the gambling and the shopping.'

'It would seem so,' Emily said. 'I haven't the heart to tell them we can't help them. Do you think we could tell them there's a job coming up in a few months' time, and hope they've lost interest by then?'

'Well, there's no need. Because it just so happens, I can help them,' he said.

'What are you talking about?'

226

'I've got a mate, Jake Lancaster, who's travelling in Australia for six months. He wouldn't mind your parents moving in and keeping an eye on the house for him. They wouldn't have to make it official or anything; they could just tell anyone who asks that they're going on a little extended holiday to London. Do you know if they get their benefits paid by direct debit? If they do, there's no problem whatsoever.'

'And this Jake wouldn't mind that they're not from an agency?' Emily said.

'Come on, of course he wouldn't mind! What's the harm in it? It's a big house, and there've been a few burglaries on that street in recent times. They wouldn't have to do anything, really – just switch on some lights at night, and so on. Keep the front garden tidy. It's only a tiny little patch, so it wouldn't be any bother for your father, I'm sure.'

'My mum is a heavy smoker,' Emily said. 'She'll stink the house out.'

'Jake is a smoker too,' Dylan replied, 'so he won't mind if she smokes.'

'When did this mate of yours go to Australia?'

'Three months ago.'

'So they'd have the house for another three months?'

'That's about it, yeah.'

'That'll be more than enough time for them to get homesick, I suppose. Actually, I would be happy if they didn't get homesick. It might do them good to make a fresh start. Oh, Dylan, this could be a great idea! Will I really tell them about this house-sitting gig, then?'

'Why not offer it to them?' Dylan said. 'Ring me back in a bit. And if it's a yes, I'll send a message to Jake. The house is about ten minutes' walk away from your flat, so you can keep an eye on them. I'll give them the spare key that Jake gave me, and they can come over to London and move in whenever they like.'

'I'm so excited. It will be okay, won't it?'

'Yes, I think so,' Dylan said. 'House-sitting generally is a simple arrangement. And Jake's place is pretty casual decor-wise; they won't be able to do much damage there.'

'Okay, I'll call you back.'

Emily dialled the number in Belfast with shaking hands.

'Hello, is that you, Emily?'

'Yes, Mum.'

'Boy, that was quick. We're still drinking our tea here. It's not bad news, is it?'

'No! It's good news; I've got something for you. A friend of Dylan's needs a house-sitter.'

'Praise the Lord. Is the house anywhere near you?'

'Yes, it's very close to my flat. It's close to the shops too. I mean, you'll be able to get your groceries home without needing a taxi,' Emily added, in case her mother thought she was referring to her shopaholic tendencies.

But her mother was too pleased to notice any veiled insult.

'Good thinking, Emily,' she said. 'I knew Dylan would be able to find us something. Good lad! Tell him thanks, won't you?'

'I will.'

'We'll be over on Sunday evening,' Emily's mother said chirpily. 'This time we're going to pack properly. Can we come to yours on Sunday evening, just to pick up the keys? We don't want to be in your way at all.'

'Of course you can,' Emily said. 'And you won't be in my way at all. You don't have to be like that about it, Mum. Look, I *am* happy that you're coming over for a while. Really, I am. Now that I've had time to think about it, it's a marvellous idea. Dad will get away from his old betting pals, and you'll have lots of new things to do. I'll cook us a nice roast beef dinner, and then Dylan can take you to see the house. Okay?'

'Okay, love, we'll call you tomorrow after we've got our tickets.'

'Okay – and say goodbye to Dad for me. Bye, Mum.'

'Bye, love.'

Afterwards Emily sat on the sofa and thought about what had happened. And she felt increasingly guilty that she'd not once thought of bringing her mum and dad to London and giving them a new role in life as house-sitters. At the very least, they'd have been able to pay their way in life – instead of rusting away on the scrap heap. She'd never thought of it, and yet Dylan had the whole thing fixed up in about two minutes. He really was a sort of guardian angel, she thought to herself. She gazed at her white Christmas tree happily. Well, this was a lovely start to December, wasn't it? The glass angels seemed to shine a little brighter this year, she fancied.

Or maybe it was because her heart was feeling

much lighter this winter?

That evening Dylan picked Emily up in his car and took her to see Jake's house. She felt very comfortable, sitting beside him in the warmth of his old BMW. In fact she almost wished they were going for a nice long drive in the country, instead of just nipping across a few streets.

'It's huge,' Emily said, totally impressed when she saw Jake's home.

'Lucky sod inherited it from his great uncle,' Dylan told her. 'It's worth about a million and a half.'

'What does Jake do for a living?'

'He runs the family business, a small brewery in Surrey.'

'Sounds like an interesting job,' Emily said.

'Yes, it is. And he loves to travel, so it's lucky for him he's got no mortgage any more. Come on, then.'

They went inside the three-storey stucco-fronted mansion. Dylan had to shove the front door a bit to get it open, because a small mountain of mail had collected on the mat. Quickly he punched in the code that disabled the burglar alarm.

'Would you look at that pile of stuff,' he said incredulously. 'I should have come round here more often. Listen, I'll sort that lot out before we leave,' he added, gently pushing the mail into a neater pile with his foot. 'I'll have a quick look and make sure there's nothing urgent, though Jake said he'd paid all the utilities before he left. Let's just make sure everything else in the place is okay before we let your parents move in, yeah?'

230

They went from room to room, exploring. The house was massive with very high ceilings, but Emily thought it was rather cold and empty-looking. Jake clearly wasn't interested in interior design – a typical man, then! Just a few cushions and a tall vase or two would have made all the difference. Dylan checked that all the windows were locked, the radiators hadn't leaked, and the fridge didn't have anything festering in it. Then he reluctantly ran the vacuum cleaner over the wooden floors while Emily gave everything the once-over with a feather duster.

'Would you look at the pair of us?' she said, laughing as she pushed a strand of hair out of her eyes.

'We're like an old married couple,' he agreed. Then he put the vacuum away and began sorting the mail as Emily attacked the fridge with a clean cloth.

'I'll come over on Sunday morning and switch the heating on; warm the house up for them,' Dylan said.

'And I'll make up the bed in the guest room,' Emily added.

'Great idea. I hope they like it here. It's very plain, though ... very bachelor pad, isn't it?'

They both gazed around at the bare white walls, the thousands of vinyl records packed into black plastic crates, and a fly-encrusted Harley motorbike just visible through the dining-room door.

'Well, I didn't like to say anything ... but this house sure could do with a woman's touch,' Emily agreed. 'We could throw a sheet over the bike. Why is it in the house, anyway? Isn't there a garage out the back?'

'Yes, there is. But Jake said the garage door was ancient, and the bike might be stolen. The house is alarmed, you see?'

'Oh yes, so it is.'

'And he never uses the dining room, so he just keeps the bike in there. You don't mind your parents coming over, do you?' Dylan asked then, setting down a stack of junk mail and giving Emily a big hug.

'No, I expect they'll get bored within a fortnight and go home again. I mean, I'm happy they're showing some initiative at last, but I don't know if they'll fit in over here.'

'It's a pity they never found their niche in life, isn't it?' Dylan said.

'Yes, I think it would have made all the difference, if only they'd found the right jobs,' Emily said.

'True. That's why I had to get out of banking before it took over my life,' Dylan told her. 'I didn't want to become addicted to easy money.'

'You'll find another passion when Sylvia can afford to hire a sales assistant for the shop,' Emily said, looking around the sitting room again.

'Yes, I will,' he agreed.

'I wonder, would Jake mind if we washed his bike?'

'I don't see any problem. I could take the bike to the car wash, if you like? I can ride a little bit – enough to go to the car wash and back, anyway,' Dylan offered.

'That'd be great. And I'll try and do something

with this room. You see, if the coffee table was placed in the centre of the room here, with the sofa there and those two chairs at either side, the room wouldn't look quite so empty. And then I'll find a couple of vases and buy some colourful flowers to brighten the place up.'

'Go right ahead.'

'Mind how you go on the bike, now,' Emily said as Jake found the keys and wheeled the motor-bike to the front door. 'And please wear the helmet.'

'Okay, you're the boss,' he said, winking at her.

While he was gone Emily rearranged the furniture, gave the leather sofa a good rub-down, straightened the curtains and found some dusty old vases under the kitchen sink. She boiled a kettle full of water, washed the vases and polished them with a tea towel until they sparkled. Then Dylan came back with a newly pristine motor-bike, and suddenly the house took on a stylish, sophisticated look.

They bought some bright red gerberas at the supermarket, and enough groceries to fill the fridge. Emily even found a dark brown wicker basket to keep the mail in.

'There!' she said, when the finishing touches had been added to Jake's cavernous house. 'What do you think?' The leather sofa was gleaming, the crates of records had been moved into a neat line, the red flowers added a much-needed splash of colour, and the gleaming Harley gave the house an eccentric but glamorous note.

'I think it's totally amazing. Jake won't know this place when he comes back from Australia,'

Dylan said approvingly. 'You're brilliant at this.'

'I should hope so, after ten years in the business!'

'No, really. In a couple of hours you've made this house a home,' he said, nodding his approval.

'Well, thank you, kind sir,' she said, making a little curtsey.

'Oh, I like that,' Dylan laughed. 'Let's go back to your place now; I fancy having my wicked way with one of the maids.'

Laughing, they set the alarm, pulled the door behind them and dashed back to the car.

18. One-night Stand

Emily and Dylan were enjoying a Saturday night drink at the Twickenham Arms, just embracing the peace and quiet before her parents arrived on Sunday evening. The pub was deliciously warm and welcoming and softly lit with orange and yellow glass lanterns. The gold tinsel strands on a huge Christmas tree were quivering in a faint draught by the door. Emily had a joint of beef marinating in the fridge back at her flat, and Jake's house was ready with the guest room all made up and stocked with a basket of new towels.

'Maybe I should stop drinking in a bit. All the cooking tomorrow will be a nightmare if I've got a belting hangover. I want to make tomorrow a nice day for Mum and Dad; it's the first time in years that they've been so excited about anything. I really hope they enjoy living in Jake's house.'

'Relax, babe, you've thought of everything,' Dylan said, his arm draped casually around Emily's shoulders.

'Did you just call me babe?' she laughed.

'Is that okay?'

'Yes, it's really nice,' she smiled.

'I'm looking forward to the dinner tomorrow,' he said then. 'Are you doing all the trimmings too? You don't cook very often.'

'No, usually I just have soup or a sandwich. But I want to make Mum and Dad feel really welcome. I think that they think I don't want them here. I should have sounded a lot more enthusiastic on the phone that time. I mean, I was pleased they'd had an idea; I just wasn't sure we'd find them anything. Of course, now they think I don't want them around in case they cramp my style. And if I overdo the hugs and the happiness when they arrive, they'll accuse me of faking it. Families, huh... I just hope I remember how to get everything ready for the meal at the same time,' she added.

'I'm sure it'll be a feast fit for a king. Are you hungry now, by any chance?' Dylan asked her.

'I'm a bit hungry, I suppose,' she admitted.

'Shall we treat ourselves to some pub grub? I fancy a steak.'

'Oh yes, let's do that! I could murder scampi and chips.'

'Right, I'll ask for a menu on the way back from the Gents,' he said, finishing his pint and standing up.

'And I'll get another round in,' Emily said, picking up her handbag.

As Emily was waiting to be served at the bar, the pub doors opened with a shudder and a bunch of rowdy guys came staggering in, almost knocking the tree over. Some of the men grabbed handfuls of tinsel and placed it on their heads, laughing uproariously. They'd clearly been drinking already; possibly for several hours. Then she realized that she knew the men, especially one of them. His name was Glenn and he'd been Alex's best man on the day of their cancelled wedding. Mercifully Alex was not with them tonight. The others had all

236

been at school with her. They were wearing football shirts, so they must all be over in London on some sort of a soccer jolly, she thought. Glenn walked up to the bar and asked the barmaid for a menu.

'Oh shit,' Emily muttered, turning away from the men.

But it was too late. Glenn had recognized her, and he came straight over.

'Well, look who it is, lads,' he said loudly. 'It's none other than Emily Reilly from dear old Belfast town. Fancy meeting you here, Emily. What's new, pussycat?'

'Shut up, Glenn,' Emily said. 'Everyone's looking.'

'Come here, you,' Glenn laughed, giving her a crushing bear hug and kissing her messily on the cheek.

'Get off me,' she said angrily, trying to push him away.

'What's the matter, pet?' he said, hugging her again.

Emily thought she might suffocate if he didn't let her go at once.

'I said, will you get off me?' Emily told him. 'I'm here with my boyfriend.'

'Oh, Emily's got a boyfriend, lads. We'd all like to meet this boyfriend of yours,' Glenn said in a slightly sinister voice. 'Is he real? I wonder. Or is he just an imaginary boyfriend?'

The other men all guffawed loudly. Emily's tragic wedding story had obviously been spread far and wide. They must all know that Alex had left her at the altar on their wedding day. She

237

wondered frantically if Glenn had given them the final detail of that most humiliating period of her life.

'Go away and leave me alone,' Emily said in the firmest voice she could muster, slithering from his grasp, paying for her drinks and turning away from Glenn and his lecherous smile.

But Glenn wasn't going to be swept aside. He followed Emily and pinched her bottom, causing her to hunch up and drop her drinks. Glasses of cola and lager hit the floor with a watery crash, and the men started laughing all over again.

A tired waiter appeared from behind the counter with a mop and bucket.

'Keep the noise down, folks,' he said anxiously.

'I'm so sorry,' Emily told the waiter as he bent down to pick up the remnants of broken glass. 'Mind you don't cut yourself.'

'What's going on here?' someone said, and Emily knew that Dylan had come back from the bathroom.

'You must be Emily's *boyfriend*,' Glenn tittered.

'Yes, I am,' Dylan said firmly. 'What of it?'

'Let's go home, Dylan,' Emily said nervously.

'Are you not going to introduce us to your *boyfriend?*' Glenn asked. 'Are you engaged yet? Are we all invited to the wedding?'

The men laughed even harder.

'Who is this idiot?' Dylan asked. 'What's his problem?'

'Leave us alone, Glenn,' Emily said, taking Dylan's hand and leading him towards the door. 'We don't want any trouble, do you hear me?'

'Would you look at Love's Young Dream,'

Glenn said, angry now at being left standing on his own in front of everybody.

His friends were all expecting a bit of a show, and he was damned if he was going to let it end like this.

'Don't go, Emily,' he shouted. 'Stay and have a drink with your old muckers.'

'Please don't say anything to him,' Emily whispered to Dylan. 'He'll only hit you, and then it'll kick off. There are eight of them, and they all enjoy a good punch-up. Glenn always did like to stir things.'

'Okay, let's go,' Dylan nodded as Emily reached for the door handle.

'You weren't ignoring me last time we met, were you, Miss Reilly?' Glenn called after them. 'You couldn't get enough of me that night, could you?'

Dylan stopped in his tracks, and turned to face Glenn and his cohorts.

'Have you got something to say to my girl-friend?' he asked in a low voice.

'No, mate, I haven't,' Glenn said quietly.

Emily was weak with relief. She tugged again at Dylan's hand, eager to be out of the pub and safely home in her cosy, lovely flat. Giving Glenn one final look of disdain, Dylan turned to go.

'I have nothing to *say* to your girlfriend, but there's definitely something I'd like to *do* to her,' Glenn said loudly.

The laughter rang out again. By this time everyone in the bar was looking at them. The bar staff were terrified that a full-scale riot was about to erupt. A load of drunken guys in football shirts, with very strong Belfast accents – what else were they to think?

'Oh please, no,' Emily said.

'Come over here and say that again,' Dylan said, letting go of Emily's hand and fixing Glenn with a cold hard stare

Emily thought Glenn would run for cover, but instead he casually strolled over to Dylan and repeated his nasty words. Before he had finished the sentence, however, and before Emily could even blink, Dylan had reached out and landed an expert punch on Glenn's sneering face. Glenn crumpled and went down like a ton of bricks, and Dylan then asked Glenn's mates if any of them would like to have a go. There were no offers, strangely enough – Glenn's friends had decided they were all too drunk to take on a man with a rugby player's build. The bar fell silent, except for Glenn's agonized moaning. A trickle of blood appeared on Glenn's top lip.

'I think you've broken my nose,' he said accusingly.

'You asked for it,' Dylan said calmly.

'We'll get you back some other time,' Glenn said to Dylan menacingly.

'Not to worry, mate. You might have your little gang with you tonight, but I have plenty of pals too; we'll be looking forward to the rematch.'

'I'll sue you,' Glenn said.

'I'll see you in court,' Dylan said, 'though if I were you, I wouldn't bother. I haven't got any money, and you were sexually harassing my girl-friend. There's no shortage of witnesses.'

The waiter handed Glenn a towel and asked

him and his friends to leave the bar as soon as Glenn was able to walk, or else they'd have to call the police. Glenn's friends then gathered round him and helped him to his feet.

'Okay, we're done here,' Dylan said, and he took Emily's hand and led her outside.

They went home to Emily's flat as fast as they could. Dylan was so angry; he told Emily he would gladly have taken on the lot of them. But Emily didn't want him to become a mere footnote in Glenn's bloke-fest booze-up.

'He's *so* not worth it,' she told him when they got back to her flat. 'People who go around picking fights like that are just messed up in the head; I mean, properly messed up. That Glenn needs a whole team of psychiatrists to sort him out. He'd rather get his nose broken by a man than be civil to a girl. He's crazy.'

'Scumbag! I hurt my hand hitting him,' Dylan said, flexing his fingers.

'I'll put some ice on it,' said Emily.

She quickly wrapped some ice cubes in a tea towel and handed it to Dylan.

'Cheers, babe.'

'What bad luck to bump into him,' Emily said, still furious. 'He ruined our lovely evening.'

She couldn't sit down, and had resorted to pacing up and down the sitting room.

'What's the story with him, anyway?' Dylan asked after a couple of minutes.

'You could say he was an ex of mine,' Emily admitted. 'A sort of ex, you might say.'

'Well, it must have been beer goggles, then. Tell

me, did he hit you?'

'No, Glenn was always getting into brawls. But as far as I know he doesn't beat women,' Emily said quietly. 'I ran into him a while after the wedding fiasco. I was at a hen party at this hotel in Dublin, and he was there too on a stag weekend. And to my eternal shame, well, we had a one-night stand.'

'Is that all?'

'I'm so embarrassed.'

'Don't be, we've all been there, done that,' Dylan said ruefully.

'Still, I should have known better,' Emily said heavily. She felt incredibly embarrassed. 'Even though I was tired and emotional, I should have known better.'

'He seemed like a right lowlife,' Dylan said, mystified.

'I know. He is. He always was.'

'So what happened? Were you on drugs when you kissed that particular frog?' Dylan joked.

'No, I was feeling sorry for myself and incredibly drunk. And he was just very nice to me,' she said simply. 'We got talking in a quiet corner of the hotel bar, and he was all sympathetic about the wedding being cancelled. He said Alex was a right fool and that one day he'd bitterly regret not marrying me. Looking back, I think he faked the sympathy to get me into bed. And it worked. I got a bit emotional and started crying my eyes out, we went up to his room and, well, basically we had a five-minute fumble on top of the bed. And then we fell asleep. We were both plastered. We didn't even take our clothes off. It was awful,

242

really – it was a pointless encounter from start to finish. I've never gone in for one-night stands, I swear to you, and that night reminded me why.'

'Listen, Emily, I told you – I'm not judging you, babe.'

'Okay, okay, I'm sorry, I know you aren't.'

'So that was the end of it?'

'Not really. The next morning he was all keen to do it again, now that he was sober and everything. The room had a walk-in shower, and he thought it'd be fun to, you know, get frisky in there.'

'And you didn't fancy it?'

'No, I did *not* fancy it. I felt completely disgusted with myself. I just wanted to go home and forget I'd ever spoken to him. He's so immature, he turns my stomach. I told him I never wanted to see him or speak to him ever again – and he wasn't very pleased, I can tell you.'

'He didn't try it on with you, did he?' Dylan said, his face lined with worry.

'Thank heaven, no, he didn't,' Emily said, shaking her head. 'I said I wasn't the type of girl who slept around, and he called me a tease and a bitch. Said it was a bit late to be saying that. I grabbed my shoes and left the room, and I got the hell out of that hotel as fast as I could.'

'Sounds like he could have turned nasty.'

'Yes, I know ... and I hoped I'd never lay eyes on him again. To tell you the truth, he's an awful bully; he always was. I really have no idea why I went anywhere near him that night. I should have known he was only faking the sympathy to take advantage of me. I should have known he'd tell his stupid mates about it. No doubt he told them

I was a right tart.'

'I'm sure all his mates know he's the kind to exaggerate.'

'I hope so. Why do some men think that just because you spent five minutes with them once, when you were at your very lowest ebb, you'll now be available to them for all eternity?'

'Search me. All I know is, that creep better not come near you again,' Dylan said.

'I hope he doesn't press charges,' Emily said.

'No, he won't do that, I could tell. He won't go to the police, because he knows you could have him charged with sexual harassment. That bar was full of witnesses – and, thanks to his big mouth, they heard every word pretty clearly.'

'Remind me not to drink in the Twickenham Arms for a very long time. Hopefully that's the end of it now,' Emily said. Then she got up and went towards the bedroom. 'I still have the outfit I was wearing that night,' she called out to Dylan.

She unlocked the wardrobe and took out a short black dress and matching jacket, a pair of five-inch black stilettos and a tiny black handbag. She brought her things back to the sitting room to show him.

'I don't want to keep these around any more,' she said.

'That's understandable, but I don't think we should sell them in the shop in case they bring bad luck to their new owner,' Dylan said. 'I'm not superstitious – but then again, you never know.'

'Agreed. I'll just bin them now,' Emily said, and she folded the outfit neatly and placed it in her kitchen bin. 'Do you know that the wardrobe is almost empty now?'

'You've done a lot of de-cluttering these last few months,' he said, putting his arm around her.

'I have, haven't I?' she agreed. 'All I have left in there are a few power suits and some pairs of court shoes that I thought would be just the ticket for the magazine industry. Before I found out that most of the photographers and stylists wear casual clothes. They nearly died laughing the first day I turned up for work. How naive was I, Dylan? I've done nothing but make mistakes my whole life.'

'You haven't made mistakes your whole life.'

'Trust me, I have.'

'Only until you met me?' he said, kissing her tenderly.

'Until I met you,' she said, kissing him back.

19. Christmas in Appleton

'Oh, Dylan, I hope they like me,' Emily said, checking her make-up in the passenger-seat mirror.

'My family is really nice, Emily. They just want to meet you; they won't bite you or anything. And we really can't put this off any longer. Mum has been begging me to bring you to meet them all for months and months now. If we didn't agree to this dinner, they'd have come to London in a minibus looking for you.'

'I know,' Emily said, patting her fringe – even though it didn't need patting.

'You've nothing to worry about, babe. They'll love you just as much as I do,' he said tenderly.

'Yes,' she smiled. But she wasn't fully convinced.

Emily almost wished they could get a flat tyre, or that the motorway would suddenly be closed for repairs, or that there'd be a genuine emergency back in London and they'd have to do a U-turn. She glanced into her handbag at her mobile phone, but it stayed resolutely silent.

'It's a pity your parents couldn't come with us,' Dylan said.

'Yes, isn't it?' Emily agreed. 'But they'd already bought the cinema tickets.'

And then she felt a wave of guilt, for she'd warned her parents that she'd kill them both in cold blood if they accepted Dylan's offer to bring them to Appleton to meet his family. And the guilt was doubled when Emily remembered that her father was still due a visit to see Sylvia's stables, which were en route to the village. But Emily knew in her heart that she'd have enough to worry about without her parents disgracing her at the dinner table. She'd have her hands full just trying to put on some semblance of being a normal, happy human being Mind you, they'd been behaving quite normally recently. Maybe she should have brought them along for the company? But then again, it was nice to have Dylan to herself for the drive to Appleton.

'Why are you jittery about today, anyway?' Dylan asked.

'I have no idea.'

'It'll be fine.'

'Maybe I was born this way?' Emily said. 'Maybe my parents were born anxious, and I inherited a double set of anxiety genes? I don't know.'

'Look, I promise you that five minutes after you've met them, you'll wonder what all the fuss was about.'

'I do hope so.'

'I think it'll be fun to celebrate Christmas early, don't you think?'

'Yes, yes,' Emily muttered. 'I hope they like the gifts I got them. That chocolate shop was half empty by the time I got through the list.'

She stared out at the green fields flying past her window. Some of the distant hills were topped with snow. Dylan's mum and dad were going away skiing for Christmas, and his three sisters were spending the day with their in-laws. So Mrs

Shawcross had come up with the great idea of having a big turkey dinner on the 17th of December.

Emily had bought gifts for everyone, and she was wearing her best jeans and one of Arabella's designer jackets. But all she wanted to do was open the car door, roll out on to the hard shoulder and walk all the way back to her flat in the city. She wouldn't mind the lofty ceilings and the freezing sitting room tonight, she thought to herself, if she could only curl up in bed with a good book.

'I do love you even more than I did already for doing this,' Dylan said, caressing her knee.

'You're welcome,' she said, giving his hand a little squeeze and then placing it gently back on the steering wheel.

'Nicely done,' he said, laughing. 'But I can hold the wheel with one hand, you know. I've been driving round the farm since I was fourteen.'

'Have you really?'

'Yeah, I can drive a tractor too. I can do hand signals and everything!'

'I sometimes wonder what it'd be like to be a more confident person,' Emily mused.

'What do you mean?'

'Well, like you are. I'd love to be like you – you know, the way you just do things without a lot of over-analysing. You just decide to do something, and then you do it. And I bet if it didn't work out, you'd just laugh it off and forget about it.'

'Well, sure I would. You only live once; why bother with regrets?'

'Some of us must be hardwired to hang on to our regrets. I wish I could be like you for just one day, Dylan.'

'You're not that bad.'

'I am, though, I am that bad. Sometimes I annoy myself, because I get so annoyed about silly things – and certain people. I wish I could just sail through life oblivious to all irritations. And that's why I love my job – because it's got nothing to do with people.'

'You interview people all the time,' Dylan pointed out.

'Not really; I ask them a few set questions, and then I compliment their home and take a sip of tea. And they're usually so exhausted from staging their houses, they've barely got the energy to talk to me or look at me. On a good day I'm out of the place in less than an hour. I spend more time choosing pictures for the magazine than I do actually talking to anyone.'

'But you're a lovely person, Emily. It's only you who thinks you're not good with people. Arabella thinks the world of you, and so do I. The only person who doesn't like you is Jane Maxwell. And that's only because you're so nice and friendly, you make her feel like a sour old bossyboots by comparison. Which she is, of course...'

'Well, thanks for that very lovely vote of confidence. I'll do my best to chat to everybody. Have you got a dog at the farm?'

'Yes, we have five dogs,' he told her.

'Oh good, I like dogs! Maybe we could take them for a walk?'

'Well, they might not want to let you out of the door... You know, I must say, your parents seem to be totally loving their stay in Jake's house,' Dylan said then, eager to distract Emily from her

249

pre-meeting nerves.

'Aren't they just? I've never seen them so ani-
mated. They're guarding that house as if their
lives depended on it,' she agreed. 'They're obsessed with the burglar alarm, did you notice that? I
think Dad holds his breath until he's pressed in
the code. And Mum even bought fresh gerberas
out of her own money when the first lot died. She
thinks they're a mandatory part of the decorating
scheme.'

'And the entire house is immaculate. I thought
you said your mum never did any housework?'

'Oh, she never did. But she says that was because
her own house was a hovel, and she had no heart
in it. Now that she's living in a mansion, it's a
different story altogether.'

'It was very nice of Jake to send them a bit of
money for Christmas, wasn't it? Maybe we can
find them another gig when Jake comes home,'
Dylan suggested.

'Yes, maybe. I think my mother is praying every
night that Jake will go to India next, for a year...'

'You know what? He just might do that. He says
he can run the company from his laptop.'

They chatted on about Emily's parents and their
Great London Adventure, and the rise and rise of
Sylvia's shop, until they reached the turn-off for
Appleton. The motorway was suddenly replaced
by an old narrow road with high hawthorn hedges
on either side. Then the flat, ploughed fields gave
way to lumpy, grassy fields full of sombre-looking
dairy cattle. In no time they were pulling up outside a stone-clad double-fronted farmhouse with a
massive conservatory at the side. Dylan's parents,

250

his sisters and their husbands and children were all inside, setting the table for dinner, patting the dogs and generally being very normal and family-like. They waved excitedly when they saw Dylan's car arriving.

'Well, they have been busy. They've hosed down the yard specially,' Dylan told her proudly. 'And would you look at the size of that Christmas tree in the conservatory? Usually they have a small one in the porch, but that beauty must be ten foot tall.'

'They've gone to so much trouble,' Emily whispered.

'Come on, now,' Dylan said encouragingly. 'My mum is probably more nervous than you are.'

'Why would she be?'

'Because you're a big fancy stylist from London, and she's a humble farmer's wife from the country, that's why. I bet she has big bunches of flowers in every room to distract from the saggy cushions and Dad's dusty old collection of pewter tankards.'

'Okay, let's do it,' she said as he jumped out of the car and raced round to open the passenger door.

'They'll love you,' he said again.

Then everyone was coming out of the conservatory door and hugging Emily, saying how gorgeous she was. The dogs were licking her hands, and the snow was making everything seem prettier and even more significant and sentimental than it might have been. And Emily knew it was going to be all right. They bundled her inside as she tried not to feel too guilty that she'd denied her poor parents this lovely day out. But then Mrs Shawcross was asking her a thousand questions about her work, and Mr Shawcross was taking photos. Sylvia was pouring her a glass of wine, and Dylan's other two sisters were admiring her very stylish 1950s-style fringe. And they were all asking her what she saw in Dylan, and exclaiming that he must have cast a spell on her. Which was a joke, of course, since Dylan was the most gorgeous man Emily had ever seen. But it was very funny to pretend that Dylan had had to enchant Emily to get her to go out with him. Emily noted that Mr Shawcross was simply an older version of Dylan, and she could see why his wife still adored him after more than three decades of marriage.

Within ten minutes they were all seated around the table, tucking into the most enormous plate of Christmas dinner.

'Me and you'll go to the pub for a quick pint later, Dylan,' Mr Shawcross said after dessert had been served. 'Let the women here have a good old gossip.'

Emily held her breath. Was she ready to be left alone with the girls?

'Sorry, Dad, not this time,' Dylan said cheerfully. 'I promised Emily we'd go for a walk round the village, just the two of us. Maybe a couple of the dogs can come with us? I want to show her where I grew up – my old school and everything. Is that okay?'

'Of course it is, lad,' Mr Shawcross said at once.

He smiled at them both, and then winked at his wife. They both knew this was no casual romance.

'I think I can hear wedding bells ringing,' Sylvia teased.

'I think you can hear bells ringing inside your head most days,' Dylan replied dryly.

'Uncle Dylan is madly in love with Emily. Mummy said so,' said one of Sylvia's young daughters.

'Shush, you little rascal,' Sylvia scolded.

'You started it, Sylvia,' her father reminded her.

'So I did,' she admitted.

'And Mummy said Uncle Dylan was definitely going to marry Emily,' the little girl said excitedly. 'Are you going to marry Emily, Uncle Dylan? If you *are* going to marry her then I want to be a bridesmaid. And I want to wear the pink dress with red roses on it. It's in the window of the Cath Kiddy shop in the village. So it won't be hard to get me ready for the wedding.'

There was a moment of dead silence, and then the room erupted into raucous laughter. Even the dogs knew there was something exciting going on, and they leapt out of their baskets and did a few laps of the dining table.

'Well, let me see,' Dylan said eventually, rubbing his chin like a character from Dickens. 'I was hoping to marry you one day, Molly. But if you'd rather be a bridesmaid then I suppose I shall just have to settle for second best and marry Emily instead.'

'Yes, I think you should,' Molly said gravely. 'You're getting very old now, and I really want to wear that lovely dress. If we wait for me to grow up, you'll be *far* too old.'

'Okay, then. It's settled,' Dylan said.

'Go on, then. Ask her,' Molly urged, wanting everything settled immediately.

All eyes were on her; Emily thought she was going to faint.

'I'll ask her later,' Dylan said gently, 'when nobody's watching.'

Emily's face was as red as a beetroot. She tried to take a sip of wine but knocked her glass over with a loud clatter instead.

'Oops,' she said, dabbing at the wine with a linen napkin. 'Oh no! Have I ruined this lovely napkin now too?' she added.

'Shall we go for that walk?' Dylan said, getting up from the table.

He thought Emily deserved a break now.

'Oh yes, what a good idea. I'll fall asleep if I don't get some air, I've eaten that much. Thanks for a delicious dinner, Mrs Shawcross,' Emily said graciously.

She stood up and nodded a temporary goodbye to everyone at the table.

'We won't be long,' Dylan told his mother.

'That's all right,' Mrs Shawcross said. 'Take as long as you like, and we'll crack on with the washing-up.'

'We're still giving out the presents after supper, aren't we?' Molly said.

Everyone laughed again.

'I want to get my presents first, because I have to go to bed at nine o'clock,' Molly added.

'This one is a born manager,' Sylvia said proudly. 'We'll not go far wrong with Molly in charge.'

Outside it was still snowing but, by the looks of it, it wouldn't lie. Dylan and Emily put on their coats and ventured out into the icy afternoon with the two oldest dogs. The Christmas-tree lights cast beautiful shadows across the newly cleaned yard.

'So what do you think?' Dylan asked Emily, giving her a tender kiss by the garden gate.

'I love them all.'

'I knew you would. So will we stay the night? I don't think anybody noticed that I didn't touch my wine. So I can still drive, if you feel a need to escape.'

'I think I can manage one night in the country, okay,' she smiled.

'Great! We're staying in my old room. You would have had the guest room all to yourself, but with everybody staying over tonight it wasn't possible.'

'I'd rather stay with you,' she said.

'Right, let's crack on; I've loads of things to show you before it gets dark,' Dylan began, taking Emily's hand and setting off down the lane at a brisk pace.

The dogs were delighted with the extra walk, and they skittered along obediently behind their favourite member of the family. Already the moon was visible in the sky. Emily thought she had made a reasonable impression on the Shawcross clan. She began to relax and even enjoy herself.

Sometimes it was annoying having so many feelings, she thought to herself. Because when the feelings were negative, they were very draining. But when they were good, they were very good indeed.

She wanted to ask Dylan if he'd been joking about the marriage proposal, but then she decided that particular topic could wait for another day.

20. Arabella's Party

It was the 20th of December, and Arabella was throwing the Christmas party to end all Christmas parties at her Chelsea town house. She'd invited all her friends and everyone she had ever met in the magazine publishing industry, even Jane Maxwell. She'd also invited all the neighbours on her street and half the staff at Liberty, Selfridges and Harrods. Luckily many of her biggest pieces of furniture had been sold off, and most of the floors were tiled, so she wouldn't have to worry too much about spilt drinks and dropped cigarettes. To make the house appear less empty, Arabella had placed a fresh Christmas tree in each of the main reception rooms and decorated the branches with pink ribbons, threaded through cinnamon cookies, and iced gingerbread men wrapped in cellophane. Each tree bore a handwritten note, encouraging people to help themselves to the goodies attached. The guests were due to arrive in about an hour.

Arabella was looking fabulous in a silk jacket with a massive diamanté brooch pinned to the collar, and a zany print skirt from Get Cutie. Emily thought she looked about ten years younger in the silk jacket than she ever had in her fur coat.

'I'm moving out next week. I got the date yesterday,' Arabella told Emily as they loaded up the dining-room table with a staggering amount of savouries, pastries and pretty cupcakes – all home-made by Arabella herself, to save money. She was living on a budget now, so hiring expensive caterers and florists was a thing of the past.

'How do you feel about that?' Emily asked carefully.

'Not quite as bad as I thought I would,' Arabella said, rearranging the plates so her gorgeous cupcakes could take centre stage. The delicious scent of the buttercream frosting was calling to her. But she'd eaten three already that morning, so she didn't dare have another one. The zip might burst on her skirt if she kept on nibbling.

'Oh good,' Emily said gently. 'I'm so pleased.'

'You should be. It's all down to you that I didn't take an overdose when the solicitor told me I would have to sell my beloved house and settle out of court – or stand my ground and face a possible prison sentence. You talked me round to the idea of letting go of this house; you made it seem almost fun to be poor.'

'Firstly, I hope you're joking about the overdose?'

'Relax, Emily; I only considered it for about five minutes.'

'And secondly, when did I ever say it was fun to be poor? Not that I am actually poor as such.'

'Oh, you know what I mean. All your tales of walking hand-in-hand in the snow with Dylan, and watching DVDs on the sofa for hours, and eating fish and chips on the promenade that day the two of you went to Brighton. You know ... the simple things I'd forgotten about after being married to David for so long.'

'Well, okay, when you put it like that, I suppose I do sound a bit thrifty,' Emily grimaced.

'I didn't mean to insult you, my darling,' Arabella said, lighting a cigarette and wafting the smoke away from the food. 'Yes, I know that you're paying off that loan you took out to rescue your father. And yes, I know Dylan isn't being paid for his work in the shop. Let's go into the kitchen and have a glass of champers in peace before the stampede begins. At least, I hope there'll be a stampede.'

'There will be huge crowds here, don't you worry.'

'I'm not coming back to work after Christmas, if nobody from the magazine turns up at the party,' Arabella declared, leading the way to the kitchen and taking a bottle from the fridge. 'I mean, ever since they found out what I did to David's house, they might all be afraid of me. Damn that reporter for spilling the beans.'

'*Everyone* at work is coming; they've been talking about it all week. And nobody blames you for starting the fire, I promise. I think they were all rather impressed, as it happens. I mean, it was fine once they knew that you'd checked the house was empty first. I hear Jane might even bring her new boyfriend along,' Emily said, accepting a tall flute of bubbly.

'Who is he, do you know yet?' Arabella asked, checking her lipstick in her compact.

'No, we still don't know his name, but she's been a bit weird lately,' Emily said.

'She's always been a bit weird. That hair of hers; it's far too long. And she wears far too much

258

make-up. Too much lippy – and, coming from me, that's saying something,' Arabella said, puffing away nervously.

'Well, she is still in her twenties, Arabella. That's the look for women of that age, don't you know? Now … don't quote me on this, but I think our Jane's going out with some sort of a celebrity,' Emily said conspiratorially.

'No way! What makes you say that?'

'Well, Jane said something to me the other day in the kitchenette. She said she wouldn't be larking about with stupid coffee tables and candlesticks for much longer. And she was caressing her precious silver bracelet when she said it. You remember that bracelet I told you about? She's always playing with it at meetings. Oh, this champagne is so delicious. It's the one thing about this winter that I don't mind being stone cold.'

'Thanks, it'll be my last great extravagance. After this I'll be shopping at Asda and Primark, for I'll have a mortgage to pay.'

'I'm so sorry,' Emily soothed.

'Don't be. I'm looking forward to it, Emily. That little house I managed to buy – it's heavenly. I mean, it's all dark and poky at the minute, but I'm going to do it up in white with distressed mirrors everywhere, and ornamental birdcages hanging from the rafters.'

'I can't wait to see it when it's finished,' Emily said approvingly. 'We'll photograph it for the magazine maybe?'

'Um, let's not. The readers might start asking what happened to my old house,' Arabella said meaningfully.

'Oh yes, you're right. Let's not bother.'

'It was only thanks to yet another political scandal that I was dropped from the front pages last Sunday. Imagine trying to claim back the cost of seventeen massages!'

'Yes, here's a toast to our hardworking MPs. Bless them,' Emily said.

'Cheers.'

'Cheers. Between the shopping, the travelling, the bunk-ups and the massages, it's a wonder they get any work done at all.'

'Here's to the Mother of Parliaments!' Arabella declared, making a wobbly salute while trying not to drop cigarette ash into her drink.

The two friends laughed heartily.

'Seriously, thank heaven for those pompous old twats in Westminster for keeping the hacks busy. I can see the headline now, if it'd been me,' wheezed Arabella. *Loony Wife Burns Down Ex-husband's Love Nest Before Downsizing To A Labourer's Cottage.*'

'No, that's far too long. It'd be something like *Interiors Queen Torches Mansion.*'

'Quite,' Arabella rolled her eyes.

Then she laughed again and reminded herself that she was supposed to be throwing a party tonight.

Just then the doorbell rang.

'Half an hour early, who on earth can that be?' Arabella said in an excited voice as Emily went to answer the door. 'Nobody arrives at parties early. At least, nobody I know does. How very common...'

Emily opened the door to find the entire staff

from *Stylish Living* standing on the steps – all thirty-five of them, except Jane Maxwell.

'We know we're early, but we just couldn't wait any longer,' Petra explained. 'We've already been in the pub for an hour and a half. None of us have ever been to Arabella's house before, and the curiosity is simply *killing* us.'

'Come on in,' Emily laughed. 'Come on in, and you're very welcome.'

Meanwhile, Arabella had switched on the stereo and was frantically lighting a dozen pink candles on the buffet table. Everyone trooped in and waited in the hall to be told what to do next.

'Give me your coats, and go in there,' Emily said, pointing to the candlelit dining room. 'I'll be through in a minute with drinks.'

Arabella was standing at the fireplace with one elbow resting awkwardly on the mantle when she finally came face-to-face with her colleagues. She looked so nervous at seeing them again, Emily felt sorry for her.

'Arabella, thanks for inviting us to your lovely home. We've missed you so much,' Petra announced, handing Arabella a small silver box. 'We all chipped in to buy you this. It's a cocktail ring, and it reminded us of you – larger than life, and twice as much fun. Merry Christmas, *darling* Arabella!'

Arabella laughed out loud with relief and began to hug everybody. Emily could almost see the anxiety melting away from her face. Arabella's staff still respected her, and that was all that mattered now.

The doorbell rang again, and another couple of

dozen of guests from the industry filed in. Then the neighbours turned up, all bearing gifts of wine and chocolates. Arabella was worn out with kissing and hugging everyone and telling them all how happy she was to see them at her party. They were soon crowded around the buffet, sipping champagne and delicately nibbling the fabulous cupcakes, when Jane and her mystery boyfriend pulled up outside the house in a yellow Ferrari. The distinctive purr of the engine was easily heard above the music on the stereo. Some people ran to the windows to look out. Jane and her new man were kissing passionately in the front of the car.

'Isn't that the American producer guy...?' Arabella began. 'Douglas Doberman.'

'Doug Liebermann,' Emily corrected.

'Do you know, I think it is him,' Petra gasped. 'He's fifty-three.'

'But it can't be,' someone said. 'He's engaged to that awful bimbo.'

'Yes, and they only got engaged a short while ago,' Petra muttered. 'Not that our Jane would care very much either way.'

'It *is* him,' Arabella said triumphantly as Jane's mystery man came up for air.

'He's Daisy Churchill's fiancé,' Emily said needlessly.

'Make that Daisy Churchill's *ex*-fiancé,' Arabella laughed.

'Oh Jane, what have you done?' Emily said.

'Daisy'll gut the two of them like fish,' Arabella trilled, running out of the room and down the hall to greet them.

'Isn't he meant to be worth about a hundred million dollars?' Petra said begrudgingly.

'Yes, he owns lots of big TV shows in America,' Emily told her.

'Well, this should be interesting,' Petra said, refilling her glass and putting a grilled prawn in her mouth. 'Talk about a gold-digger.'

'Petra, I'm sure it's a genuine love match,' Emily said, rolling her eyes as they all turned to face the door.

Arabella's lovely party quickly turned into a Doug Liebermann autograph hunt. Though not an actor himself, he had every actor in LA on speed dial. He owned a disgustingly large mansion in the hills with an infinity pool and three guest cottages. And to top it all, he was six foot four with a blond mullet and shoulders like the Incredible Hulk.

Emily and Arabella sat on a window seat, nursing two glasses of champagne but forgetting entirely to drink them. They watched Jane with fascination as she hung off Doug's arm like a handbag, her casual office clothes now replaced with the tightest, shortest dress imaginable. Her hair had been bleached to a platinum waterfall, and her lips looked a bit fuller than they'd been the previous week.

'Do you think he's good-looking?' Arabella asked.

'He's not my cup of tea. But he's not bad, I suppose,' Emily said quietly.

'I reckon I'll soon be reading Jane's resignation letter,' Arabella whispered.

'If it lasts beyond the weekend,' Emily said.

'I wonder how she ever hooked up with him?' Arabella asked idly.

'They must have met at Daisy's house when she was staging the shoot,' Emily offered. 'She did a shoot there, but we didn't use it in the end.'

'Oh yes, of course; that must be it. Jane's a bit younger than Daisy, isn't she?' Arabella mused.

'Yes, and she looks it. Poor Daisy; all that plastic surgery and tanning must be very hard on the skin in the long term.'

'Not to mention very hard on the wallet,' Arabella added, newly conscious of monetary matters. 'Are you jealous?'

'What of?' Emily asked.

'Of the lifestyle Jane will soon be enjoying in LA? I am!'

'No way; I love London and I love my job. I couldn't bear to live from day to day, just hoping to get another few months out of it before my rich boyfriend trades me in for a better model,' Emily said. 'Oh, I'm so sorry. I didn't mean that the way it sounded,' she added, thinking of Arabella's ex-husband and his new family.

'You're all right, darling; I know exactly what you meant, and you're quite right. I'll never get married again, not as long as I live. I'll never invest so much time and energy in a man again. Never!'

'But you might meet a truly nice man some day,' Emily said.

'There's no such thing as a truly nice man,' Arabella said darkly.

'Yes, there is,' Emily countered.

'No, some clever men *pretend* to be nice. But

264

they're still only being manipulative.'

'That's a very cynical thing to say,' Emily said.

'It's true, my darling.'

'Dylan is lovely. He's taking my parents out to a show tonight; he bought the tickets especially so they'd be fully occupied tonight. So I wouldn't be worrying about them turning up here and doing their *Father Ted* routine.'

'You really do focus too much on your poor, dear parents,' Arabella said affectionately. 'Secretly you're a bit of a snob, aren't you? Well, don't worry. I'm sure they'll go home to Belfast soon.'

'I am not a snob! How dare you! I didn't want them to come tonight, because they'd be out of their depth – that's all. And people might laugh at them and hurt their feelings. If you must know, I'm getting used to them living in London. They're so happy here. I'm not used to seeing them this happy.'

'Well, that's lovely. Will you help me to heat up some more savouries, sweetheart? The food is disappearing like nobody's business.'

'Sure.'

Arabella and Emily made their way through the chattering crowds towards the kitchen and were very surprised to find Petra, sitting on a chair by the back door, crying her eyes out.

'What's the matter, my love?' Arabella said, rushing across to hug her.

'It's Jane – she just told me she's engaged to Doug,' Petra sobbed. 'Can you believe it? They've only been dating for about five minutes, but he's told her she's *the one*.'

'She must be having you on; I didn't see a ring,'

Arabella said.

'They haven't announced it yet,' Petra told her.

'I wonder why not?' Emily asked. 'I mean, Jane would just love to be in all the gossip magazines, wouldn't she?'

'Doug's lawyers told him they need time to check whether Daisy can sue him for pain and distress,' Petra explained, dabbing her tears away with a pink napkin. 'Apparently, Doug promised Daisy he would give her a starring role in one of his soaps. But now he wants nothing more to do with her. He says she has a temper on her like a volcano. She threw half his clothes in the pool last week, because he kissed Uma Thurman on the cheek at an awards do. But never mind all that! He's with Jane now, and Doug's so rich that Jane'll never have to work again. And here's me twice-divorced – with negative equity, a rubbish car and a set of clothes from the Ark.'

'And your dignity, my darling; don't forget you've still got your dignity. I'm *so* glad I'm single, I can tell you,' Arabella said. 'They all do the dirty on you in the end, the faithless brutes.'

Emily thought of Dylan and said nothing. After all, it was Arabella's party – and she didn't want to argue with her.

'I'll do the savouries, shall I?' she offered.

'Would you? I'd be so grateful,' Arabella said, handing a cigarette to Petra and taking one herself. 'Cheer up, old thing,' she said to Petra, flicking her cigarette lighter open. 'There's not a single man on this earth worth ruining your mascara for. And it doesn't matter how much money you've got when you're lying awake at

night, wondering what the hell they're doing –
and who they're doing it with.'

'I suppose so,' Petra said.

'That's my girl,' Arabella soothed.

'I despise men,' Petra said.

'Me too,' Arabella replied.

'They're all perverts,' Petra declared.

'Absolutely,' Arabella nodded.

Emily said nothing.

She set two trays of mini-quiches in the oven,
refilled the chips-and-dip tray, then went back to
join the party.

21. Election Special

It was the 22nd of December. Emily and Arabella stood outside the imposing apartment door and tried not to giggle; they were so excited they could hardly speak. Arabella was practically hopping from one foot to the other with delight. She was wearing enough make-up to open a cosmetics company. Emily had pinned a silk hydrangea to the lapel of her denim jacket.

'I cannot believe we are doing this,' Emily whispered.

'I know. Me neither,' Arabella whispered back.

'Why are we whispering?' Emily whispered again.

'I don't know,' Arabella mimed.

The two women clutched each other in silent mirth.

'What a posh wreath,' Emily said, sniffing the cinnamon bunches on the lavish wreath attached to the door knocker.

'I know,' Arabella agreed.

'You ring the bell,' Emily said quietly.

'No, you do it. I'm too nervous,' Arabella replied.

They both looked at the bronze buzzer with its barley-twist detail and started giggling all over again.

'I don't think I can bring myself to touch Jeremy's buzzer,' Emily said eventually.

'Oh, listen. No double entendres today, please – or I'll die laughing,' Arabella squeaked.

'I think I need the loo,' Emily said anxiously.

'Why don't you ask Jeremy if you can use his?' Arabella said. 'I hear it's made of solid gold!'

'I reckon it's only gold-plated. Would you pull yourself together, and stop making me laugh? I knew it was a mistake to let you come with me today,' Emily hissed.

'Are you kidding me? I wouldn't miss this tack-fest for the world,' Arabella said, rubbing her hands together with anticipation.

'Well, listen. We've got to keep up some pretence of good manners,' Emily warned her friend solemnly, 'even if we never use the pictures, right?'

'Right,' Arabella agreed.

'This will probably be a massive waste of time,' Emily said crossly.

She was feeling giddy, cross, irritable, nervous, excited and terrified all at the same time. This was their highest-ever reader profile.

'No, it won't,' Arabella told her. 'We'll get a jolly good laugh out of it, and we'll have something to talk about for the next five years. This man could be Prime Minister some day. And we'll be able to say we were in his bedroom. Go on, push the button.'

Emily pushed it with a shaking finger.

'Emily just touched Jeremy's buzzer,' Arabella said softly. 'How did it feel, Emily?'

'Shut up! I mean it – we've got to behave professionally.'

'I should never have let you be editor that time,' Arabella said sadly. 'The power has gone to your

269

head completely.'

The door swung open. Both women stood up straight like soldiers on parade.

'Good morning,' said a handsome young man with three shades of blond highlights in his gelled-up hair. He was wearing an expensive lemon sweater, impeccable grey slacks and neat grey sneakers. His tan was glowing and golden, and his teeth were gleaming white. His eyebrows had definitely been shaped in a beauty salon.

'I see you've met my partner, Julian,' said a fiendishly sexy voice from behind them.

Emily and Arabella wheeled round to find Jeremy Cavendish MP standing in the corridor, holding a paper bag full of pastries from the most upmarket deli in London.

'Jeremy, how absolutely lovely to meet you at long last,' Arabella trilled.

'Thank you so much for the invitation,' Emily added.

Jeremy shook both their hands, and there was a bit of air kissing and bowing and hugging.

'We've all heard what a keen decorator you are...' Arabella said brightly.

'And we're so flattered you'd like to be in *Stylish Living*,' Emily finished.

'What an enchanting double act you are,' Jeremy smiled.

'I've made coffee,' Julian told them, beckoning both women into the hall.

'Shut this door and keep the heat in,' Jeremy added, coming in and closing the heavy front door behind them.

'I hope our humble home meets with your

approval,' Jeremy said, hanging up his scarf and coat in a cupboard with its door painted to match the hall walls.

Arabella and Emily couldn't help craning their necks to see into the cupboard; it was all neatly laid out with Perspex shoe racks and a brass rail for the coats. No clutter to be seen, there was even a small painting of a pair of shoes on the wall, with a picture light above it.

'I'm speechless,' Arabella said, and for once it was true.

The apartment was beyond amazing – soft grey walls, solid wooden floor laid out in a parquet pattern, two old-gold chandeliers and an Impressionist-style artwork hanging above the console table. Two high-backed antique chairs stood sentinel on either side of the table, and there was a massive stone angel that must have come from a Victorian cemetery standing by the stairs. One entire wall was lined with custom-made bookcases; all the books seemed to be about art and sculpture. And that was just the entrance hall.

Arabella and Emily glanced at each other; this was not what they had been expecting. Rumours had been circulating around London for years that Jeremy Cavendish lived in a glorified gay disco full of pink scatter cushions, cheap silk flowers and modern art prints. But this apartment was so perfect, it was on a par with Coco Chanel's boudoir.

'Mr Cavendish – I mean, Jeremy – this is breathtaking,' Emily said at last. 'You have got to tell us the name of your decorator.'

'Yes, please do,' Arabella added.

'You're looking right at him,' Jeremy said, nodding at Julian.

'I don't believe it. This delightful young man can't be more than twenty-five,' Arabella purred. 'He can't possibly be responsible for such perfection.'

'That's right, he is; he's just out of college,' Jeremy said affectionately. 'An MA in Fine Art, but he makes a living doing interiors. He did all this, from top to bottom. And that's one of his paintings there above the table. He's the love of my life, ladies. We're having a civil partnership next year.'

Arabella almost passed out. Could the UK really be in line to have a married *gay* PM some day? And married to an artist, no less; it was all so gloriously perfect!

Nobody mentioned the fact that Jeremy Cavendish was fifty-two. He was a good-looking man, and it was known that he went jogging every day to keep fit. And age-gap love affairs were all the rage nowadays, obviously, Arabella thought bitterly. David was twelve years older than Mary, after all. And look at Jane and Doug – a twenty-five-year gap between them. Still, all that stuff was behind her now; she was a single woman and the editor in chief of a prestigious magazine. And she was just about to get the scoop of her career.

'Did somebody say coffee?' Arabella asked politely.

'Follow me,' Julian said, striding down the beautiful hallway towards the kitchen.

'I really can't take it all in,' Arabella said as Emily got out her camera and began lining up shots.

The kitchen was composed of six freestanding, distressed dressers. Each one was loaded with all-glass dishes, jars of wooden spoons and rustic bottles of olive oil. The table appeared to consist of two more cemetery angels with a glass top laid above them.

'I'll get a plate for the buns,' Jeremy said, 'and you two ladies, please be seated.'

'I love that shade of green; so evocative,' Emily said, indicating the olive-coloured walls.

'I'm *so* over white,' Julian said modestly.

'Me too,' Arabella replied, making a mental note to have her own home repainted as soon as possible.

Greys and greens were the new whites, or so it seemed.

'Where did you get the statuary?' Emily asked, flicking out her notebook. She was afraid to reach for a pastry. The tall, chocolate-covered confections looked as if they cost ten pounds each.

'The statue came from a reclamation yard in Austria. Help yourselves to the buns, please,' Julian said, setting out green glass plates and cups.

'I think I've died and gone to heaven,' Arabella said as she gingerly scooped up a pastry and bit into it.

'I say that to myself every night,' Jeremy said mischievously, blowing Julian a kiss from across the table.

'Concentrate, you naughty boy,' Julian scolded, though he did blow a kiss back.

'He loves to boss me about,' Jeremy laughed.

'His coffee is beyond delicious,' Emily said quickly.

Her face was starting to blush. Jeremy was clearly obsessively in love with his new boyfriend.

She wondered if a twelve-page feature on their fabulous home would propel Jeremy Cavendish straight into political history, or bury his career for ever under six feet of homophobia. Well, that was Arabella's call. She accepted a pastry, and began to eat it delicately with a small silver fork. Then she picked up her camera and took a few snaps of her plate. She got a lovely picture of some of the spilt icing sugar on the glass table, with the statue's face in the background.

'Don't mind our Emily, she's devoted to her work,' Arabella said proudly.

'I loved your brochure on de-cluttering,' Julian said kindly.

'Thank you,' Arabella said graciously. 'That was Emily's handiwork. Tell me about the apartment.'

'I bought it last year, just before I met Julian, and he kindly offered to decorate it for me. And that's it, really,' Jeremy smiled.

'Can we say what the place cost?' Arabella asked. 'Or maybe we shouldn't mention cost? I don't want to drop you in it regarding the MPs' second-home allowance.'

'No, my darling, it is not my second home,' Jeremy said sweetly. 'Do you think I'd have let you in the door today if it were? This is my one and only home, and I paid for it myself. Well, okay, I paid for it with an inheritance, thank you very much. It was £750,000. I can't deny there's some old money floating about in the Cavendish family coffers. But that's not a crime, is it?'

'Not at all,' Arabella assented. 'I wish some dear old aunt would pop her clogs and leave me a load of money.'

'Indeed,' Jeremy smiled, pouring more coffee.

'At least I've invested my windfall in property and helped the economy,' Jeremy added. 'I could have nipped off to the Bahamas with it and left dear old Britain behind. This place hasn't warmed up in years.'

'That's true,' Emily admitted.

'I'm almost afraid to ask this question, but do you think you'll be PM some day?' Arabella said, patting some chocolate sauce from her crimson lips with a paper napkin.

'We will, of course,' Jeremy said confidently. 'I have no doubt of it. And then we shall set about making this country great again.'

'So do you think we should focus on politics with this feature, or on your forthcoming happy union with Julian?' Arabella wanted to know.

'Both,' Jeremy replied at once. 'I think it's time to put this country back on the map – both as a centre of art and culture, and as a country that respects committed relationships of all kinds.'

'Bravo! Hear, hear,' Julian said happily. 'Let me show you the bedrooms, and then we can round off the tour with the sitting room, the study and the TV den.'

Arabella and Emily were out of their seats in a heartbeat.

'Our bed is a reproduction four-poster, and it has twenty-eight pillows and cushions on it,' Julian said proudly. 'It takes half an hour each morning to make the bed. We had to sleep in the guest bedroom last night, because I knew there wouldn't be time to stage our room for your visit.'

Oh boy, Emily thought to herself as the four of

275

them went prancing up the stairs. This is going to be good.

And it was.

She got a super picture of the two men sitting rigidly on the bed together, holding hands but staring straight ahead like something from an art-house film.

Arabella was positively giddy for the rest of the day. She bought everyone in the office a box of luxury chocolates, and took them all to Pizza-Express for supper. She even gave Jane Maxwell a hug, and told her she was doing great work as a stylist.

'Emily,' Arabella said triumphantly to Emily in the taxi home that night, 'we have arrived.'

'We have?'

'Yes. Not only will I be putting Jeremy and Julian and their bed on the next front cover of *Stylish Living*, I will also be relaunching the magazine as a truly upmarket celebrity style bible.'

'Are you sure about that? What if we can't find a celebrity for every issue?'

'Are you serious? They'll be queuing up to be in it. I'm sure Jane will be able to get us lots of big names now she's partying with Doug and his pals. We might even go global, start shipping issues abroad. We'll get more advertising, and you and I can go on junkets to Nantucket and Moscow. Oh, Emily, this is going to be huge.'

'Welcome back to the wonderful world of *Stylish Living*,' Emily said dryly.

Arabella just threw back her head and laughed until the tears were running down her face.

22. House-hunting

It was the 23rd of December. Emily and Dylan were lying in bed together. They'd been in bed all day. There were two duvets on the bed as well as a fake fur throw. They were both wearing paisley flannelette pyjamas (as a joke) and they were still slightly cold. They'd been watching old Miss Marple DVDs on the portable TV, dozing occasionally, making love, and drinking cups of hot chocolate to keep warm. Although it was still early in the evening, it was already pitch dark. The sky outside the bedroom window was the mottled silvery colour of black grapes. It looked as if it might snow again too. Emily said if it didn't stop snowing soon, she was going to move to the North Pole and be done with it. At least that way she could finally bid farewell to hope and just resign herself to everlasting icicles and chilblains. It seemed as if one fall of snow had only just been swept away, or melted into slush, when it was replaced with another layer. They could hear some partygoers in the next building, raucously singing all of Slade's greatest hits. Neither of them had done a single bit of Christmas shopping.

'Are your parents coming over for Christmas dinner?' Dylan asked.

'Yes, I asked them yesterday,' Emily said. 'Get ready for the time of your life, kiddo.'

'Come on, it'll be lovely.'

'Yes, you're quite right. And I'm going to be nice to them from the minute they walk in the door until the minute they leave. If my mum says the turkey is dry, I'll offer her more gravy. And if my dad says there's nothing good on the telly, I'll invite him to tell us riveting tales about Christmas past. You know, when they got a satsuma and a walnut in their stockings, and they had to walk fifty miles to church, wearing a coat made from a wheat sack and shoes lined with old newspapers.'

'He probably isn't exaggerating about the shoes. Listen, good for you for asking them for dinner. And I'll do the washing-up.'

'You're a living saint, do you know that? I invited Arabella too, but she's going away to some hotel spa in Spain for a couple of days of pampering. I told her she was a lucky thing, but I get the feeling she might be a bit lonely there.'

'Maybe. But she can always come home, if she is. Why don't we go late-night shopping this evening, and get your mum and dad a whole bunch of nice little things?' Dylan suggested.

'Like what?' Emily asked nervously. She didn't want to remind Dylan she was counting the pennies these days. Everything in the fridge was a 2-for-1 from the supermarket. Every time she looked in there, she thought she was seeing double.

'Well, like scarves, gloves, chocolates, biscuits, socks, soap, shower gel, coffee, books, jams, wallets and slippers for a start?'

'Steady on, I'm hardly Simon Cowell,' she joked.

'I know, but we could go to BHS and Primark and Tesco ... and get loads of stuff. We could wrap lots of little things, and pile them up on the dining table on Christmas Day.'

'Have you been reading my old magazines?' Emily laughed. *'Christmas Style on a Shoestring Budget.'*

'Maybe I have,' he admitted shyly, 'when you were having a bath last night.'

'What did you get for your family, by the way?' Emily said, sitting up and reaching for her dressing gown.

'Vouchers – I just get a load of vouchers every year and give them to Mum. She slips them into her own Christmas cards, and adds a note that the vouchers are from me. Actually, I don't even buy the vouchers myself; I give Mum the cash and she buys them.'

'You lazy sod,' Emily scolded him

'I know. But it's what my sisters want, trust me. They all have children and mortgages, so they'd rather have vouchers than scented candles.'

'Fair enough. So will we hit the shops tonight, then?' Emily asked.

'Yeah, might as well – it'll only get worse on Christmas Eve,' Dylan yawned.

'Okay, I'll jump in the shower,' Emily said, getting out of bed.

'I'll make breakfast,' Dylan offered. 'Or should that be supper? You've made me lose track of time, you temptress.'

'Dylan, what would you like for Christmas?' Emily said suddenly.

'Oh, nothing much. A kiss under the mistletoe with my true love would be more than enough for me.'

'Seriously; stop larking about for a second.

279

What would you like? It's our first Christmas together. So even though I'm not exactly minted at the moment, I'd like to buy you a nice gift.'

'Do you want me to tell you the truth?' he said quietly.

'Of course I do. Why wouldn't I?'

'Right, then – you asked for this. I'd like us to move in together.'

'Wow.'

'Yes, big wow,' he laughed. 'What do you say?'

'You mean, you'd move in here – to this flat?' she asked, looking around the room. 'I suppose it could work. The wardrobe is empty now, so there'd be room for your things.'

'Don't get too carried away, will you?' Dylan teased, pulling her back on to the bed and kissing her tenderly. 'There's a lot more to moving in together than a roomy wardrobe, you know.'

'I'm sorry, it's just taken me by surprise a bit,' she laughed.

'Why don't we get the shopping done, and then drive around the city checking out affordable neighbourhoods? If we find a nice area, we could park the car and just walk around looking at all the Christmas trees in the windows. I always think you can tell that a place has a good sense of community, if it has lots of Christmas trees. Or is that an old-fashioned thing to say?'

'It's a bit old-fashioned, yes. But more important than that, it's freezing outside.'

'It might be nice to move house – or even buy a house – around Christmas time, though,' he replied. 'And it's a buyer's market at this time of the year, because nobody is really looking. And none of the sellers are expecting an offer, so they might accept a bit less than the asking price.'

'You soppy old romantic,' she teased him, suddenly filled with Christmas joy.

'That's my girl. So will we go house-hunting, then?'

'Yes! Oh, wait a minute... I owe the bank my wages for the next ten years, and you're doing unpaid work for Sylvia. How are we going to pay the rent, or the mortgage? Say we did find anything remotely decent and halfway affordable?'

'I'm going back to work,' Dylan said then.

'You mean, you're going back to banking?' Emily asked, puzzled.

'No, I'm going to apply for something in accounting. I can do that as well as banking. It's a bit boring, but it pays well enough. And it doesn't have the same terrible stigma as banking.'

'An accountant... When did this happen?' Emily said excitedly.

She had a sudden vision of Peter Diamond, sitting in his lovely office in the Doll's House while his wife cleaned and dusted and mopped and vacuumed her days away.

'You never told me you were thinking of going back to work.'

'I just decided last night,' he told her lovingly. 'When you were sleeping last night I just lay awake thinking about my future, and I realized I can't see a happy future for myself without you in it. And why should we bother with a ten-year courtship if we know already that we're meant to be?'

'Oh well, now,' Emily said, moved to tears by

such a tender revelation.

'So what do you think? Do you fancy a duplex, a semi, a loft, a new-build, a cottage, a mews, a tower block or a warehouse?'

'I'd like a small, cosy Victorian terraced house, with white window frames, sills deep enough to carry window boxes, and a dark green door. And a tiny patio garden out the back where I could grow daffodils and red tulips in reclaimed chimney pots. And I'd like the sitting room to have deep alcoves on either side of the fireplace where I could have built-in bookcases. And I'd like a kitchen with open shelving, so I could display lots of crockery and storage jars instead of hiding them all away in cupboards. And I'd like it to have room for a tumble dryer, so I never have to go to work in damp socks ever again. And I'd like the house to be near the Tube station, so I can take the train to work – if the traffic gets any worse than it is already. And I'd like it to be near a deli, because I'd love to be able to say, I'm just nipping out to the deli for a baguette and some Swiss cheese, but I won't be long.'

'How delightfully specific; I can tell you've given this subject plenty of thought already. And I think I know several streets that might fit the bill. I used to read the property pages during my lunch break at work.'

'Why did you never buy a house before this?' Emily asked him. 'If you were in such a good job, it would have been better to buy than to rent, surely?'

'I knew there'd be a massive slump, that's why,' he said sheepishly. 'I'm the only one from my old

282

office who hasn't got at least forty per cent negative equity nowadays. Bless them; why did they ever think a terraced house was worth two million quid? I just knew it wouldn't last.'

'My, you're the clever one,' Emily said, nodding her head in admiration.

'Mind you don't tell anyone,' Dylan laughed. 'I like to portray myself as a rather endearing idiot.'

'In your dreams... This is so exciting,' Emily cried. 'Let's go right now! We can always do the shopping tomorrow.'

'Hooray!' Dylan laughed. 'Yeah, let's go now. And we can pick up a couple of bacon rolls at some coffee shop.'

Three hours later, Emily and Dylan stood arm-in-arm in front of their dream house. It was exactly as Emily had described it to Dylan – right down to the window boxes planted with winter flowers, and the dark green front door.

'How did you know?' she said breathlessly.

'I didn't. I just thought I remembered there were some Victorian terraces around here, that's all.'

'It's my dream house,' Emily said, pointing at the yellow-coloured brickwork. 'There's the date set above the bay window, look.'

'And there's lots of lovely big Christmas trees in this street too,' Dylan added, 'which means there's lots of young families around here.'

'Pity the house we want isn't for sale,' Emily said sadly.

'Not to worry,' Dylan told her, pulling a notebook and pen out of his pocket.

'What are you going to do? Make them an

offer?' Emily asked him.

'Might as well, if it's really the house you want. I'll not make an offer just yet; I'll just tell them we're interested, yeah? Give both parties a chance to do some thinking and look at current market prices for this neighbourhood. I also need to get a job.'

'Oh, Dylan, I can hardly believe it,' Emily cried, throwing her arms around his neck.

'It's pretty normal stuff – getting a job and buying a house,' he laughed.

'I know it is, but I never thought it would happen to me,' she said. 'Most of my friends in the office have given up on ever owning their own places.'

'Ah, but they aren't dating a financial whiz kid, are they?'

'No! Lucky old me...'

Just then the front door of the house opened, and a little old lady in a purple tweed coat came teetering down the steps, complaining bitterly to herself about the cold. Suddenly, as Emily and Dylan made to walk away, the elderly woman slipped on a patch of invisible ice and almost lost her balance. She clung on to the garden wall for support and dropped the paper bag she was carrying. Half a dozen cherry scones tumbled out of the bag and rolled in all directions.

'Bugger it and bollocks,' she cried. 'All blinking afternoon it took me to make those things. Damn this winter to the pit of hell.'

'Are you all right?' Emily asked, rushing over to help.

'Wretched winter,' the woman said crossly. 'I was

taking some home-made scones over to my friend Ida. She lives on the other side of the street.'

'Shall we walk you across?' Dylan asked her. 'Or would you rather we brought the parcel for you?'

'I shouldn't tell you my business,' the old woman said carefully, 'but I like the look of you, so I will. My pal Ida is going into a residential home to-morrow, and I'm really going to miss her. The home is miles away, so visiting will be a real problem for me. But Ida's not able to manage on her own any more, and that lazy daughter of hers can't be bothered coming round every day. No, she'd rather go ballroom dancing with that idiot lover of hers. Nobody cares about old people any more. Well, I do. So even though it's late, and perishing cold to boot, I wanted to sit with Ida for a while.'

'Come on, then,' Dylan said, proffering his arm. 'Lead the way. I'm Dylan, and this is Emily. We were just doing a bit of house-hunting.'

'And I'm Enid. Oh, this one is good-looking, isn't he?' the lady said brightly. 'If I were fifty years younger, I'd give you a good run for your money, young Dylan.'

'I bet you would,' Dylan said, winking at her.

'So are you looking to buy in this area?' Enid asked as they made their way slowly to Ida's house. 'This is a good, quiet neighbourhood. But we don't get a lot of interest from young people like yourselves, as there's not a lot of off-street parking. Most young ones can't walk to the corner shop.'

'Oh, I didn't think of parking,' Emily said, glancing round.

'I've got a good-sized garden round the back that could be converted into two spaces,' Enid said brightly. 'Say you used those porous bricks?'

'How do you know about porous bricks?' Dylan laughed.

'My late husband was a landscape gardener,' Enid told him sharply. 'So I know all there is to know about porous bricks, thank you very much. I might be on the wrong side of eighty, but I've still got all my marbles.'

'Sorry, Enid,' Dylan said contritely.

'So how much are you looking to spend?' Enid asked them.

'Do you mean on a house?' Emily said.

'Yes, on a house. I don't need to know what you spend on groceries, do I?' Enid quipped.

'No, of course not, silly me. Well, let me see. As far as our budget goes ... well, that depends,' Emily smiled.

'What on?'

'Lots of things: the decor and the fittings, and so on,' Emily faltered.

'I might be putting my place on the market one of these days,' Enid said suddenly.

'Are you really?' Dylan and Emily asked in unison.

'Yes. I don't think I can let Ida go into that home by herself; you hear all sorts about residential homes these days. Corners being cut and rough types hired. They'll give anybody a uniform – or so it seems – and do the checks whenever they get round to it. Country's gone to the dogs, and no mistake. It looks a nice enough place. I'm not saying it doesn't look nice, but I can't help worrying about poor Ida.'

'I'm sure it's fine,' Emily said kindly.

'It'd better be fine, for not much gets past me,' Enid said firmly.

'Well, look, if you're serious about selling, here's my number,' Dylan told her. He scribbled his name and number on a piece of paper and gave it to the old woman. 'I wouldn't want to take advantage of you, though, just because you're feeling sad about your friend moving away.'

'Dear me, this one is a keeper,' Enid said softly, brushing a tear from her eye. 'I'll tell you what. You pair come over to my house at lunchtime on Boxing Day, and I'll show you round. The whole place needs to be gutted from top to bottom; no point lying about it. There's a damp patch in the scullery, and the stairs creak like a sinking ship. My late husband was a terrific gardener, but he couldn't do a scrap of DIY. Mind, I'll knock a fair bit off the asking price, if you're keen to do business. I don't want a lot of fuss at my age, and I don't want a lot of smooth-talking estate agents in fancy suits waving their clipboards in my face.'

Emily and Dylan exchanged ecstatic glances; could it really be happening that they'd found the house of Emily's dreams on their very first day of house-hunting?

A few tiny snowflakes tumbled out of the darkness and settled on Enid's collar.

'Bugger it,' Enid said.

'Looks like another night of snow,' Emily said. 'They did say it was going to snow tonight.'

'Will you be able to get home again?' Dylan asked.

'I'll call a taxi,' Enid said, rolling her eyes at the cost of it.

'Well, here we are,' Emily said as they helped Enid up the steps of Ida's house.

'Yes, here we are. And that settles it,' Enid said sharply.

'That settles what?' Dylan said.

'I'm not spending one more winter shivering in that house. The home where Ida's going is like a furnace day and night. I'm going to ring them tomorrow and ask if there's another room going spare. The wallpaper would make you weep, it's that bland. But at least the heat will keep my arthritis at bay. Don't forget to call round on Boxing Day, though, for when I decide to do something, I don't hang about.'

23. All that Glitters

On Christmas Eve Dylan was very jittery and jumpy. All day long he was looking at his watch and forgetting to finish cups of tea. Emily knew there was something going on with him, but she didn't like to ask in case he was thinking about Enid's house.

She supposed he was having second thoughts about having to work as an accountant so that he could afford the mortgage. But she knew that if the price was too high, they could always decline to put in an offer – and then Dylan wouldn't have to sell his soul in some anonymous accounting firm in the City. She knew she would survive losing the pretty little house. After all, it looked gorgeous from the outside, but Enid had told them it was falling apart on the inside. And perhaps it was too soon for them to be moving in together or buying a house. But then she had a vision of herself and Dylan, sitting on two deckchairs in the little yard, pouring wine beside the tulips and daffodils, and she almost had a giddy spell of her own.

In the afternoon they went shopping for small but exciting gifts for Emily's mum and dad. They both knew Dylan could have chipped in with a contribution, but Emily wanted to pay for the gifts. And subconsciously they were both thinking of the deposit on Enid's little terrace.

They had such a lovely time trawling the shops for last-minute bargains, they barely noticed the time passing. Then Emily spent two hours wrapping everything beautifully in textured white paper, adding long white ribbon curls and perfect white glitter swirls to the petite parcels. She made a little tower of gifts on each parent's plate, then wrote out their names on pieces of crisp white card. Meanwhile, Dylan prepared the vegetables for dinner the following day, did a quick tidy of the flat, phoned his family and made a large plate of chicken sandwiches. They had decided not to cook on Christmas Eve, as they didn't want to mess up the kitchen.

'They'll love all this,' Dylan said approvingly when everything was finally ready.

'Do you know, I think they will,' Emily smiled.

'Shall we watch TV in here this evening?' Dylan said, handing Emily a mug of piping hot tea. 'Give the bed a rest?'

'If you like,' Emily smiled.

'It's snowing again,' Dylan grimaced. 'But it's wet-looking snow; I don't think it's going to lie for long. I'll pick up your parents tomorrow, anyway, and bring them over. I know your mum doesn't like the cold.'

'Thanks, love. You've been so good about looking after them. They're having a great time over here; I haven't seen them for a week. I think they went into town today to spot celebrities on the red carpet at some premiere or other. They might go shopping too, spending the money Jake sent with the Christmas card.'

'Good man,' Dylan nodded.

'I'll just get my fleece,' Emily said then. 'It's so cold in here with these high ceilings.'

'Could you fetch my sweater while you're in the bedroom?' he said casually. 'It's in the wardrobe.'

'Sure.'

But when Emily opened the wardrobe door she couldn't see any sweaters, or even any clothes. All she could see was a small grey velvet box, sitting all alone in the bottom of the wardrobe.

It must be a pair of cufflinks or something, she thought to herself.

She closed the wardrobe door again and started hunting for Dylan's sweater under the bed and in the wicker hamper. But then it dawned on her.

'Is this a ring for me?' she whispered. 'No, it can't be for me...'

But then she remembered what Dylan had said about not being able to see a happy future for himself without her in it. She went back to the wardrobe and opened the door with trembling hands. She lifted out the little velvet box and held it in her hands for a minute before gently prising open the spring-loaded lid. A diamond engagement ring winked back at her. Quite a large diamond.

'No, it can't be for me,' she said again.

For how did she know this ring was for her? It could just be a family heirloom or something. But then again, Dylan knew only too well the significance of Emily's wardrobe and what it had symbolized. All of her past had been stored within its ancient dusty heart. Now the wardrobe was empty, and Emily's future was a blank page just waiting to be filled. Was Dylan offering to co-write Emily's future?

'Will you marry me?' he said, appearing in the doorway.

'Oh!' Emily gasped.

'Will you?'

'How long have you been standing there?'

'Long enough to start to wonder if you're going to turn me down...'

'Is this ring really for me?'

'Yes, it is ... if you want it. Will you marry me, please? I'll be good to you always, I promise.'

'I can't believe you've proposed!'

'I love you, Emily,' he said, crossing the floor in two strides and holding Emily in his arms as if he would never let her go.

'I love you too,' she said.

'So it's a yes?' he said.

'I do love you very much,' she said.

'But you think it's too soon?' he asked.

'Not too soon, no. Well, maybe just a little too soon,' she conceded.

'But we're perfect together.'

'Yes, we are, aren't we?'

'Of course we are!'

'And you're not just asking me to marry you because you feel sorry for me?'

'Why would I feel sorry for you, you dope?'

'Because Alex stood me up,' she said.

'That guy didn't deserve you,' Dylan said, kissing her tenderly.

'Can I have a few days to think about it?' Emily asked.

'Yes, but I'm a bit hurt you need to think about it,' he said.

'Well, it's not that I need to think about it as such. I just want to enjoy the moment,' she explained.

'Okay,' Dylan said, letting her go and walking over to the window.

'I'm sorry, Dylan. It's just that I've worked so hard to get used to being on my own. I never thought I'd be getting married – ever! And then you come along and sweep me off my feet, and you've been so good to me... My emotions haven't quite caught up.'

Dylan nodded, as if he understood. But then he said he remembered something he had to do at the shop, put on his coat and went out. Emily was left alone to consider her beautiful engagement ring. And it didn't take her too long to realize that the flat seemed horribly empty without Dylan in it. Yes, getting married was a big step. But she was ready for it.

If she wasn't ready to trust Dylan now, after all the things he had done for her, she never would be.

Throwing on her own jacket, she raced over to the shop to tell him she would love to marry him.

The rest of the evening passed by in a delicious, happy, hopeful haze.

Emily didn't phone all her friends to tell them the good news. She wanted to keep this precious moment just for herself and Dylan. She wanted to remember always this wonderful Christmas Eve with the diamond flashing on her engagement finger and the snow falling silently all across the city. She wanted to remember the delicate white

Christmas tree and the two little bundles of white-wrapped gifts on a perfectly tidy table. She wanted to savour the peace and quiet of the city as it counted down the last few hours until Christmas Day. And, most of all, she wanted to bask in the warmth of a stable and supportive relationship – without all the doubt and drama she was used to.

'Are you happy?' Dylan asked her as they fell into bed sometime after midnight.

'Yes, I am,' she said simply.

'I'll apply for jobs the first Monday after the holidays,' he told her.

'So you're serious about buying Enid's house?'

'Of course I am. Do you still want it?'

'With all my heart. But only if you want it too,' she said.

'I'm okay with any style of home,' he yawned. 'We can't realistically afford anything bigger right now, anyway.'

'I hope we get the house and never leave it,' Emily said happily. 'We can always convert the loft, and add a conservatory-kitchen at the back.'

'True,' he agreed.

'It's a lovely street,' she added.

'Do you remember the day we met?' he said then.

'Yes.'

'It was Christmas Eve,' he said.

'I know. I was de-cluttering this place,' Emily smiled. 'Who'd have thought Arabella's pasta maker would have brought us together? And now we're engaged, Arabella is getting divorced, my parents have become house-sitters, you're going

294

to be an accountant – and we might be buying Enid's house.'

'I know; it's strange the way things happen sometimes. Well, merry Christmas, baby!' he said, kissing her softly on the lips.

'Merry Christmas,' she replied.

And, snuggled under several layers of blankets and duvets, they quickly fell asleep.

24. The Wicked Fairy

'Hi there, how did the holidays go, my darling?' Arabella asked, breezing into the magazine offices and dropping a heavy stack of rival magazines on to her desk. 'I don't know about you, but I was half starved in that damn spa. Nothing but fruit and muesli for three days straight; I could absolutely murder a latte and a strawberry muffin, actually.'

'No problem. I'll run down to Starbucks for you now,' Emily said brightly, finishing off a short article on her computer. 'I might treat myself to a sandwich too. I fancy something with lots of cheese in it.'

But as Emily reached for her coat, her engagement ring caught the light and Arabella did a double-take.

'Wait a minute, Miss Reilly. Is that a sparkler I see on your finger? Nobody mentioned an engagement to me on my way through the office.'

'Indeed it is! I was just about to tell you! Oh, Arabella, we got engaged on Christmas Eve; it was so romantic,' Emily said happily. 'I haven't told anyone yet. I was going to tell them all at lunchtime. You know, after they've had time to settle back in to work?'

'Show me the ring,' Arabella commanded.

Emily held out her hand obediently.

'It's huge,' Arabella said quietly, and her face

296

darkened like the sky just before a summer storm. 'I do hope it's insured, petal? Better not wear it, if you go into any dodgy areas.'

'I never thought of that,' Emily faltered. 'Thanks for the advice.'

'Don't mention it; I don't want my best features writer to get her poor little engagement finger ripped right off by feral drug addicts, now do I?'

'I suppose not,' Emily said, thinking of Sarah Diamond. 'I'll go and get you that latte.'

'Thanks, darling.'

Arabella didn't seem to notice that Emily was on the verge of tears.

'Emily, are you sure you know what you're doing?' Arabella asked suddenly.

'What do you mean?'

'Well, you've only known Dylan a year. Are you sure you know him well enough to marry him? Or is this going to be one of those tediously long engagements?' Arabella asked, flicking on her computer and tapping some keys impatiently.

Emily was lost for words. She knew Arabella was still hurting after David's departure to Italy with his new family, and she knew Arabella was trying to put a brave face on the loss of her gorgeous Chelsea town house, but her attitude this morning was downright frosty.

'Oh, I think we'll muddle through,' Emily said tightly. 'He's not got any illusions about me, and I think he's the nicest man I've ever met. We haven't set a date yet, but it's going to be within the next twelve months. Definitely.'

'And how will you pay for this dream wedding

of yours?' Arabella asked briskly.

'Dylan's job-hunting as we speak. And it won't be a dream wedding, or anything of the sort. You know it won't be a big wedding, Arabella. It's going to be a tiny affair, whenever it happens – just a handful of close friends at the nearest registry office.'

'Not a church wedding?'

'No, and I'm not going to wear a full-length wedding gown. We might not even have a formal reception. I thought a couple of tables in a nice restaurant would be fine.'

'Cheap and cheerful, huh?' was Arabella's dismissive reply.

'Of course, it'll be cheap and cheerful ... just like me,' Emily said, allowing a touch of sarcasm into her voice.

'Hey, I know! You could get married wearing chimney sweep's outfits, and then go to Burger King for the reception.'

'Maybe we will, Arabella. Maybe we'll get married on a London bus and hand out packets of crisps to the other passengers.'

But Arabella didn't answer. She was busy trawling through her emails for anything remotely interesting.

Emily picked up her coat and bag, and walked quietly out of the office. Her hands were shaking with anger, but she couldn't bear to start a row with Arabella on their first day back at work after the Christmas holidays. She had never known Arabella to be so hurtful and cruel. Arabella knew Emily was heavily in debt. So how could they afford a big wedding? And she knew Dylan was a good man. So why had she expressed doubts about him?

And things had been going so well for them all at work too. The de-cluttering booklet Emily had designed for the January issue had been a massive success; they'd sold by far the most copies ever of the magazine last month. And the Jeremy Cavendish feature was destined to catapult *Stylish Living* to the top of the league in the interiors publishing scene worldwide. A gay MP and his artist-designer lover; it was interiors gold. Jane Maxwell's relationship with her TV mogul was going so well, there was even talk of Jane relocating to LA and becoming their North American correspondent. (Good old Jane knew this was her only hope of getting invited to lots of 'A' list pads.)

So why the hell was Arabella on such a downer?

'I won't give her a fight,' Emily told herself as she pushed open the door of Starbucks and inhaled the swoony aroma of coffee, cream and chocolate. 'I won't be her punching bag.'

There was a very long queue at the counter. Emily estimated she'd have to wait about twenty minutes or more to reach the front of the line.

'Well, serve Arabella right,' she said to herself. 'Let her starve back there. And then maybe she'll think twice about what she said to me.'

But when Emily returned to the offices Arabella's mood seemed to have become even worse. She didn't say thank you when Emily set her snacks in front of her, or offer to pay for them.

Emily shrugged off her coat and flung it over

the back of her chair.

'So are you going to move the Sun King into your Twickenham love nest?' Arabella asked absent-mindedly as she sorted through the backlog of snail mail in her in tray. 'Or is he taking you to live with him in some fairy-tale castle in the clouds? Don't tell me he's secretly worth millions and only working in that charity place for a laugh? Don't tell me he's minted up to the eyeballs and was only pretending his folks muck out cattle for a living?'

'Okay, what's the deal with you today?' Emily said carefully.

'I'm sorry?'

'Arabella, whatever is the matter with you? I didn't get engaged just to annoy you, you know. I didn't get engaged just to rub your nose in it. You seem positively spooked by my engagement. And I've no idea why.'

'I am not one bit spooked. How funny you are! I think it's very sweet and lovely,' Arabella soothed.

She didn't look up at Emily. Emily's breath was coming out in small gasps of rage.

'It is not sweet and lovely at all; you're being utterly patronizing. Look, it's a proper, grown-up relationship,' Emily snapped. 'Deal with it.'

Arabella looked Emily straight in the eyes then. She seemed so angry, Emily was almost frightened of her.

'Are you okay, Emily? There's no need to be so defensive.'

'I am not being defensive,' Emily said. 'You are being rude.'

'Are you serious? I have no idea what you're talking about – really, I haven't. Are you annoyed with me just because I made that throwaway little quip about Burger King? Come on, Emily, where's your sense of humour?'

'Okay, then. So we're joking around today, are we? So is it all right to have a good laugh at the crazy woman who burned down her ex-husband's house in a fit of jealousy, and then lost her own house as a result? Let's all have a good old giggle at Mrs Arabella Harrington, the arsonist, shall we? Don't leave your matches lying around, everybody – Arabella might be tempted to do it again.'

'That's a bitchy thing to say.'

'Takes one to know one,' Emily replied.

'Is that the best you can do? That's a very lame reply.'

'It's how I feel,' Emily said through gritted teeth.

'Well, I can't help feeling a bit jaded where romance is concerned,' Arabella told her bitterly. 'So don't expect me to put out the bunting for you.'

'You know I deserve this chance to be happy, Arabella. I did my time in a lousy relationship – ten years of it. I've been stood up at the altar, and I'll be in hock to the bank for years to come because of it. And yes, I know I have nobody but myself to blame for being such a fool over Alex. But that's all behind me now. I've seen the light. And I thought you'd seen the light with David too? You said it was over a long time before he met Mary, didn't you? I thought you'd be pleased for me. I was going to ask you to be one of my

301

witnesses at the ceremony. Why are you being so mean about Dylan and me getting engaged?'

'I'm just being realistic. It's too much, much too soon. I think you're rushing into this marriage because you're still mortified at having been stood up before.'

'Arabella, you could just have said congratulations and left it at that... What's it to you, if I get married on a tight budget? Or even, if it works out for us in the long term? Honestly, after all the support I gave you when David left you, this is just ridiculous.'

'You didn't give me any support when that man bailed out on me without so much as a note on the kitchen table,' Arabella cried.

'I did, Arabella – I listened to you complaining for weeks and weeks. I advised you to seek legal advice, and I told you not to do anything stupid. Didn't I? Well, didn't I?'

'All I know is, I wouldn't have burned down his stupid house if you'd stayed with me that evening instead of running away to have a silly chat with that reader.'

'You know I had to keep that appointment; people spend days staging their homes for our visits. And besides that, I'm not your mother, Arabella,' Emily seethed. 'If I'd stayed with you that night, what's to say you wouldn't have started the fire the following night, or the night after that? I couldn't be with you every hour of the day and night. That is a totally ludicrous thing to say.'

'Nevertheless, it's how *I feel*,' Arabella shouted.

'I thought you were okay with selling the house? You said it was fun living in a smaller place.'

'Oh, grow up, Emily. I was only saying that, because I know you live in an attic flat. Did you really think I could be happy living with one bathroom and no walk-in wardrobe? I can't stand living in a house that feels smaller than my old bedroom used to be. How could anyone be happy living in a shoebox?'

'So it's my fault you lost your home?' Emily demanded.

'I'm not saying that at all.'

'You *so* are.'

'I'm not.'

'You're as good as blaming me outright! Look, if I had the money, I'd give it to you.'

'Whatever,' Arabella said. 'I'm sure I'll get used to it eventually.'

By this stage everyone in the office was straining to hear every word. Pens were frozen in mid-air, hands were hovering above keyboards and coffee cups were suspended only inches away from open mouths. Emily Reilly had been stood up at the altar! Arabella was now living in a humble one-bed house! This was world-class gossip. This was far better than a mere house fire.

'So what are you saying to me, Arabella? Do you want me to resign from the magazine? Am I nothing to you but a reminder of the house you lost? Because if this is going to be thrown in my face every time you get PMS, I'll clear my desk and leave right now. I am not going to go on working here, if you are going to make me feel like a failure. I'm not going to be the focus for all your disappointment from now on.'

'Don't be so juvenile, Emily. I think you should

see a shrink, do you know that?'

'Why?'

'Because every single thing you do has to be related straight back to your idiot parents – Mr and Mrs Reilly and their long-term train-wreck of a marriage. You're not the only person in the world with dysfunctional parents, you know? In fact I don't know anybody whose parents are remotely sane! You really ought to get over yourself, Emily. You're a five-star drama queen, and I'm getting very tired of it.'

A collective gasp went up from the office. Somebody spilt their mug of tea all over the photocopier. It made an angry stuttering noise, and then fell eerily silent.

'Now look what you've done,' Arabella said flatly. 'You've upset the entire office, and we've only got a few hours to wrap up the next issue.'

'Right, that's it,' Emily said in a thin, high voice. 'I'm taking the rest of the day off, and possibly the rest of the week too. I'll be in touch.'

'You can't go home now, Emily; I need you to finish writing up the Jeremy Cavendish feature today. That's our lead piece.'

'Do it yourself,' Emily said rebelliously. 'I'm not in the mood.'

'If you leave this office today, you're fired,' Arabella said, panic-stricken.

She hadn't banked on Emily taking her barbed comments so hard. But there was no way she was going to say sorry in front of the staff.

'You can't fire me,' Emily said quietly. 'I resign. And you can stick your two weeks' notice where the sun doesn't shine.'

304

Emily put on her coat again, and walked out of the office with her head held high. Adrenaline surged through her veins, making her thoughts dance wildly and her knees wobble alarmingly.

How dare Arabella speak to her like that in front of everybody!

How dare Arabella be so vile about her engagement!

How dare Arabella make her feel like a silly little girl playing brides and grooms!

Even her own parents had been delighted when she'd shown them the ring on Christmas Day. And they'd opened all their modest little gifts with genuine delight and happiness.

'Bitch, bitch, bitch,' Emily said venomously, jabbing the lift buttons hard with her index finger. 'Arabella Harrington is a vicious old harpy from hell.'

Emily drove home in a trance. She walked up the stairs, let herself in and sat at the breakfast bar with her coat still on. After half an hour had passed, she made some chamomile tea and sipped it very slowly. Her stomach felt as if it had been torn right out, kicked up and down the street by Vinnie Jones, and then put back the wrong way round.

At lunchtime Dylan phoned to say he'd been offered a job with a large accounting firm. With their combined salaries they'd be able to put in an offer on Enid's house immediately. Even though they wouldn't actually be using any of Emily's salary, of course – that all had to be set aside to pay for Mr Reilly's poker debts. And a Vera Wang frock and the gourmet food at Belfast Castle.

'Darling, it's all happening,' Dylan said excitedly. 'What did they say at work when they saw your engagement ring? I bet it was mad, was it? Is Arabella going to be your bridesmaid? I bet all the girls were queuing up to be bridesmaids, were they?'

Emily cradled her mobile phone against her cheek, and closed her eyes.

25. Fashion Destination

Sylvia rang Dylan and Emily in a state of high excitement on Saturday morning.

'Brilliant news!' she squeaked. 'You are not going to believe this!'

'Tell us, then,' Dylan laughed.

He'd been making tea in the kitchen when Sylvia rang. Emily was still hiding under the duvet, refusing to listen to Dylan's affirmations that Arabella would be begging for her forgiveness in the very near future. He had also tried in vain to convince Emily they could still afford to buy a house some day soon. And failing that, they could just move to the suburbs and rent a bigger flat. Emily was fed up on all fronts. She had switched off her mobile – and warned Dylan that, if he let Arabella into the flat, there might well be an assault committed.

'Okay, drum roll please... The shop is going to be featured in *Vogue*,' Sylvia trilled.

'Do you mean *Vogue*, as in the magazine?' Dylan asked.

'Yes! What else?' Sylvia laughed. 'Our little shop is going to be a fashion destination! Hooray!'

Emily rolled her eyes. Her life seemed overwhelmed with magazines these days.

'I think this is something you girls might prefer to talk about,' Dylan said, handing Emily the phone. 'The shop's going to be in *Vogue*.'

307

Emily shook her head and kept her hands under the blankets, but Dylan simply dropped the phone on the bed and walked away. If anyone could talk Emily out of her mood, it was Sylvia. Sylvia was famed for her infectious laugh.

'Hello? Emily?' Sylvia said. 'Are you there, Emily?'

'Yes, I'm here,' Emily said, reaching out from beneath her duvet of doom. 'How did this amazing thing happen?'

She forced some enthusiasm into her voice for Sylvia's sake.

'One of their stylists was passing the shop a few months ago, and she thought it looked really nice with the peacock-blue shelving. So she took some photos, and – to cut a long story short – she did a fashion shoot here this morning.'

'You didn't say anything about this before. And Dylan didn't say anything about it either,' Emily said, puzzled.

'Dylan wasn't in the shop the day the stylist was passing. And I didn't tell you both about this morning's shoot in case they decided not to use the pictures. The stylist did say that most of what they take never gets used, you see. Anyway, she's just texted me to say the feature has been approved already, charity shops being very *in* this year, and the shoot is going to cover eleven pages. We're going to get a big mention. Isn't that the most amazing news you've ever heard in your whole life?'

'Indeed it is,' Emily said.

'Well, maybe not your whole life,' Sylvia admitted.

'No, this is fabulous news, and you've worked so hard. Good for you!'

'I'm stunned,' Sylvia said. 'Just stunned...'

'What month will the magazine be out?' Emily asked.

'October, I think,' Sylvia said wistfully. 'All the waiting will kill me.'

'Yes, October sounds about right,' Emily agreed. 'They do have a long lead-in period. I'm so happy for you, Sylvia. You deserve a break more than anybody.'

'Thanks, Emily, but I couldn't have done it without your advice on colour, and Dylan's expertise with a hammer and nails.'

'Don't mention it,' Emily smiled.

Dylan came into the room then. He handed her a mug of tea and a plate of toast. They had only the ends of the loaf left, so Emily's slice of toast was about an inch thick.

'We'll call into the shop later and say hello,' Emily said, taking a bite of the buttery doorstep. It was the first thing she had eaten in twenty-four hours.

'Okay,' Sylvia said happily. 'I'm interviewing new sales assistants later on today, by the way. Now that Dylan's joining the white-collar brigade again, I'll need a bona fide assistant here to cover for me when I go to look after the horses. But hopefully, with the shop taking off the way it is, I'll be able to afford to pay someone to work full-time.'

'I'm looking for work at the moment,' Emily half joked.

'What are you talking about?' Sylvia asked.

'I resigned from the magazine this week,' Emily

309

told her sheepishly.

'For pity's sake! Why?'

'I had a row with my boss.'

'Did you indeed! What was it about?'

'She seems to think I only got engaged to stick it to her,' Emily said sadly. 'She's divorcing at the moment.'

'Yikes, the green-eyed monster strikes again, huh?' Sylvia groaned. 'Dylan has that effect on some women. They tend to look at their own partners and feel short-changed. And as his *woman*, you're bound to cop a bit of the flak.'

'Yes, I think something like that might have happened,' Emily said. 'Mind you, she never seemed to be jealous of me. I always thought she cared more about interiors than relationships, anyway. She's way more glamorous than I'll ever be. I'm still in shock, really; we were best friends for years.'

'What a shame.'

'I know. And to think I only met Dylan when I came into the shop to donate a pile of Arabella's old gifts to me. You could say she brought us together.'

'Swings and roundabouts,' Sylvia said. 'Is there no hope of the pair of you making up?'

'No way,' Emily said firmly. 'I'll never trust her again, and I'll never work for her again. In fact, I'm beginning to think everything nice she ever said to me was a lie.'

'Oh, Emily, I'm sure it wasn't,' Sylvia said in a motherly voice.

'Spilt milk,' Emily said sagely.

'A tenner says you'll make up again,' Sylvia said.

'Okay, but now I'm putting you back on to

Dylan. You mustn't let anything spoil your big moment.'

Emily handed the phone back to Dylan. She sipped her tea as Sylvia told Dylan all the lovely things the *Vogue* stylist had said about the shop. Then Emily suddenly remembered she hadn't told her own parents yet that she'd left her job. She wondered why that was, and assumed it was because she didn't expect they'd give her any sympathy. They'd only tell her to go out and get another job – as if ten years of friendship, and thousands of hours of unpaid overtime, counted for nothing. But then she reminded herself to think of them as children, and it did actually help her to think of them more fondly. Emily also thought longingly of her days pottering in Sylvia's shop, ironing the new donations and playing about with the window displays. It had reminded her of playing in the Wendy house at primary school. Even then, Emily had enjoyed putting the pots and pans in a neat row on the kitchen shelf. She reached out her hand for the phone.

'Sylvia, I wonder... Would you consider taking me on for a while?'

'Are you serious?'

'Yes. I quite liked working in the shop, actually – the few times I did it,' Emily said. 'There's a lovely atmosphere in there since it was all fixed up. It's like a little treasure trove, full of dark corners and secret alcoves. I did enjoy setting out the new things and chatting to the customers. It was nice chatting to ordinary people, instead of the ones who were half mad with keeping their homes in perfect order all the time.'

311

'Tell you what,' Sylvia said kindly, 'you're far too talented to work in a charity shop. And I'm only offering to pay minimum wage. But if it gets you out of the house, you can work here for a month or so. And if any of my applicants are suitable today, I'll tell them they can start here in a month's time, okay? Just so you don't end up staying here for a year, right?'

'Thanks, Sylvia,' Emily said in a small voice. 'I'll be there first thing on Monday morning.'

'Okay, bye. Say bye to Dylan for me.'

She hung up.

'Don't tell me you've taken over my old job?' Dylan said, shaking his head at her.

'Only for a month,' Emily assured him. 'Just for a month, until I decide what I'm going to do next...'

'That's what I said,' he murmured, sitting on the bed and kissing Emily's neck as she devoured the tea and toast. 'And I was there for more than a year.'

'Oh wow, you're right,' Emily laughed. 'Well, I can promise you now that I will only stay for one month. Not a minute longer. I need a rest and a bit of down time, and I don't want to go rushing into the first job that comes along. And besides, the shop is a worthwhile cause – and we've all those hungry horses and ponies to think of.'

'I said all that too – almost word for word. That shop has a magical hold on people with kind souls.'

'Oh dear, I suppose you're right. But it's all arranged now. I don't want to back out again.'

'Right, missy. Get out of that bed. You need a

treat, so I'm taking you to the cinema.'

'What are we going to see?' Emily asked him.

'Anything – it doesn't matter what. I fancy some popcorn, and I fancy a burger afterwards. And I fancy a night out with my beautiful fiancée. We're getting obsessed with work. We need to remember that we have lives to live too.'

'And you're not mad at me for packing in my job?' she said.

'Of course I'm not. I know how it feels when you come to the end of one path, and you want to start again.'

'And you don't mind that Enid agreed to sell her house to that other couple yesterday?' Emily said, her eyes filling up with unexpected tears.

'Hey, come on. Don't cry. We wouldn't have got our paperwork done that fast in any case. The wily old bird wasn't joking when she said she didn't like to hang about. She had to move fast to get that room next to her friend Ida, anyway. There'll be other houses, baby. London is full of houses. And some of them might even have stairs that don't creak like a sinking ship.'

'I love you, Dylan.'

'I love you too.'

'You're a lovely man.'

'Yes, I know it.'

'And so modest too...'

'What's the point in false modesty, I always say?'

Emily laughed, and threw a pillow at him.

'Give me twenty minutes,' she said. 'I just need to jump in the shower and blow-dry my hair... I quite fancy a bucket of popcorn tonight myself.'

26. The Home at the Top of the World

Dylan had been right about many things: the sudden drop in property prices, the right way to deal with Mr and Mrs Reilly, and the prediction that he would not be sued by Emily's ill-fated one-night stand, Glenn. But he was wrong about one thing: Arabella didn't come round to Emily's flat and beg for her forgiveness. And she didn't ask her to come back to the office. Instead, she accepted Emily's resignation in a letter sent the day after Emily walked out of *Stylish Living* for ever. And she gave Emily's job as chief features writer to none other than Jane Maxwell. Senior stylist Petra Dunwoody told Emily all about it over a cup of tea in a new café near the magazine's offices one blustery afternoon at the end of January.

'We were all stunned when Arabella made the announcement,' Petra said in a grim voice. 'Honestly, you could have heard a pin drop for about twenty seconds after she'd finished speaking. We were all sitting around the table as usual, waiting for the weekly meeting to begin. And she just told us coolly and calmly that Jane was now her second-in-command. She never mentioned your name once. Not once. Stunned, we were.'

'I bet you were,' Emily said. 'I still can't believe I don't work there any more.'

'We had to clap and pretend to be delighted

and congratulate Jane, of course. But it was so muted, it was embarrassing. Arabella's always disliked Jane, and everybody knows it,' Petra said sadly.

'Tell me about it! Arabella's been dreaming of firing Jane for years,' Emily agreed.

'But now that Jane is dating that orange-faced *billionaire*, Doug Liebermann, the two of them are glued together 24/7. We all thought Arabella would be dead jealous of Jane, but she seems delighted by it all. I wonder... Is she planning to seduce old Doug the minute Jane's back is turned?'

'I don't think so. Arabella is the classy type, and Doug seems to go for the airheads.'

'Look, I feel awful even telling you this, Emily, but Jane and Arabella are going to LA together next week to shoot some homes there. We're bringing out our first ever American Homes issue in May, apparently. And Jane and Doug are going to be in it, announcing their relationship to the world. As if the world cares about some sleazy guy with a pot belly and dark glasses, and his giggling blonde bimbo gold-digger...'

'Ah well, it doesn't matter to me any more,' Emily said. 'It was becoming quite stressful, working at *Stylish Living*. I mean, I love my home. But beyond buying the odd set of new mugs and embroidered cushions, I don't lose any sleep over it. In recent years most of the readers I've interviewed have been slightly bonkers. Half of them can't sleep at night for worrying about anyone putting a scrape on their cantilevered staircases, and so on.'

'True. It is a bit shallow.'

'Jane's always wanted to have more celebrities in the magazine, and now she'll get her wish,' Emily added.

'But Arabella always said the magazine was about real homes, not celebrities,' Petra complained. 'I don't like the way things are going, to be honest with you. We'll end up taking close-ups of Z-listers wearing white shirts. They'll be plugging their latest project, and we'll be Photoshopping out their plastic surgery scars rather than showing the readers their actual homes.'

'Probably,' Emily nodded.

'I'd resign myself, if I didn't need the money so badly. And we are in a recession and all...' Petra said bitterly.

'I'll tell you this much, though,' Emily said brightly. 'There is one thing that Jane was good for – she gave that silly old cow Daisy Churchill a taste of her own medicine.'

'Oh yes! She surely did that.'

'How many marriages has that woman wrecked during her *glamour* career? About six that I can think of, off the top of my head... Yes, at least three footballers and three pop stars have ended up in the divorce courts because of Daisy and her airbags. And now she's been chucked herself, for our very own Jane Maxwell. It's the most perfect, poetic irony. I laughed my head off when Daisy Churchill was arrested for breach of the peace yesterday.'

'So did I – we all did.'

'I know it's *so* mean to take pleasure in anyone else's misfortune, but Jane was lucky she got away with only losing a fistful of her hair extensions. She might have been murdered. Hell hath no fury like a woman scorned, and all that.'

'I know – isn't it the truth? Jane's got twelve magazine covers out of this *romance* so far, so she was well pleased when Daisy attacked her outside the Ivy. I think *OK!* magazine were on the phone to her this morning. Now Daisy has been truly humped and dumped, and Jane is the new gossip favourite in town.'

'Well, it wouldn't be London without a bit of juicy celebrity gossip, would it?' Emily smiled. 'It wouldn't be London, if you couldn't be a humble magazine stylist one day and the darling of the tabloid media the next. If Cheryl Cole can be described as the Nation's Sweetheart just because she got cheated on, there's hope for us all.'

'Well, listen. Anybody who can knock Daisy off the front pages for a week or two has got to be welcomed. Do you miss us at all, Emily?' Petra asked.

'Of course I do,' Emily said, pouring more tea. 'I miss everybody at the magazine, even Arabella and Jane. But I'm having such a lovely time at the charity shop. The sales assistant who was supposed to replace me found another job, so I'm staying on for a while. Just until I figure out whether I want to find another job in magazine publishing, or try something new altogether.'

'And how is Dylan keeping?'

'He's fine, thanks for asking. He's working hard and generally treating me like a princess. We're thinking of buying our own place soon.'

'Are you really?' Petra said excitedly.

'Early days, but yes... I'm going house-hunting today, actually. Just having a tootle around on my own. I like to spend my days off looking at houses. It makes a lovely change – looking at properties for myself and Dylan, instead of interviewing the readers. We won't be able to afford much. Maybe a studio flat? But I'll be working again soon, and we can start slogging our way up that old property ladder.'

'I really thought Arabella would say sorry to you,' Petra said tearfully. 'We all did.'

'It doesn't matter,' Emily smiled. 'She's been through such a hard time recently, with the divorce and then having to downsize. And I dare say I could have picked a better time to get engaged.'

'But you were such good friends always,' Petra added, dabbing her eyes with a napkin.

Nobody at the magazine had realized how much they liked Emily until she wasn't working there any more. The cosy atmosphere that Emily had created with her tea and biscuits had now been replaced with a frosty, target-driven regime. And the write-ups that were once packed with delicious domestic details were now just crisp notes slotted in around the pictures.

'I do wish Arabella all the best... Maybe we'll make up again some day?' Emily said generously.

But they both knew this would never happen. Arabella had moved on, and it was time for Emily to move on too. *Stylish Living* had changed; Emily didn't want to be a part of that world any more.

'So where are you going today?' Petra asked.

'I thought I might try Hampstead,' Emily said.

318

'I thought I'd start at the highest point in London and work my way down.'

'Why not? That's as good a plan as any,' Petra nodded, leaving a small tip for the waitress. 'I can only afford a pound, but every little helps,' she smiled. 'Thanks for lunch, Emily. It's been so lovely to see you again.'

'Well, keep in touch, won't you?' Emily told her. 'You have my mobile number, and I'll let you know if we ever find a place we can afford. You'll have to come to the housewarming party.'

'Try and stop me.'

The two women hugged briefly outside the café door, and then Petra returned to work while Emily jumped on a Northern Line train in the direction of Hampstead.

While she was sitting there, half hypnotized by the clickety-clack of the train, she got three calls on her mobile phone.

One was from a very emotional Peter Diamond – to say that his wife, Sarah, had gone out of the house for the first time in ten years, to rescue a small grey cat that had caught its foot in a shrub in their garden.

'I'm so pleased for you both,' Emily said, tears of happiness welling up in her eyes.

'Yes, Sarah saw the poor thing struggling in the bushes. I was out of the house that day on business, and after a while she could bear it no longer, so she went outside and plucked the cat to safety.'

'How amazing! I did notice a cat's paw prints in the snow the day I visited you. I wonder if it's the same cat?'

'We seem to have adopted it, anyway,' Peter Diamond said. 'Ever since Sarah rescued it, it won't leave our kitchen. We went out for a short walk that very evening, Emily. I think Sarah may be on the road to recovery.'

'That's wonderful news.'

'Yes, it is. Well, take care.'

'Yes, you too…'

The second call was from her parents – to say that Jake Lancaster was coming home early from Australia, but that a friend of Jake's had offered them another house-sitting gig in a nearby street. They couldn't decide whether to take the job and give up their old house in Belfast, or go home again and settle down to the quiet life. Emily was amazed to discover she wanted them to stay in London. She told them to think about it for a day or two, and that if they ever felt they were getting bored with house-sitting, she would help them find another place to live – either in Belfast or in London.

Then she told both of them that she loved them dearly, despite knowing that lots of people on the Tube could hear what she said.

'We love you too, Emily,' Mr Reilly said.

And Emily knew that he meant it.

The third call was from Dylan – to say that his old bank had agreed to give them an exclusive deal as a well-regarded former employee: a hundred per cent mortgage if they ever wanted one. Only up to the sum of £300,000, but it was a great start. So all they had to do now was find a place of their own.

'And I have to find a job,' Emily grimaced.

'You will,' he said confidently.

'I'll do my best.'

'Where are you, anyway?' Dylan asked.

'On the Tube, going to Hampstead,' she told him.

'Any particular reason?' he said.

'Just looking at property; I hear the views are pretty good in Hampstead,' she smiled.

'Okay, I'll see you later,' Dylan said tenderly. 'Take care. Love you.'

'Love you too,' she said.

Emily got off the Tube and walked towards the Heath. It was a sunny day, though still very cold, and she went in that direction purely because the sun seemed to be shining a little stronger there. She bought a takeaway cappuccino at a café, and sipped it slowly while strolling along pretty streets lined with red-brick Victorian houses.

She turned into Parliament Hill, then remembered someone telling her once that Parliament Hill was where the members of the Gunpowder Plot had gathered to watch the Houses of Parliament burn. The area had stunning views across the city.

And then she saw it: a small but perfectly formed second-floor flat with a For Sale sign in the front window. The front door of the house was painted dark green. On the doorstep was a reclaimed chimney pot – empty now, but in Emily's mind it was brimming over with red tulips. She set her cappuccino on the garden wall and rang the number of the estate agent. They answered on the first ring; they were obviously having a quiet day at the office.

'Hello? My name is Emily Reilly, and I'm calling about the second-floor flat in Parliament Hill,' Emily began.

'Would you like to see it today?' a woman said.

'Yes, please,' Emily said, amazed. 'I'm standing right by it now, actually.'

'I'll send someone over right away,' the woman said.

Five minutes later, Emily was climbing the stairs with her heart in her mouth. The communal hallway was bright, clean and airy. And when the estate agent opened the door to the flat, Emily felt dizzy with excitement. Although small, the flat had stunning views of the Heath and the city beyond. She felt as if she were standing at the top of the world.

'Stunning views,' she said breathlessly.

'Indeed,' the agent smiled.

'I like it,' Emily told him, noting the brand-new carpets, the spotless kitchen and the built-in storage in the bedroom. All of it done up in white to maximize the feeling of space. There was no garden – not even a balcony for her reclaimed chimney pot. But she could make do with a vase of red tulips on the window sill. And with the Heath on their doorstep, they didn't really need a garden of their own.

'Any offers on it yet?'

'A couple of offers, yes, but the owner is holding out for the asking price.'

'What is the asking price?' Emily, said, trying to sound nonchalant.

He told her.

It was just within the budget Dylan had mentioned.

'Can I have another look around, and then phone my fiancé?' Emily asked quietly.

'Sure. I can come back later today, if he wants to view the property.'

The agent went out to the communal hall to make some phone calls. Emily gazed out of the wide bay window and then selected Dylan's mobile number with a trembling hand.

'I've found our first home,' she said.

'Have you? Wow! Where is it?' he asked.

She told him.

'Do you like it?' he said.

'I love it, baby.'

'You called me baby,' he laughed.

'We have got to buy this place,' Emily said.

'I'll come over and see it now,' Dylan said.

'Can you just leave the office?' she gasped.

'I'll ask the boss, and then call you back,' he laughed. 'I'm sure he'll say yes.'

'Okay, I'll wait for you outside,' Emily said.

The agent came back into the flat. He was looking at his watch. Emily knew this was just another day at work to him.

But to her it was the beginning of something wonderful.

27. A Winter's Wedding

One year later...

All year long Emily had been praying for snow on her big day. She was probably the only adult in the entire city who was yearning for the long, icy fingers of winter to come creeping across the rooftops once more. And Emily's prayers did not go unanswered, for on the morning of the wedding the air was filled with countless millions of floating, falling, tumbling, silent flakes of white.

'I don't believe it,' she cried happily, looking out of the window of their flat on Parliament Hill.

'Be careful what you wish for,' Sylvia laughed, handing her a mug of hot chocolate and a glass of pink champagne. 'We won't be able to feel our feet come lunchtime. I don't know which one to give you – hot choccy or champers? So you might as well have both.'

'Can I have pink champers?' Molly asked, resplendent in her flowery frock and polka-dot wellies. 'Just a little glass? I am a bridesmaid, after all.'

'No, you certainly can't,' Sylvia said, rolling her eyes. 'And don't forget to take your pumps with you for when we get to the party.'

'I have them all ready,' Molly said crossly, holding up a pale pink dolly bag, 'and my tissues and the box of confetti. I'm not stupid, Mummy.'

'No, you're not stupid at all; you're the most gorgeous bridesmaid that ever was,' Sylvia laughed again.

She scooped the child up into her arms and waltzed round the room with her.

'I'll go and get dressed now,' Emily said. 'Thanks for doing my make-up, Sylvia. Do you know, my heart's suddenly gone all fluttery?'

'That's to be expected,' Sylvia told her gently. 'It'll be fine when we get there. And the beauty of a civil service is ... it only takes ten minutes.'

'Oh yes, I forgot about that. Thanks, Sylvia; that helps me a lot, actually.'

Emily went into the bedroom to put on her dress. The soft layers of palest pink tulle moved a little bit in her slipstream as she approached. The glittery bodice sparkled like a handful of diamonds. She wondered what Dylan was doing, and thinking, at that exact moment. He was getting ready in Jake's house, as were her parents. Arabella and Jane had not replied to their wedding invitations, and Emily was rather relieved they hadn't. She'd sent them out on a whim, but there'd been no RSVP in the post. Petra had also been invited but as it was her sister's wedding on the same day she couldn't make it. Now she was glad she had made the gesture, and glad it had not been reciprocated. The only guests at the wedding today would be Emily's parents, Jake and his Australian girlfriend, and Dylan's immediate family. Strange to think that Jake's girl would be there, a person she had never met before. Yet Arabella and Jane would not, and she had worked closely with them both for ten years.

'Ah well, that's life,' she said.

Emily sat down at her small, antique dressing table and took the large roller out of her fringe. She combed her long brown hair into a smooth ponytail, then clipped the silk rose on to it. A spritz of perfume on both wrists, and she was ready. She looked at her reflection in the mirror; Sylvia had given her grey, glittery eyeshadow and palest pink lip colour. This was a good thing, Sylvia said, because she wouldn't be worrying all day about smudging red lippy.

This time tomorrow she and Dylan would be on their honeymoon, bare feet toasting on hot sand.

'I can't believe I'm getting married,' Emily told herself as she slipped out of her dressing gown.

The wedding dress fitted her beautifully. She could hardly feel it against her skin. It felt like cobwebs, or a whisper, against her body. The kitten heels were perfect with it. She was like a princess in one of Molly's picture books.

'What do you think?' she asked, coming back into the sitting room.

'Oh, Emily, you're a vision,' Sylvia said, patting down her own gown – a more grown-up version of Molly's.

She was standing by the window, looking down at the street 'I see the car has arrived. Shall we go?'

'Might as well,' Emily said nervously.

'Don't forget the bouquets,' Molly said.

'Oh wow, I nearly did,' Emily gasped.

'Here you are,' Molly said importantly, handing over the bride's bouquet – a small, neat posy of fresh white roses. 'And here is yours, Mummy. And this one is mine.'

'You're the best,' Emily said, kissing her on the head.

The three of them went gingerly down the stairs in their wedding finery, and climbed into the vintage car that Dylan's parents had insisted on paying for. It was only a small wedding, and only a short distance to the ceremony, but they wanted Emily to feel special.

And she did.

At the registry office, Dylan was pacing up and down the foyer in a black suit and pink tie. There was a pink rosebud in his buttonhole.

'Relax, mate,' Jake told him.

'She's two minutes late,' Dylan said, checking his watch.

'It's snowing, mate. They might be clearing the windscreen of the car.'

'What if she's not coming?' Dylan said.

'Mate, she's coming.'

'Will you please stop saying *mate*?' Dylan asked him.

'Sorry, mate.'

'Jake!'

'Sorry, that's the thing about having an Aussie girlfriend.'

'She's here!' Dylan said happily as the silver and black classic Bentley drew up.

Jake and his girlfriend Priscilla shook their heads as Dylan ran down the steps to greet his bride.

'Did he really think Emily would do a runner?' Priscilla asked.

'I can't think of anyone less likely to do a runner,' Jake said. 'They're crazy about each other.'

'Ah, the little one is so cute,' Priscilla said. 'We'll have to ask her to be our bridesmaid when the time comes.'

'Are you proposing to me?' Jake said nervously.

'Relax, mate,' she laughed. 'I'm only joking. I think I can do better!'

Jake laughed too, but then he became rather thoughtful. Maybe it was time he settled down? He put his arm around Priscilla and kissed her on the cheek.

Emily and Dylan came into the foyer again, brushing snow out of their hair.

'Emily, you look lovely,' Mr Reilly said, coming up the corridor,

He'd been calming himself down with a swift cup of tea in the café. He was wearing a neat black suit, and both his shoes and his hair were gleaming. Emily was delighted that Dylan had managed to coax her father into a stylish outfit for the first time in his life.

'Hello, Dad. You look fantastic! Where's Mum?' Emily said excitedly.

'She's coming, love,' her father said quickly. 'She just had to nip over the road to get something.

Emily's face darkened.

'Has she gone shopping?' she asked.

'No, she has not gone shopping. I told you, she saw something – one thing – in a shop on the way here, and she just wanted to go back and get it.'

'We don't want to be too late,' Dylan added.

'Here I am,' Mrs Reilly said, coming up the steps of the registry office.

She was wearing an immaculate grey suit and matching hat. She was carrying a small leather

328

handbag ... and a big, plastic, silver horseshoe on a ribbon. She held the horseshoe out to Emily. Everyone else held their breath. All of Dylan's family had heard about Mrs Reilly and her impulsive purchases. Even little Molly could see that the old-fashioned silver horseshoe would spoil Emily's minimalist outfit entirely.

'For good luck,' Mrs Reilly said quietly. 'I know that you don't like clutter, but you can't get married without a silver horseshoe for luck.'

'Thank you, Mum,' Emily said. Her eyes were full of tears. 'I'll keep this horseshoe for ever.'

'Don't cry, Emily,' Molly warned. 'You'll ruin your make-up.'

She handed Emily a tissue from her dolly bag and gave Mrs Reilly a stern look. Molly knew that Emily's mum and dad currently worked as house-sitters in Mayfair, and she half wished they'd stayed at home today. Imagine, spoiling Emily's perfect dress with that tacky old thing!

'No, its fine. I'm only crying because I'm so happy,' Emily said.

She took the silver horseshoe and looped it over her wrist. Then she hugged both her parents – and everyone else as well.

'Come on,' she said then, shooing them all into the wedding hall. 'Let's get this show on the road!'

'Just a minute,' Mrs Reilly said. 'I've got something else for you. A certain someone who arrived here an hour ago...'

'Mum, we really must get on,' Emily told her. We're a bit late already.'

'This won't take long,' Mrs Reilly said. 'Okay,

you can come out now!' she called.

A door at the back of the foyer opened and Arabella appeared, looking very sheepish. She was wearing an oyster-coloured jacket and skirt, and an enormous hat with a swirl of oyster-coloured feathers on it. In one hand she was clutching a small, rhinestone-covered clutch bag, and in the other hand she had a pretty pink basket filled with prettily wrapped gifts.

'Congratulations, Emily and Dylan,' she said quietly. 'I hope you have a brilliant day today, and I'd be honoured if you'd let me come to your wedding. Please.'

Emily could tell she'd been rehearsing that line for quite some time.

'Get over here, you idiot!' she said.

Arabella rushed across the foyer, and she gathered Emily into her arms. Her large hat almost fell off in the process.

'I'm so sorry for gate-crashing, but I couldn't resist! And I'm so sorry for all those awful things I said; I didn't mean any of them... Petra persuaded me to come. Everyone at the office sends their love. And these gifts,' Arabella said. 'And, of course, we'd all love you to come back to work. It hasn't been the same without you.'

'Oh, Arabella! I'd love to come back! Thanks so much!'

'I'll make you deputy editor, naturally. That de-cluttering brochure of yours was the nicest thing we ever produced. And finally, Jane says hello,' Arabella continued in a breathless voice. 'She'd love to have been here today, but sadly she left London yesterday for a new life in LA.'

'You mean she's not with the magazine any more?'

'No, she doesn't need us now she's finally landed herself a ticket to the Big Time,' Arabella said meaningfully. 'She and Doug have set the date. Please say you'll come back to work right after the honeymoon, Emily? We desperately need your vision. I don't want to run after celebrities any more; they're only using our little magazine for self-promotion. You were quite right about that. I want to get back to basics now, to the way it used to be. I want to focus on people who love their homes, no matter how humble or tiny they are.'

'Um, we are supposed to be getting married today,' Dylan said, tapping his watch and smiling at Arabella.

He could tell Emily later on that evening that Enid had been in touch with him – to tell him that her old house was back on the market, if they were still interested. He hadn't been going to tell Emily that the house of her dreams was once again available, now fully modernized inside! But if she was going to be working at the magazine again, they just might be able to afford it.

He would also tell Emily later that he'd managed to buy the old wardrobe from her Twickenham flat as a wedding present for her. They'd both felt very emotional about leaving it behind when they'd moved to Parliament Hill. It had taken ten of his old mates to get it down the stairs and into a van the night before; by the time they got back from honeymoon it would be safely installed in their current home.

The lads and their girlfriends would all be joining them later, at the wedding party in an Italian restaurant nearby.

'I'm so sorry for holding you up!' Arabella said.

'Not to worry; there'll be plenty of time for a catch-up at the party,' Mrs Reilly said happily. 'Have you heard that Pat and myself are living in London now too?'

'Is that right? How wonderful! Oh, I've missed you so much, Emily,' Arabella said, dissolving into tears.

Mr Reilly took the basket of gifts from Arabella, so she could hug Emily again.

'Come on,' he told both women. 'All's well that ends well. Now, if only we could get on with the ceremony... We don't want the registrar to think it's all been cancelled and go off home, do we? Plus, I'm about to drop with hunger here. And this jacket is cutting the neck off me, it's that stiff.'

'And I want to be a bridesmaid *right now*,' Molly said, tugging gently at Emily's dress. 'I've got itchy feet from all the waiting.'

'Would you look at the time?' Mrs Reilly said. 'Emily, love, are you ready to get married?'

'Yes,' Emily said. 'I'm ready.'

She looped her arm through Dylan's, then took a deep breath as she turned towards the marble stairs.

'Come on, Molly. Come on, everyone,' she said. 'Now that we're all here, together at last, let's make this the best day ever!'

332

Acknowledgements

I'd like to say a massive thank you to everyone at Penguin, especially Mari Evans, Clare Ledingham, Lydia Newhouse, Samantha Mackintosh and Shân Morley Jones; thank you for being such an absolute joy to work with. Thanks also for six beautiful book covers, and for the stunning bouquets that duly arrive on my doorstep each launch day.

Thanks to everyone at the Curtis Brown Agency, especially Shaheeda Sabir; thank you so much for all your patience and kindness.

Thanks to Dermot, the love of my life, who believed in me from the moment we first met in a swirl of dry ice, in a very glamorous disco, in 1984. Thanks to our wonderful daughter, Alice, just for being herself, and for designing my new website.

Thanks to all the readers who have supported me, sent me lovely messages and helped to spread the word! I hope you enjoy this story.

With warmest wishes,
Sharon

The publishers hope that this book has given you enjoyable reading. Large Print Books are especially designed to be as easy to see and hold as possible. If you wish a complete list of our books please ask at your local library or write directly to:

Magna Large Print Books
Magna House, Long Preston,
Skipton, North Yorkshire.
BD23 4ND

This Large Print Book for the partially sighted, who cannot read normal print, is published under the auspices of

THE ULVERSCROFT FOUNDATION

CHANDLER COURT

Eventide